THE
BABYSITTER'S
SECRET

BOOKS BY CASEY KELLEHER

STANDALONES

I'll Never Tell

Only Child

Mine

The Taken

The Promise

Rotten to the Core

Rise and Fall

Heartless

Bad Blood

THE BYRNE FAMILY TRILOGY

The Betrayed

The Broken

The Forgotten

THE GRIFFIN ESTATE SERIES

No Escape

No Fear

No Going Back

THE BABYSITTER'S SECRET

CASEY KELLEHER

bookouture

Published by Bookouture in 2023

An imprint of Storyfire Ltd.
Carmelite House
50 Victoria Embankment
London EC4Y 0DZ

www.bookouture.com

ISBN: 978-1-83790-083-1
eBook ISBN: 978-1-83790-075-6

Ben & Danny
You are mine, but not mine to keep.
But you keep all of me.

— JESSICA URLICHS

PROLOGUE

The noise has stopped.

The gentle splashing of the water, the sound of boisterous playing and squeals of laughter that had earlier filled the house, gone now. Replaced with a deadly silence.

She stands in the bathroom doorway unable to believe what she is seeing, as the taut air crackles, an impending feeling of doom all around her.

The sense of foreboding.

The sense of finality.

She forces herself to take a second look. She must, because she might be wrong. Her eyes might be deceiving her.

But no.

They are motionless, floating face down in the murky water. A mop of blond hair splaying out like a fan around their head.

It's a trick! That's all this is. Just a silly game.

It's not real.

They are just pretending.

GET UP!

She tries to move but her legs feel weighted, her feet stuck to the floor. Still, she drags her legs. Stepping inside the small tiled room. Stepping closer.

GET UP!

Any second now they will launch themselves upright from the bloody-coloured water and start laughing at her excitedly. Maniacally.

Spitting out mouthfuls of water.

Ha! Got you!

Only they don't get up. They don't move.

Their body remains there, floating lifelessly in the water.

The water, red?

She sees it then, the dark wound on the back of their head as the blood continues to trickle out. The gash expanding, getting bigger as it merges with the bath water.

There is so much blood.

Too much.

Splashed up the walls. The droplets that drip down from the tiles a watery, diluted pink. Trailing back down into the water, towards the body that the blood has flowed out from, as if they are being sucked down the plughole.

She is floating.

Completely numb yet feeling every single emotion intensely too. All at once. Hot and cold and panic and nothing. Oblivion.

She's in shock, she realises as her brain is trying desperately to process the horror that has unfolded in front of her. She is outside of her body, seeing it all through someone else's eyes, not her own.

Because she can't bear it.

This isn't real. This isn't happening.

No. No. No.

This is all her fault.

Oh my God. This is all her fault. She did this.

Her face is wet with the tears that run down her cheeks.

She didn't realise she was crying, until the sharp piercing scream slices its way through the silent bathroom like a rusty serrated knife, and wakes her from her trance-like state. Bringing her back with an almighty bang as she clamps her hand over her mouth to stop the noise from leaking out.

WHAT HAVE YOU DONE? WHAT HAVE YOU DONE?

Only the noise doesn't stop, and it takes a few seconds for her to realise that it is not coming from her; the screams are not her own.

That god-awful noise is not coming from her mouth, it is coming from behind her in the doorway.

It's coming from *her*.

1

EMILY

'No, No, No!' I wail as the child next door starts crying again. 'This can't be happening. Not again.'

But it is.

Her cries are even louder tonight, desperate, echoing through the thin plaster and filling up the space all around me. So loud that I have no need to do as I normally do, resorting to pressing my ear up against the magnolia painted wall as the sound radiates through the brickwork beneath.

This time it is so blatant, so obvious that there is no denying it. It is happening again.

Never laughter, only ever tears.

Why is she crying like that?

I press my hands firmly against the bedroom wall in a bid to steady myself, as the sinking feeling swirls deep inside of me. Tonight the sound is roaring and my heart plummets to the depths of my chest as I shake my head, because already I can sense it, how it will continue for hours.

I won't get any sleep tonight. I won't be able to escape it, the uninvited sound that invades my home, my space, my head.

Do something. Say something. Anything.

Anything?

Anything other than what I'm doing right now, which is standing gormlessly on the spot. Behaving like I'm nothing more than a helpless spectator. Which is exactly what I am I guess, if all I'm willing to do is stand here yet again and do nothing as the child's wailing grows louder. I feel distressed as a bolt of hot urgency jolts through me, as if it's trying to startle me into action.

A tiny voice resounding inside my head as it whispers, *For Christ's sake, Emily. You stupid woman. Don't just stand there. Check that the child is okay. Find out why she is crying.*

I should go, I know that. I should go next door and rap my knuckles hard against the front door and confront the child's mother. I should demand to know what's going on inside of those four walls. Why is the child crying so much like that?

But already I can hear it, the accusation there. How my concern would only be misconstrued as judgement. Which of course it is. What mother wouldn't take offence at that? Because I am judging her, aren't I?

No child should be left to cry like that.

What if she is a young mother? What if she is struggling? A baby raising babies, I bet. Perhaps she is so bedraggled and exhausted that she barely has the energy to deal with the crying child.

Stop making excuses! Check on the child.

I should go, I know that I should. But I'm scared, because I know what might happen if I do. The same thing that happened last time.

Only this time it's different, isn't it?

No! Don't go there. Don't get involved. Mind your business.

Besides, I can't move now, even if I wanted to. My feet are weighted to the spot on which I stand. As if the soles of my shoes have been glued to the floor. I stand here, talking myself out of the idea of getting involved, giving myself a million reasons why I should stay right here. Resigning myself to once again doing nothing at all. I am only one person. One solitary person. What difference could I make?

Don't get involved.

Ignore it.

A flush of shame rises up through me as I make my decision.

I cross the room and reach for the TV remote, turning the volume up loudly to drown the sound out. Before reaching for my bottle of sleeping pills.

One before bed.

I take two. Just in case. Because one won't be enough.

One is never enough and tonight I need them to work.

I need them to help me drown the sound out. To make it all stop. I am exhausted and I need to sleep.

Even if it's only for a little while at least.

2

SASHA

This can't be right, she thinks as she slams the door of the taxi and steps back from the kerb, so that she can get a better look at the tall, imposing Victorian house that looms high above her. The slanting high-pitched roof and huge gleaming sash windows shaped into tall, pointed arches. The sheer beauty of the place in all its grandeur makes her hold her breath.

This can't be the house that she is looking for, surely?

'Wait...' She turns to stop the taxi driver from driving off, because clearly there has been a mistake. He must have misheard her. He must have brought her to the wrong address. But he is already gone, and as she turns back, her eyes shift to the plaque that adorns the yellow brickwork, next to the brightly coloured stained glass front door.

64 Maple Street.

She looks down, then, at the crumpled piece of paper that she clasps tightly in her slightly shaking hand, to the bold, black lettering scrawled upon it. It's the same, it matches.

This is it.

Though she can't quite get her head around that because she'd imagined squalor. She thinks of her mother. How she would approve of this place. Before a pang of loss, of guilt ripples through her. So suddenly and unexpectedly that for a second the feelings floor her.

Dead. Her mother is dead.

Her body lies cold, in the ground, covered with six feet of damp, hard earth. Decorated with a shrine of decaying flowers. All of them rotting. Just like her.

She is gone, yet somehow Sasha has been pretending, imagining that her mother is simply busy at home, tending to her precious garden. Or sitting in her favourite armchair and reading her book, or waiting patiently by the phone for her daughter's eagerly anticipated phone call.

Placing her hand on the wrought iron gate, she stores those feelings away, reminding herself why she has come here as she takes a deep breath to steady herself. Adrenaline fizzing inside of her as she wrenches open the gate and steps over the pretty mosaic of red and orange leaves that have scattered down from the trees like confetti, covering the pathway.

At the front door, she reaches out a finger towards the copper bell and presses it firmly, sending a loud shrill buzz of noise through the house.

No one comes. And for a second, she is filled with relief that no one is home. Because she is unsure what she would have said if the door had been opened. Unsure of what she should tell the people inside about why she had come here.

She thinks of the newspaper article. Where would she even start? What would she say? Would she tell them how she'd always felt as if she didn't belong? Or about the anger that burns inside of her. Or maybe how the dark flashes of fractured memory sometimes float around inside her head. Tiny fragments of what she wonders might be something real.

She can't keep ignoring it.

The memories of things that had happened in her life before. Those forgotten years.

She can't keep hoping it will all go away. She'd been doing that all her life and she's not prepared to do it any more.

She knocks again, louder this time because she feels it.

The pull of the place.

Inside these walls, she'll get her answers.

Here, in this house where it all started.

3

EMILY

.

The tablets aren't working. I've taken two, so why haven't they drowned the sound out? My head is pounding, and the noise just won't stop. If anything, it's getting worse. The child isn't just crying this time, she is screaming. The sound is so loud, so magnified that it has woken me from my already fretful sleep.

I slept?

That's something I guess, though as I stare at the clock, I realise that it was only for twenty minutes at the most. I must have finally drifted off. After lying for hours staring into the darkness, tossing and turning frantically in the bed. Alone with my bleak thoughts and building anxiety.

I am wide awake now.

Lifting the covers, I drag myself up from the bed and switch the light on. I concentrate then, standing in the middle of the room, listening intently, so that I can hear the sound more clearly. So that I can dissect the screams from the cries and from the banging.

That poor child.

What is going on inside that house next door?

I am so damn tired. All I want is silence so that I can get

back to sleep. But more than that I want whoever is making that child cry, to stop.

'STOP IT. STOP IT, PLEASE.' I am over at the wall now, banging my fists hard against it. Ignoring the pain that starts in my hand, radiating its way up my forearm, as I bash repeatedly against the solid brickwork beneath. The flesh of my closed palms red raw.

THUD. THUD.

I want them to know that I can hear her. That it needs to stop. Except, the loud shrill crying continues. As do I.

I am not giving up. Hitting the wall harder, with more force.

'Stop it. Stop it. Stop it,' I shout. Resigned to the fact that sleep is done for me now. The crying won't stop.

I need to get out. To get out of this room, out of this flat. To get away from the sounds of the child's cries that radiate through the wall. Sending me crazy.

No! I am not crazy. I am not crazy.

I am better now.

Keep busy! I think. *Pretend you can't hear her.*

Tea! That's what I need. A nice strong cup of tea. I'll make it now before Louise gets here. Because she never makes it the way that I like it. She'll make it milky and cold on purpose, because she knows that I like it strong and sweet and hot. Boiling hot.

I fill the kettle up, closing my eyes with relief at the sound of gushing water as it pours from the tap and drowns out the sound of the little girl. Peace and quiet. No sound now.

Until I turn it off again and the young girl's voice continues to fill the room. I turn the tap back on. An experiment, the water flowing full blast. To check that the noise is not inside my head. That it's in this room. That it is coming through the wall from the house next door.

Louise will tell me that it's all in my head. That I'm imagining it.

But I am not.

I do not care that the water is spitting up the tiles and spraying out across the kitchen sides and floor. I do not care that it's a waste, that the water is running straight down into the drain and Louise will be angry at me for running up a higher bill. She always seems pissed off with me about something. Besides, the noise of the gushing water is the only thing helping me right now. I leave it on as I boil the kettle. Another noise to add to the mix. It bubbles loudly as a plume of steam shoots from its spout upwards into the air before coming to an abrupt stop. I pour it into the teapot, letting the steaming liquid pass through the strainer. Then I inhale a long, deep breath of the aromatic loose leaves, before I let them steep in boiling hot water. Some things are just better that way, done properly. They are worth making that extra bit of time and effort for.

Louise should take note.

This is how you make a proper cuppa and fresh tea always tastes better like this. Made right.

I sit at the table then and wait. For this is the best bit. The waiting. The anticipation. The longing. Tea always tastes stronger when it's brewed like this, and I need something stronger today, I decide as I add three heaped spoonfuls of sugar to my cup for good measure before I pour the tea, stirring it continuously. My eyes following the whirlpool that the teaspoon creates as it pushes the water around in circles.

Hypnotic almost.

I hug the hot cup tightly between my palms, and then finally I take a sip.

Perfection.

Though this morning, the heat doesn't touch me. The scalding temperature from the cup does nothing to stop the shivers that tremble through my body. Not even the fleece dressing gown wrapped tightly around me, my cold feet shoved inside my favourite fluffy slippers, can keep out the cold that has seeped deep down into my bones. This is what insomnia does to you over time, I think. It grinds you down and makes you feel weak. It makes you start caring less about silly, insignificant things such as what you look like, and instead makes you concentrate on the important things such as basic functioning. The simplest things like eating, drinking, and talking.

I take another sip, while my mind starts to plan.

I need to write everything down, in case I forget.

I need to document everything that I hear. I need proof.

Picking up my notebook, I trace my finger over the embossed line of the turquoise and gold peacock that adorns the front cover, before opening it and pausing on the first blank lined page. Fresh. Empty. Waiting for me to fill it with my words. This time, I am determined to take my time. Not to rush. Because I rushed before, didn't I? And I saw the way they had looked at me.

The doctors in the psychiatric unit. Louise. The police. When I'd shown them all the evidence of all the times I'd heard her – the crying girl. How I'd written it all in my old notebook's pages. All they saw was the mass of scrawl and scribbles that I'd frantically documented on its pages. The handwriting so unreadable that even I had struggled to read it out loud. Just frenzied ramblings of someone who wasn't in their right mind.

No wonder they had seemed doubtful. No wonder they hadn't taken me at my word. It would be hard for anyone to take the words I'd scrawled there seriously, when they had looked as if they had been written by someone who was possessed. Or crazy.

I am not crazy. Although, lately I feel as if I'm not entirely inside my own body. As if I'm a little bit lost somewhere inside my own head. I don't trust myself. Exhaustion can do that to someone, I know that all too well. How it can make you feel so tired, so manic, that you can't get your thoughts straight. Only this feels like more than that. This feels like something has been stirred up from where it has festered deep down inside of me.

I tap my pen against the blank page and take a long, deep breath before I start.

5 a.m. – Thursday, 5th October 2023

I can't tell them. I can't tell them that the child is crying again. That she is getting louder. So loud that for a while I thought she had somehow found her way through the wall and into my room.

Because they won't understand.

And no matter what they think, they won't be able to stop it.

This is my punishment. This is what I deserve.

But I can't go through all of that again, I can't go back there.

I have to keep it to myself. I have to ignore it. Pretend that it isn't happening. And perhaps she'll go away. She went away before, didn't she? She left me for a while.

I was better.

I am better.

Why can I hear her crying? Why is she back?

Signed

Emily Pickett

I lean back in the chair. Eyeing my words. How neat they sit on the page. My very best handwriting, all perfectly spaced and beautifully executed. My name is printed boldly beneath my signature. It looks formal. Properly documented. They'll have to take me seriously now. I wonder if I need to add more, if I need to elaborate, but the sound of the front door draws my attention away.

Please be Charlotte and not Louise.

Please be Charlotte.

Getting up from where I'm sitting, I shove my notepad inside the drawer of my bedside cabinet which sits next to my bed. The heavy footfall along the hallway fills me with anxiety.

It's Louise.

She always knows when I am keeping things from her. I don't know how. Sometimes it feels as if she can see right inside me, as if she can pull my thoughts straight out of my head. I go back to the table and pick up the teapot, fighting to hide the unsteady shake of my hands, and busy myself making another cup of tea.

She walks into the room.

'You're up early?' she says, her eyes boring into mine as she tries to gauge my mood, before her gaze sweeps the room.

'I couldn't sleep,' I say, before taking a sip of the tea. Burning hot. The water scalding my lips.

Do not look over at the wall.

Do not mention the little girl.

All the while I pray that she doesn't suspect that something's up and starts rooting through my private things, because she's done that before. She doesn't like it when I keep things from her. She doesn't like that at all.

4

SASHA

It feels like an entire lifetime has passed in the time it takes the woman who lives here to come to the front door. Sasha is grateful for that. For those few extra minutes she's had to compose herself. Rehearsing the lines that she recited to herself inside her head, the entire way here in the taxi.

Hi, I'm sorry to disturb you. I know how crazy this will sound but I used to live here...

And it does sound crazy. Even now, three months later, when she's had time to digest the news of her past properly. What happened in this house still sounds completely and utterly barmy, like something that happened to other people, not her. Like something off the TV. One of those true-crime documentaries. Or *Crimewatch*.

The sound of the chain as it slides across the internal lock on the other side of the door, pulls her from her thoughts and she watches as the front door is pulled open.

'Oh finally! Finally! Thank God. I was starting to lose all hope! I've got a million and one things to do today and I'm already running late, so I'm going to have to throw you in at the deep end I'm afraid...'

'Is that all you have with you?' the woman asks, nodding down to the small suitcase that sits at Sasha's feet.

'I'm not...' Sasha starts, as she follows the woman's gaze, realising that the woman has mistaken her for someone else.

She had only brought a few things with her, in case today ended up being a longer day than she anticipated. Instead of travelling home again, she could stay in a local hotel.

'Never mind, I'm sure you'll be able to pick more stuff up if you need it. One sick nanny is the very least of my problems, I'm just relieved the agency could send someone as a replacement at such short notice. You'll be okay here by yourself, won't you? An easy first day, really, once you've dropped them off at school. You can settle yourself in properly.'

Sasha is about to interrupt again, to ask the woman who she'd be dropping off at school, when the woman stops talking and lifts a hand to her mouth, almost theatrically.

'Sorry. Sorry! I'm babbling again, aren't I? I have a habit of doing that. Going off on a tangent. Don't worry we can sort all that out later. My name is Cecelia. Cecelia Clarke. I didn't catch yours?'

'Sasha. My name is Sasha Hammond...' Sasha begins, noting the woman's flawless make-up. She is dressed in an expensive-looking outfit, a shapely pencil skirt and a crisp white blouse. Faint lines branch out around the woman's eyes, telling Sasha that the woman is older than she is, by at least a decade, somewhere in her late thirties, she guesses. Her shoes are already on as if she is about to go out.

'Sasha. Lovely! The girl you're replacing was called Jenny. Do you know her? She's sick apparently and the agency told me that they'd send a replacement; but they didn't tell me your name, they just said you'd be here first thing. Though it's not really first thing, is it? I thought you'd be here ages ago.

'Do you have your references and CV with you?'

Sasha shakes her head, and Cecelia purses her mouth, her

forehead creasing to an irritated frown. She is about to tell Cecelia that she has made a mistake, that she isn't who the woman thinks, except Cecelia starts talking animatedly again.

'Honestly! I thought I was disorganised. And at the extortionate prices I'm paying to your agency for childcare services, you'd really think these things would be a priority. Still, you're here now, that's all that matters. We'll sort all the paperwork out later. I really haven't got time right now. Come through. I'll introduce you to the kids.'

The kids?

'I'm not...' Sasha starts, except she can't seem to find her voice to explain to Cecelia that she isn't here to babysit her children. Her mouth feels dry and there's a hard, bulging lump stuck midway down, inside of her throat.

'Oh bugger!' Cecelia exclaims, staring down to where a trail of cream-coloured sludge has slipped down the front of her blouse. 'Oh, great! Honestly, how Zachery manages to get more porridge down me than he does down his own throat heaven only knows. I'll have to change. Two secs. Come on in...'

She is gone. Waltzing off down the long hallway, leaving a waft of heady, floral perfume lingering in the air between them, as her sharp, pointed heels tap loudly against the clay tiles that line their way to what Sasha guesses is the kitchen up ahead. Sasha should follow her inside. She should explain, she thinks; she should tell the woman who she is and the real reason that she has come. She should tell her about the letter that her mother wrote to her. Ask her if she knew the history of what happened in this house.

Only she doesn't know where to start, because it would sound like madness to a stranger, wouldn't it? If she explained how she had turned up on the door unannounced, demanding answers to all the messed up, fragmented questions that swim around inside her head.

Embarrassed at the mix up, Sasha wonders if she should

just leave. If she should turn and slip away unnoticed while the woman is distracted. She wavers then, just for a few seconds, as she considers doing just that, turning around and walking back down the pathway that she'd just walked up. Only she is here now, and curiosity has already gotten the better of her as she stares inside the house that she once lived in.

The house where she'd spent the earliest years of her life.

The lost years that she holds no memory of.

Hadn't Cecelia just said that once the kids were at school, she'd have the house to herself today? She'd be here all on her own. It would be the perfect opportunity to have a proper look around and see if she could remember anything, wouldn't it?

Because she has so many questions swarming inside of her head, and somehow, she has a feeling that she might find some answers here. What was the harm in staying a while longer?

'I've got to be at a very important meeting today and a train to catch in half an hour, so we'll need to be quick,' Cecelia calls out, and Sasha takes that as her cue, following the woman's lead, through into what she'd rightfully had suspected was the kitchen.

'Wow! This place is huge!' Sasha says as she steps into the large open-plan kitchen and stares around at the space incredulously. The high ceilings have been opened up by huge skylights, throwing brilliant sunshine around the room, which in turn bounces from the white marble counters and stainless-steel appliances, making the room appear to be glistening with silver.

'Hmm, some might say a little too big,' Cecelia quips from where she stands at the sink. A tap is running and she's plunging a tea towel underneath the flowing water, before wiping frantically at the food that is slopped all down her top. 'Damn it, I'll have to change. Two secs,' she says before stepping into what Sasha assumes is the utility room on the other side of the kitchen. She emerges just seconds later, pulling a crumpled-looking white shirt over her head.

'This is going to have to do, I haven't got time to iron it,' Cecelia says as she tucks it into her skirt and returns her gaze to where Sasha stands, glancing around the room in awe.

'I expect I sound ungrateful, but really, the bigger the house, the more there is to do. Lately I feel as if I haven't got enough hours in the day as it is—' Cecelia stops mid-sentence as if catching the whiney tone to her voice. 'Let's just say, it's not all roses. It looks nice but it's a lot of time, money and work. The place was dire when we bought it. Needed to be completely ripped apart before we renovated it. To be honest, it probably would have been quicker and cheaper if we had knocked it down and rebuilt the place...' Cecelia wrinkles her nose in distaste at the memory of how they'd first found the house. 'It used to be a hostel for vulnerable women. Can you believe that! And let's just say the house has quite a bit of history attached to it.' Cecelia shivers then as if something has just left her feeling uneasy.

'What kind of history?' Sasha asks, feeling the heat inside of her rise to her cheeks. Because she knows what Cecelia is referring to.

She is talking about what happened here.

When she had been here last.

'Trust me, you don't want to know,' Cecelia says, waving her hand dismissively. 'The place is unrecognisable now. Sat empty for years, in complete squalor, before we got our hands on it. Reeking of damp, with mould growing up the walls and thick layers of dust and cobwebs everywhere. Anyway, here we are.'

Cecelia stares out to the garden, as if she is a million miles away, lost in her thoughts.

'Or here I am, at least,' she says finally, before looking at Sasha once more. 'Henry, my soon-to-be ex-husband, has moved out. It's for the best. Hence why I need some extra help.' She looks as if she is about to say more, but they are interrupted by high-pitched squeals that come in from the direction of the garden.

'I can't do them, Mummy!' a little girl shouts as she hobbles in through the open bifold doors and throws herself down, dramatically, to the floor.

'Annabelle! You're going to get filthy, get up, please,' Cecelia says, rolling her eyes as she watches the little girl stubbornly shake her head, as she continues to force her foot into her black patent school shoes to no avail.

A little boy trailing in behind her.

Younger than the girl. Three at the most. He screeches excitedly as he runs through the kitchen, his paper aeroplane high in the air above him, before he throws it, the sharp point of the cockpit striking his sister in the face.

'Zachery! Stop it,' Annabelle says, getting up and pushing her brother as he reaches down to retrieve his plane. In order to teach him a lesson. To get him back for hurting her. Only she pushes him too hard, and the boy falls forward. Landing in a heap on the floor, his plane squashed beneath him.

'WAAAAAAA!' The little boy is crying now.

'Idiot!' Annabelle mutters.

'Annabelle! Don't say idiot. It's rude. Say sorry to your brother, we do not push, and we do not call each other names!'

'But he is an idiot...' Annabelle retorts sulkily, well aware that Sasha is taking this all in as she plays up to her new audience.

'I haven't got time for this, Annabelle,' Cecelia says, ignoring her daughter's comment and picking the boy up from the floor herself, before checking that he isn't hurt.

'She didn't mean it, Zachery. It's okay.' Then looking down at the now-crooked plane, Cecelia adds, 'How about we ask Sasha if she will make you a new one. Would you like that?

She's going to be minding you. Because Mummy has to go, I'm very late...'

'You're leaving already?' Sasha asks, a horrified look on her face as she stares from a flustered-looking Cecelia to a stern Annabelle and a crying Zachery.

The realisation suddenly hitting her that she is going to be left alone in this woman's house.

Alone, to look after these two small children.

'Don't look so scared. I'm sorry that you've walked into complete and utter carnage today, but I promise you, once they're at school, you can relax a little until you need to pick them up again.' Cecelia laughs already making her way across the room and picking up her bag and keys, before she heads towards the kitchen door. 'You can take the guest bedroom, upstairs. It's the back bedroom that overlooks the garden. Please make yourself at home. There's a list on the side with the children's schedule for the day. The times, addresses and contact numbers of the places they need to go this week. It's only school today, so it's a 9 a.m. start and a pickup at 3. I'll call the school and give them your name, you'll just need to the use password I've written on the note when you collect them. And I've left my mobile number at the bottom for emergencies too.'

Sasha hears the way that Cecelia places the emphasis on the word 'emergencies', making a subtle point to Sasha that she is not to call her under any other circumstances while she's at work.

She should tell her, she thinks. There's been a mistake. That looking after the children isn't why she has come here. Only before she realises it, Cecelia is kissing each of her children on their foreheads and she's out the door.

Gone. Her heady sweet perfume that lingers in the room the only clue that she'd been here at all.

'Right then, kiddos. I guess it's just you and me.' Sasha smiles at the two expectant faces as the children stare back at her. Trying to look as if she knows what she is doing. That somehow, she is still in control. When the reality is, this is complete and utter madness.

She is an imposter. A fraud. Though she didn't intend for any of this to happen. But here she is. Cecelia has been careless enough to let a complete stranger into her home to look after her children.

All Sasha did was go along with her.

5

EMILY

I recoil at the sight of myself in the bathroom mirror, as two bloodshot eyes, my pupils like sharp pins, reflect right through me. Right back into my very soul.

I look awful.

It's no wonder that Louise keeps looking at me so suspiciously, the way that she does.

I can hear her now as I dry my hands on the towel. How she is pacing my flat like a ravenous dog sniffing out a meaty bone. I imagine her eyes darting around the room at all my personal things as if searching for clues.

Normally, she would have left by now, but today she is lingering like a bad smell. Because she knows that something isn't right. She can tell. She always seems to have a knack for that, for being able to read me like an open book. She may be lot of things, but stupid isn't one of them. I need to be smarter too.

I splash cold water against my face, wincing at the shock of the coolness against my skin. Though my complexion remains grey and sallow only highlighting the exhaustion there. It's pointless. No amount of water on my skin will help me look more human. But I must at least try and stay composed.

'Are you sure you're all right, Emily?' Louise asks me when I finally come out of the bathroom.

I nod my head because I'm not sure how convincing the lie will sound as it leaves my mouth. I guess that the nod doesn't appease her either. She doesn't look reassured.

'Let's have some tea,' she says, busying herself boiling the kettle, while my heart plummets inside my chest.

I know to do as I am told though. Keep my head down and stick to the rules.

Her rules.

Bracing myself for what's to come, because when Louise wants 'a cup of tea and a chat' what she really means is an interrogation. She wants to carefully dissect the truth from me. To pick apart every word I say, poking at me until I finally give in and confess what's really going on. Only if I tell her what is going on, I know what will happen.

She'll send me back to the unit again. She'll lock me away.

She'd love that, wouldn't she? Forcing me to go back to that dreadful place with all of those loud, confused people.

Crazy people.

I stare at the front door, my eyes fixed on the silver handle. Still unable to get my head around the fact that if I want to, I can simply get up now and leave. The door here is not locked.

I think back to the very first day I moved in, after Louise had left. How I had stood there opening and closing the door repeatedly. Yanking at the handle. Slamming it loudly on its hinges, until one of the neighbours had shouted at me to stop.

I had smiled obligingly and done as they asked. Closing it behind me before standing up against it, full of the newfound sense of freedom.

Freedom. Ha! I've been here for just over two weeks now and though I am allowed to come and go as I please, I choose to stay.

Part of me is still unable to pluck up the courage to leave, because it is safe here. And part of me is still unable to bring myself to go back out there, into a community that once, so viciously, turned their back on me. Besides, where would I go?

I prefer it in here. Hiding away in the sanctuary of these four plain, boring, magnolia-painted walls of this tiny studio flat. A space all of my own.

Louise is my only real visitor, and the new girl, Charlotte. That's it, other than the occasional agency carers that sometimes have to cover their shifts. Louise and Charlotte do their daily checks on me. For now. Until I can show them that I am capable of doing things on my own. Of feeding myself regular meals and remembering to take my medication on time.

I am trying.

There are checklists and makeshift charts pinned to the inside doors of my kitchen cupboards. There are Post-it notes stuck to the giant cork board that fills almost an entire wall. Here, I can watch whatever I want on TV without being interrupted by the constant chatter of others. The mad people they locked me up with. Louder than me, angrier than me. Crazier than me.

I am alone, but I am never lonely.

Here, my beloved books are my friends. They are my companions. Through them, I managed to escape the locked doors of the psychiatric unit. Through them I have lived a million different lives. If I'm ever capable of feeling genuine happiness again, I guess this is the closest I'll come to it. Being here.

Until *she* started to cry again and ruined it all for me once more. I can hear her now, her cries radiating through the walls, and I bristle. Don't look. Don't acknowledge her.

Louise catches my movement. I see the way her head turns and her eyes flicker. Though she doesn't comment; instead she pretends not to notice, turning back and concentrating on pouring the tea into the pot.

'How come you didn't sleep?' Louise asks, finally, as she places the pot down on the table and sits opposite me. Pouring tea into the cups and passing mine to me. Her eyes don't leave mine.

'I don't know,' I say, offering a slight shrug to play down my answer.

Pretending that it wasn't a big deal. Lying awake all night tormented by a crying, screaming child. That I simply just couldn't sleep. She sits there and drinks me in, her eyes burning through me as she scrutinises me closely. Reading my body language and studying my facial expressions the way she always does.

So, I study her right back, noting the tiny line in the middle of her brow that creases there, a tell-tale sign that she is still not convinced.

'I felt a bit sick,' I lie in a desperate attempt to make her believe me. 'I still do,' I say again, hoping that perhaps the thought of catching my sickness bug will make her want to leave.

She doesn't though.

'Maybe it's something you've eaten?' she says finally.

I nod my head. Telling myself all the while to keep my eyes on her.

Do not look over at the wall.

Ignore the girl. Pretend you can't hear her cries.

'Maybe,' I say then, tight-lipped.

Needing something as a distraction, something to do to take my mind off the child, I pick up the cup and drink the tea down in one.

Not flinching as the liquid scalds my lips and burns at the back of my throat. The heat of my face and the watering of my eyes gives me away, and Louise is up off her seat.

'Whoa! Easy. You'll end up doing yourself some damage...' Louise says, in an effort to stop me, but it's too late. The tea is already gone. Besides, I like it like that. Burning hot to the point when it's almost unbearable. I like how the searing heat pulls me out from being inside of my own head. How for just a few seconds there is nothing else.

Nothing. Not even the noise.

How the burn of it helps me to distinguish between what is real and what is not.

The tea is gone; but I can still hear the crying.

'Do you want another?'

I narrow my eyes but nod despite myself. Wondering all the while: why is she being so nice to me? She is normally so closed off, so cold. Staring at me with such contempt in her eyes when she talks and speaking only when she has to. I am used to this. To the way that professionals have dealt with me. How they simply go through the motions and do their job, despite their real feelings towards me. Tight-lipped, hard stares, no real compassion for me. The way that they sometimes talk over me, to each other, instead of talking to me.

As if I am not really here, as if I don't matter.

As if I don't deserve to be treated any other way. And I understand that.

Louise pours me another cup. Adding extra milk this time. So much, that she almost fills the cup with it. She smiles then, as she sets the tepid, milky-beige cup of liquid down in front of me. Letting me know that she's done it on purpose. That she is proving a point. That I can't burn myself this time because she won't let me. She is the one in control, not me.

I take a sip without complaint. Without saying a single word. Without showing an ounce of distaste. Because I'd never give her the satisfaction of thinking that she had won one over on me.

The crying continues, louder now. Filling the room, and for a second, I wonder how on earth Louise can't hear the child crying too. How is she managing to simply ignore her? Or can she hear her too? Is this why she is still here?

Maybe this is all just a test. That's why she is pretending to be so nice to me, as she waits so patiently for me to confess that I can hear the noise that floats in from the room next door. She is seeing if she can trust me to tell the truth, to not hide things from her. Should I tell her? I wonder as I inadvertently stare over towards the wall.

'What is it, Emily? Tell me.'

I hear it then. How there is something there, in her tone. A conceitedness, a knowing that makes me realise that I am wrong. She doesn't want to know for my benefit: she wants to know for hers. She's been waiting for this moment, relishing it. She doesn't believe that I deserve to be here, in this flat. She doesn't believe that I deserve to have my freedom again.

She wants to send me back there.

Stupid idiot! I almost caved. I almost confessed.

I hold the cup up to my lips like a shield, gazing back at her over the china rim and drink her in.

'You know you can talk to me. Tell me. What is it?' She is smiling warmly at me. But I'm not falling for that. If I didn't know her better, I'd think that the jagged edges of her spiky personality had been replaced with something more kind, more genuine.

But I do know her.

She is cold and hard and impatient.

I say nothing. Instead, I drink the milky warm piss that passes for tea down again in one. Because if I don't distract myself by drinking it, I might laugh at Louise's best efforts to try and be nice to me. To befriend me. It doesn't suit her.

'Emily, I know that it must be hard for you. Moving here. You're still finding your feet, and it is such a huge adjustment.'

I place the empty cup back down on the table. I wipe my

mouth with the back of my hand before staring her straight in the eye. Stay strong. You can do this.

Lie.

'I'm fine. Really. I told you. I just didn't get much sleep last night. I was too hot, it felt like there was no air in the room.'

Don't look back over at the wall. Pretend you can't hear her.

'Okay, well, if you're sure. Charlotte will be here later,' she says tightly as she stands up and puts the teapot and the cups on the tray. Bored of trying to prise the truth from me. She doesn't believe me but she's giving in for now, biding her time. Well, two can play at that game.

I should know. I've been biding my time for what feels like my whole life.

6

SASHA

Closing the front door behind her, Sasha stands deadly still, her back pressed up against the stained-glass window as she revels the silence. She soaks it up. Breathing in the stillness of the place. How the peace and quiet calms her bubbling stomach, lessening the anxiety and replacing it with excitement. She feels it. The thrill of being here, inside someone else's house when she knows she shouldn't be.

She's glad that she's alone. The children are finally at school. That in itself had been a mission. Not used to being made to walk, they'd both excessively whined the entire way. They'll moan to their mother about it too, later. When Cecelia is summoned to the school to collect them at the end of the day, when Sasha fails to turn up.

Cecelia would know then, wouldn't she?

When Sasha simply disappeared into thin air, never to be seen again, that she wasn't who Cecelia had mistaken her for. That she hadn't come today to look after the woman's children. She'd come for this. The chance to get a look at the house she once lived in. The house that she sometimes dreamt about.

Part of her still can't believe that she is here, finally. That she is all alone inside of it. Safe with the knowledge that she has the place to herself for the rest of the day. That she can take her time now.

And she does take her time.

Wandering slowly around each room as she tries to gauge a proper feel for the house.

She starts in Cecelia's office. The smaller room at the foot of the stairs. Unable to help herself as she reaches out her hand and sweeps her palm over Cecelia's large mahogany desk, before she fiddles with all Cecelia's fancy belongings. A collection of expensive-looking objects. Accessories and ornaments that she has used to dress the room.

Sasha pushes at the golden globe of the world with the tips of her fingers so that it spins on its axis, before she picks up the sparkling amethyst paperweight, feeling the hefty weight of the slab of crystal in her hand, then she sits it back down on Cecelia's desk.

Making her way over to the large bookcase that runs the height and width of the entire back wall of the office, Sasha pulls one of the old, musty-looking books out from where she'd doubted it had ever been moved since it had been placed there, before she thumbed its dated, yellowed pages.

Charles Dickens. A classic. Cecelia has the entire collection. Of course, she does. Though Sasha suspects that these books are only for show. Strategically placed on bookshelves like ornaments, just like everything else in Cecelia's home. That makes her feel sad. How they would sit there like that, for eternity. Unloved and bursting to tell the stories that they kept buried inside their pages.

Sasha puts the book back, her eyes scanning the sheer height that the shelves climb. Twisting their way up to the vast ceiling above her. A pretty, ornate plaster ceiling rose that blooms above her as its centrepiece. Nothing in this room jogs any of her memories. There's nothing familiar in the kitchen or lounge either.

Sasha takes the stairs. Her feet sinking into the thick, luxurious carpet. She tries to imagine the steps bare under her footing. The walls damp and the wallpaper peeling. The squalor that Cecelia had told her that the house had been in, when they'd bought it.

Sitting derelict for years after being used as a home for vulnerable women.

All traces of the run-down hostel that once was, gone now. All traces of her.

She can see why Cecelia is so successful at what she does. She has great taste. Expensive taste. She's decorated the house to such a high spec. Having made her way back from the school through the bustling streets of Battersea, Sasha could tell how the area was up and coming too now. Full of luxury, high end boutiques and trendy bars and coffee shops. The house must be worth a fortune.

Making her way across the hallway, Sasha glances into the two smaller bedrooms that sit side by side. A pink and purple, pony-themed room that she guesses belongs to Annabelle. While the bright blue and orange room next door, with space rockets up the walls, must belong to Zachery.

Making her way along the split-level landing, with all its misshaped bow windows, she passes what must be Cecelia's room now. A huge super-king-size bed in the middle of the room. A mirrored dressing table cluttered with jars and bottles of expensive skincare and perfumes. That same heady sickly smell of the woman's perfume lingering here.

Sasha keeps going. Only stopping when she reaches the bedroom at the back of the house. The guestroom that Cecelia had mentioned would be hers. As soon as she steps into it, she sees the dark green furniture. The bed and the matching dressing table chair. The thick cream carpet underfoot. The ceilings high and airy, and she instantly feels how welcoming and cosy it feels.

Making her way over towards the huge arched window, Sasha stares out to the long, twisting, narrow garden. Her eyes fixed on the cute brightly painted treehouse that is built around the main trunk of the large apple tree that sits at the very back of the garden.

She wonders if Annabelle and Zachery play there. The adventures they must have, the games that they could play.

She feels sad then. That the house hasn't jogged her memory.

That she has no recollection of her life here before.

Perhaps, all of this was pointless.

Being here. Wandering around inside these vacant rooms while Cecelia and her children aren't home.

Because so far, she can't seem to conjure a single memory of ever being in this house before. Not even the vaguest notion that she'd ever been here at all. Which was strange, wasn't it? Because this was the kind of home that you couldn't simply erase from your memory.

You'd remember being here once, wouldn't you?

You'd remember living in a house like this.

Though the house hadn't been like this when Sasha had lived here.

Cecelia had said it herself, hadn't she? How the house had been renovated. How it was completely unrecognisable to what it had once been. Unrecognisable, even to her.

She moves her gaze from the treehouse, her eyes scanning the branches of the apple tree that surrounds it. The leaves turning yellow and brown at the edges ready to fall and leave the branches bare.

Something stirs inside of her at the sudden glimpse of something vague. A real memory hanging just out of her reach.

Red wellington boots sinking into wet mud. Bruised apples at her feet.

The image is gone as quickly as it had come. The thought so fleeting that she was second-guessing herself now. She had felt it, hadn't she? That feeling of nostalgia. Of being here before. Something about that apple tree. Or perhaps she is so desperate to remember something in this house, maybe it's just wishful thinking. She is simply willing her brain to fabricate a memory.

She shivers. A crackle of something electric in the air, something sinister and cold all around her. Leaving her shaking. Unable to move from where she stands as she wraps one arm tightly around herself, the hand gripping on to the thick sash window frame, as if to keep her from losing her balance and falling. To help stop her legs from giving way beneath her.

You're being overdramatic, Sasha! she tells herself, *because this is silly, isn't it?* she thinks as she steps back from where she stands and stares around the room. She had thought that this would be so easy. That all she had to do is come here, back to this house, and she would find the answers she seeks.

As if they would just jump out at her, right here in this very bedroom.

She was so certain that the house held all of its secrets. That they are buried somewhere here within these very walls. Only suddenly she realises that she has been foolish. What if there are no memories here for her?

What if this is all just one big waste of her time?

The shrill of the doorbell interrupts her thoughts. Sasha stands deadly still, ignoring it. Only when it rings for a second time, longer now, more desperate to be heard, she worries that it might be something important. Perhaps Cecelia has forgotten her key. She'll be wondering why Sasha isn't answering.

Sasha takes the stairs.

Opening the front door to a well-dressed woman with a large suitcase at her feet.

'Hi, I'm so, so sorry that I'm so late. The trains are all on strike and it took hours longer than expected. You must be Cecelia. My name is Gabby, I'm from the agency. Your temporary cover...' The woman holds out her hand, and Sasha shakes it, realising as she does that she is staring, open-mouthed, as she takes in the woman's flustered look on her face, how her cheeks are glowing red, even though she is smiling warmly at her.

'Here, this is my CV and my references. They are glowing. Honestly, I hate to give you such a bad first impression...'

When Sasha doesn't reply, Gabby continues, 'I really am so sorry. I hope it didn't cause you too much of an inconvenience?' Her eyes glistening with tears as she speaks, she sounds genuinely apologetic.

Sasha almost feels sorry for the girl. For a second, she wonders if she should do the decent thing and reassure her that this isn't her house. That she isn't Cecelia and that the children are not her kids. She doesn't care how late this woman is. She should let her in and allow her to take over. Cecelia and the children would have their real nanny then. Only as she goes to speak something stops the words from forming inside her mouth.

Her mind going back to the apple tree in the garden. How seeing it had triggered something inside of her. A faint feeling of familiarity.

Autumn leaves, coloured and curling, falling at her feet. The tree's branches bare. Bruised apples.

The vague notion of a memory of seeing that tree before.

Had it been real?

She wasn't sure.

Part of her feels so disappointed that she hasn't found any solid answers yet, but then, she has only been inside the house for a few hours. Maybe she just needs more time.

Recalling Cecelia's clipped tone when she'd first opened the door to her earlier, how flustered she'd appeared when she'd mentioned that this wasn't the first time that this agency had let her down, Sasha says sternly, 'I'm sorry but being this late isn't good enough! This is the second time this month I've been let down. I'm afraid it's just not acceptable. I'm sorry you've had a wasted journey, but I've already found a replacement for you. I'll call the agency myself and tell them that I won't be requiring their services, or yours, any more going forward.'

'But—' the woman starts.

Only Sasha cuts her dead.

'I have two young children to think of. I can't leave them in the hands of someone who can't even turn up on time. What kind of a mother would that make me?'

Sasha slams the door. A trickle of guilt running through her as she imagines the disheartened woman pulling her case back down the front path and making her way back to the train station. Her trip here, wasted. It was selfish of her to do that; she knows that deep down. Only it feels as if she has no control now. She needs answers and somewhere deep inside of herself, she is still convinced that this is where she'll find them.

In this house.

She stares down at the paperwork that she's still holding tightly in her hand. The woman's CV and a letter from the childcare agency, with their logo emblazoned at the top. Paperwork that Cecelia had mentioned earlier that she would require from her. Sasha has it now. The paperwork that she needs. All she has to do is to add her own photograph and change the name.

Maybe she could really do this? Buy herself some more time.

She could call the agency right now and pretend to be Cecelia, couldn't she?

She could terminate the contract with them and tell them she's found someone else more permanent. That way, she could stay.

She could look after the kids and the trade-off would be that her days would remain empty whilst they were at school. She could still tend to all the other things she needed to do. She could spend time here too. In this house. While she pieced the early years of her life together again.

While she got the real full story of what had happened back then.

What difference would it make to Cecelia who is here looking after her children, as long as someone was here to drop them off and pick them up from school?

It couldn't be that hard a task, surely. What harm would it do if she stayed for a few days?

7

EMILY

'Woah, Emily! The TV is so loud, I can hear it all the way out in the hallway,' Charlotte says as she crosses the room and turns the volume down on the TV, which is blaring loud now.

I jump, startled by her sudden appearance. She's right, the TV is so loud that I didn't even hear her come in. Standing there now, her fluffy yellow cardigan still on, the strap of her bag still hanging loosely from her hand.

'Leave it. I want it right up,' I say, with a little more force than I mean to use as I too cross the room and turn the TV back up. I have been too abrupt, which is mean of me, I don't want to be mean. The look on Charlotte's face changes to an expression of pain, as if she's just been physically slapped. The girl is young, and she only means well. She's not like Louise. She is softer, kinder, more patient.

Right now, I'm not thinking about any of that, of how nice she is. I'm only thinking about me. About the ways I can stop the sounds of the crying girl from penetrating my head. I am losing it. I can't bear it for another second. The noise of the child constantly crying is like sharp nails being dragged down a chalkboard, the high frequency of her tone making me wince in pain.

The blare of the TV is not enough. I can still hear her as she gets louder with the sound.

She is relentless in her need to punish me. As if she knows. As if she is doing it on purpose.

I cover my ears with the palms of my hands.

Eyes pinched tightly together; jaw clenched shut.

I need to make it stop; I need to drown it out. Because it feels as if it is slowly driving me crazy.

'Stop it. Please stop!' I scream.

'Emily? What on earth is going on? Stop what?' It's Charlotte I hear now. Her voice is etched with concern, but it's also distorted. As if it's coming from somewhere way off in the distance.

Far away from me.

I can't get to her. I am here, alone with the child.

The sound is twisted now. As if it is no longer coming from the other side of the wall. It's as if somehow it is here, close now, creeping around this very room in which I stand, as I push my hands tight against my skull and cup my ears to stop the sound from penetrating them; only somehow it can still squeeze its way in through my ear canal. Before it nestles somewhere inside of my head.

The pain is unbearable, making me double over in agony.

Suddenly I am down on the floor. Beating at my ears with two closed fists. Anything to try and make it stop.

I want it gone. I want it gone.

But even that doesn't work.

'Can't you hear her too?' I shout over the constant drone of crying. My own voice loud, so that it carries over the raucous noise that the child is making. So that Charlotte can hear me.

'Hear who?' Charlotte asks and my heart sinks.

She can't hear her. She can't hear the girl.

How can that be?

Why am I the only one that can hear her.

You know why! You KNOW why!

I start crying, whimpering loudly whilst shaking my head, because I don't want to accept my fate, that it has started up again. That the noise is not coming from next door, it is not inside of this room. It's coming from inside of my head.

Taunting me. Haunting me.

'Please, you won't tell her, will you? You won't tell Louise. Please, you mustn't. You mustn't!'

'Tell her what? What is it, Emily? Please, tell me. I'm worried about you!'

I am crying. The look of concern that flashes across Charlotte's face too much for me to bear. I crumble.

Rocking back and forth rhythmically on the floor.

'About the crying girl. Don't tell Louise that I can hear her again. Make her stop. Please just make her stop,' I scream.

But I know that Charlotte can't make the girl stop.

Nobody can.

8

SASHA

'I'm so sorry to do this to you, on your very first day, Sasha...' Cecelia's voice sounds frantic at the other end of the phone, as she explains how late the meeting is expected to go on for tonight. 'It just wouldn't make sense to come all the way home from Manchester tonight, only to have to come back here again first thing in the morning. I got here late today as it is and then I somehow managed to forget my portfolio too, so it's taken me ages to get myself organised for this client. I can't let them down again. I already look so disorganised and unprofessional.'

'Please don't worry! It's fine, Cecelia,' Sasha says. 'I've got everything under control here. Annabelle and Zachery have had their dinner and they are just about to have a bath before they get all snuggled up in bed. I might have to keep them distracted with a mug of hot chocolate and lots of stories though. What do you think?'

Sasha grins as the children cheer excitedly in the background, their obvious excitement making Cecelia laugh loudly too.

The relief in her voice is palpable when she speaks again.

'Oh, you are a star! Thank you so much for doing this, I am so sorry that I keep throwing you in at the deep end.'

'Seriously, Cecelia. Don't worry. That's what I'm here for. We'll see you tomorrow,' Sasha says, letting the children wish their mother good night, before she hangs the phone up.

'Right, first one up those stairs and ready for the bath gets to choose the first book,' Sasha says as the children squeal with delight once more, before they make a run for it. Sasha follows them upstairs, glad in a way that Cecelia won't be back tonight. She'll have her first evening at the house to herself, once the children are asleep.

Running the bath, Sasha perches on the chair in the corner of the bathroom, while the two children clamber into the bath. Oohing and aahing as they lower themselves down into the warm, bubble-filled water.

'Can you wash my hair, please, Sasha?' Annabelle asks, dipping her head into the water and re-emerging with a mountain of white bubbles piled high on her head. Zachery squeals with laughter at this. Patting bubbles onto his own head too. And Sasha can't help but join in. Taking her hand and skimming the water's surface, before placing a huge handful of bubbles onto her own head. The three of them giggling so loudly as they all bob their heads about, sending the bubbles all over the room.

'Okay, it's getting late. If you want a story, you're going to need to get out now,' Sasha says, realising the first thing she'll need to do once the kids are asleep is come back in here and dry the walls and floor properly from where the three of them have soaked it.

Annabelle makes it to the bedroom first, the two children dressed in their pyjamas now, before diving under her covers and snuggling in close together.

'Okay, I've put a splash of extra milk in these so they shouldn't be too hot,' Sasha says as she hands the children their mugs of hot chocolate. 'Annabelle, you get to choose our first book.'

'I want you to read *The Little Mermaid*, please.' Annabelle beams smugly, while Zachery pouts, clearly unimpressed by his sister's choice of book.

'But *The Little Mermaid* is for girls. Can't we read something else? What about the one about the naughty dog?'

'No! I won fair and square,' Annabelle says haughtily, as if repeating words she's heard directly from a grown-up's mouth. 'I want *The Little Mermaid*.'

'Not fair!' Zachery cries.

'Hey. Come on, you both get a story. Annabelle just gets hers first. Then we can read your one, Zachery. Besides, mermaids are not just for girls, you know. Boys can be mermaids too. Well, technically they are called mermen.'

'Mermen? Woah, really? And they can do everything that mermaids can do?' Zachery gasps, sounding impressed, as Sasha nods her head.

'Of course.'

'I'm going to practice being a merman next time we have a bath!'

'Okay!' Sasha laughs, glad to see that both children seem happy with her here, as they settle back against the pillows, eager for their story now.

She'd thought that this job would be harder than it is. That the children wouldn't settle. That they'd be pining for their mother. But so far, it is as if they haven't even noticed that Cecelia isn't here. They are having far too much fun for that. It pleases Sasha enormously.

Reading the books animatedly, she finds herself enjoying the stories just as much as the children, as she puts on funny-sounding voices for each different character, pausing in all the right places, to ensure that there is enough tension to keep them both from getting bored.

When she is finished, she realises her grave error. How she has done such a good job in keeping them entertained, that instead of making them tired and ready for sleep, she has somehow managed to hype the children up.

'Can we have another one? Pretty please?' Annabelle pleads.

'I've got a few things I need to do tonight...' Sasha says, thinking about the CV and references that she still needs to amend. So that when Cecelia comes back and mentions them again, she won't be suspicious when Sasha passes them off as her own.

She needs to clean the bathroom too.

Though a few more minutes wouldn't hurt, would it? She had all night.

She sits with them for a while longer. Though instead of a story, they begin chatting about their day, mainly about school, until Annabelle is quiet for a few minutes.

'We wish Mummy would tell us stories like you do, Sasha,' Annabelle says, finally breaking her silence. 'She never has time to read. She always says she's too busy with work.'

'Yeah, busy on her 'puter,' Zachery chimes in, nodding animatedly in agreement with his older sister.

'Well, your mummy works very hard so that she can buy you lots of nice books and other things...' Sasha opens her hands as she glances around the room. The children seem to have so many toys and books. 'You want all these nice things, don't you?' she begins.

'Yeah, but what's the point of buying so many books and toys if she never has time to read or play with them? It's a bit stupid, isn't it?' Annabelle says, sounding ahead of her years once more, and Sasha realises that she doesn't have an answer for that.

Because to be fair to the child, Annabelle does have a point.

Sasha can tell that Annabelle has been feeling this way for a

while, because the little girl already told Sasha how their
mother barely ever sat at the dinner table with them and ate
their dinner, the way that Sasha had done tonight with them.
Annabelle had said that her mother always ate alone, while she
worked late into the night. Glued to her laptop.

'And sometimes...' Annabelle starts with caution, 'she gets
cross with us. If we don't stay in our beds. Sometimes Zachery
gets a bit scared and wants to sleep in with me, but if she hears
our voices, or our footsteps on the floor, she shouts at us.
Because she says we're interrupting her from doing her work.'

Sasha can hear how the resentment in Annabelle's voice
builds when she speaks about her mum. She can see the seed of
animosity that has been sown there, in Annabelle's mind. How
her mother doesn't have time for her. How she's always too busy
doing something else. Something more important.

Already the girl seems so much older and wiser than her
years. Since Sasha has arrived here at the house, she's witnessed
it herself, how Annabelle constantly takes care of her brother as
if it's her natural role. Checking that he's eaten his dinner, and
that he's warm enough now that he's in bed, as she pulls the
duvet tightly around them both. 'Well, I'm sure she doesn't
mean it when she shouts, she just wants you to get a good
night's sleep that's all. That's what a mummy's job is. To look
out for her children. To keep them safe and make sure that they
are sleeping properly when they go to bed,' Sasha says, her voice
quietening as her sentence tails off.

Annabelle and Zachery are luckier in ways that they'll
never truly understand. Cecelia may not be completely present,
but she means well. She is hard-working and caring. They all
live in this beautiful house. The children's bedrooms are immaculately decorated and full to the brim with toys. She sees it on
the children's faces though. How they have everything and
nothing all at once. How they have been spoiled with just stuff.
Plied with things to appease them in place of time with their

mother, in a bid to keep them occupied and busy. In a bid to relieve Cecelia of the burden of her guilt, for all the time she spends away from them.

For paying a nanny to do the job that she is too busy to do.

Sasha is sure that Cecelia means well. That she thinks that she is doing all of this for her kids. To give them a better life. The best life. Only in doing so, the woman is missing out on her children's precious early years.

Missing out on all the important bits that really count.

'I'm tired now,' Annabelle says, with a big yawn. Her words pulling Sasha back from her thoughts and she realises that she's been daydreaming. Her mind wandering off as she thought about her own mother. How she too had tried to give Sasha everything when she'd been growing up. All the latest clothes and toys. The endless classes and after-school clubs, in a bid to keep her entertained and out of mischief.

She had been the very same at Annabelle's age and beyond, and hadn't appreciated her mother's efforts at the time either.

Zachery is already asleep, and Sasha can see by the way that Annabelle's eyes are closing that the little girl won't be long behind him. Sasha kisses them both gently on the head.

'I like you being here,' Annabelle says, her voice muffled as she snuggles down further under the blanket and closes her eyes, giving in to sleep.

Sasha stands at the door for a few seconds. Surprised at the girl's words and the unexpectedly profound effect they have on her. For the protectiveness she feels towards the children in such a short space of time. She feels sad for Cecelia. How the woman is missing out on so much. How the children are too. They are only young once.

A pang of loss for her own mother now. In the ground. Dead.

They need their mother.

Sasha should know.

9

EMILY

'I've made us a nice pot of tea. I cleared the fridge out while I was at it, it smelt a bit funky. I think something might have gone off in there, you know. The milk's okay though. That's the main thing!' Charlotte says with a warm smile.

And I know what she's doing. As I sit on the edge of the bed now. My face burning with humiliation that I allowed myself to get so wound up by it all. So consumed by it all. By her.

The crying child.

She's trying to act normal. As if nothing has happened. As if me breaking down in tears in front of her was nothing to worry about.

But I am worried. I am embarrassed too, that Charlotte was here to witness it all. Me, at my lowest ebb. Spiralling back there.

To that place I've worked so hard to get away from.

Louise would have told her of course, she would have filled her in. Telling her all the sordid details of my history and why I'd been held at the facility in the first place.

She'd have told her what I'd done.

She'd know about my treatment too, though, wouldn't she?

Which meant she must know how much progress I've made since then. Because they wouldn't have moved me here otherwise. If they didn't think I was able to manage it. And I am. They don't put people in low-secure housing unless they are certain that they are no longer a threat to society.

I'm no longer a threat. I am better now. Aren't I?

Or at least I was.

'I've made it strong. Just how you like it,' Charlotte continues; her smile is warm and encouraging, her tone soft as she attempts to coax me into the chair.

Which, of course, works. I lick my dry, cracked lips at the thought of it. A nice hot cup of tea would help. Tea always helps. I am parched.

I smile as I reach the table and take a seat. Noting the effort that Charlotte has gone to, to make my tea just the way that I like it, how she's brewed it in my favourite green china teapot.

I am grateful for that. For the way she listens to me. How she really hears me.

Unlike Louise.

I am grateful for some company this afternoon too. A real person to talk to. Maybe sitting here with Charlotte would be enough of a distraction to enable me to drown out the sound of the girl. Because she's still here. Her voice grating on my last nerves.

'Here, let me,' Charlotte says as she pours the tea, before she hands me the cup and saucer, standing back and eyeing me with a satisfied look on her face, that I'm more settled now, that my outburst is over.

'I added an extra sugar. So it's nice and sweet. It will help,' she says, watching as I take my first sip.

The heat of the drink burns my mouth, tongue and throat and that's the bit that I relish the most. I drink it back in one big gulp. She is right. Tea always helps.

'Woah!' Charlotte laughs. 'I like mine hot, but even I can't drink it straight from the pot!' Then after a few seconds of silence she adds, 'Are you okay, Emily? I mean, like, really, okay?'

I nod my head. I am okay, aren't I? Now. With a cup of tea in my hand and Charlotte sitting just across the table. Better than okay, as I thank my lucky stars it was her who walked in on me having my breakdown tonight and not Louise.

I was lucky this time.

I can't afford to let it happen again.

'Are you sure, only you're very quiet? You don't seem yourself at all?' Charlotte says, her voice softer now, quieter. I see the look of concern on her face, as if she is as shocked by the change in me as I am. But then, she has only known me since I've lived here, in this flat. For two short weeks.

She only knows the me now.

She doesn't know the me from before.

When they'd locked me up in there. If she did, she probably wouldn't like me either. She'd be just like the rest of them. The staff barely tolerating me, speaking at me through gritted teeth, their eyes directed anywhere but at mine as if they couldn't even bear to look at me.

Charlotte's never looked at me like that.

She holds my eye. She reads my body language, she notices my tone. She seems as if she genuinely wants to help. As if she sees something in me that isn't all bad and dark and bleak. But I still don't know if I can trust her.

'You won't tell her, will you?' I say suddenly, unable to sit here for a second longer without telling her what is on my mind. 'She'll send me back there again, to that horrible place. They'll lock me away.'

'I'm sure they won't...' Charlotte begins, only we both hear the uncertainty in her voice. She isn't sure either.

But I am. I know how these things work. I know exactly what Louise will do the second she thinks that I'm spiralling back there again. Nothing would give her more satisfaction, I think to myself.

'Louise doesn't like me,' I confess, staring over at the door, checking that she isn't about to come through it, that she can't hear me. 'None of them like me, because of what happened.' I clear my throat. 'Because of what I did.'

I search Charlotte's eyes then. For a clue, an inkling of what is going on in her thoughts behind them.

Only she gives nothing away.

She must know though, surely? Louise would have told her; she would have given her every single detail. Only Charlotte is purposely not reacting. She is making a point to not judge me.

'If you tell her that I can hear the girl again, she'll send me back there. To the secure unit. They'll lock me away. With all the mad people. And I'm not mad...' I say.

The child is real.

The child is real.

'Louise only wants the best for you... We all do...' Charlotte says again, only for her words to be cut short as I slam my cup down hard on the table. Making her jump.

'NO!' I shout. 'Louise does not want the best for me. You don't know her the way that I do. If you tell her about the girl, she'll put me back there again.'

'Who is she? Who is the girl you hear?' Charlotte asks as she looks at me blankly, as if I am talking in riddles.

'The little girl on the other side of the wall. The one who is always crying,' I say, and I see her shift awkwardly in her chair. Her eyes following mine as I look around the room. My eyes stopping where the noise comes from. Through the wall that joins this room to the property next door.

'Is she crying now?'

'Can you really not hear her?'

I stare at Charlotte as she concentrates, narrowing her eyes as she listens intently. She can't possibly hear the girl, because if she did, she wouldn't need to strain to listen. The girl is loud. Her cries fill the room.

'Maybe? I'm not sure...' Charlotte says eventually. Her words are spoken with care. As if she's almost worried to say them out loud. 'It's very faint...'

I look at her. Her cheeks flushed pink, her wide eyes almost exaggerated.

'You can't hear her, can you?' I say, still seated. My hands clasped tightly together on my lap. She is being kind, I realise. She is trying to make me feel as if I am not going mad. When in fact, maybe I am.

'Who is she, Emily? You can tell me. I won't tell Louise,' Charlotte whispers now, her hand clinging to mine as if to offer me some kind of hidden strength. To help me find the words that are there, lingering in the back of my throat.

'Is it them? Are they the ones that you hear? The little girl and boy from back then...'

Charlotte's eyes search mine and I know immediately that she knows it all. Louise has told her everything about what had happened back then. In that house. With the children.

'No,' I lie as I pull my hand free from hers.

Charlotte's spell is now broken. I am not ready to talk about any of that. I am not ready to talk about them. Charlotte might mean well, but she is one of them and I know deep down that I can't trust her. I can't trust any of them.

If I tell her what happened, what really happened, what would she think? She'd be just like Louise then, wouldn't she?

She'll think that she knows it all, but she doesn't, she can't.

Because they weren't there.

They only know what they were told.

What I told them.

10

SASHA

'Wow! Hello, er, where are my children? I've only been away for two days, what happened? Have aliens landed and replaced you both?' Cecelia laughs as she walks into the kitchen, an expression of surprise on her face to see the children sitting nicely at the breakfast bar, finishing their breakfast. 'Washed and dressed already, huh! Well, this is a lovely surprise.'

'Mummy!' the children chorus, having not seen the woman for two days now.

'Hello, darlings!' Cecelia says, making her way over to where they both sit before she gives them a kiss and a hug.

'They've been as good as gold, the pair of them! How was your business trip? I did wait up last night, but I must have fallen asleep by the time you got back?' Sasha beams as she pours Cecelia a fresh cup of coffee and hands it to her. Wanting to show the woman that she could more than handle the responsibility of minding her two children.

'Oh, thank you! I could get used to this,' Cecelia says with a warm smile as she cradles the hot mug in her hands gratefully. 'I got back very late last night. And I am utterly exhausted this morning but, alas, I've got another manic day, I'm afraid. But I guess I've just got to do it while the work's there. I mean, there are worse things to complain about than a new business taking off, isn't there?!'

'Are you going away again, Mummy?' Zachery asks, pouting as if he's about to cry.

'Only for one night this time, sweetie. I thought that I'd get everything done while I was there, but I've got to get back to Manchester again, later today, and it's going to be another late one. Will that be okay with you?'

Sasha nods in agreement, watching as Cecelia glances at the calendar then and visibly winces as she reads the handwriting scrawled on the box marked today's date.

'Oh, no! Annabelle. I'm so sorry, honey! Your school garden project is due in today. How on earth did I forget that?!' Cecelia shakes her head crossly with herself, before catching Sasha's eye. 'She's been pestering me for weeks to help her with it, and I meant to, I just totally forgot. The days are just all merging into one...' Cecelia starts to explain. Mumbling her words apologetically as she glances over to Annabelle, an expectant look on her face. Waiting for the tantrum that she knows is coming. That she fully deserves too.

But the response from her daughter is far worse than that.

She is met only with indifference.

'Never mind! It doesn't matter any more because Sasha did it with me, yesterday, before dinner.' Annabelle shrugs, her tone unconcerned, not bothering to look up from where she's spooning the last few Shreddies from her bowl into her mouth.

'She did?' Cecelia asks, relief evident in her voice. 'You did?'

Sasha nods before adding, 'But only because I saw that you'd marked it on your calendar. I asked Annabelle about it, and she wasn't sure if we'd have time to put it all together, but somehow, we did. I hope that's okay?'

THE BABYSITTER'S SECRET 55

Sasha makes her way to the utility room, returning with a huge painted cardboard box in her hands.

'This is the masterpiece. Annabelle worked so hard on it,' Sasha says, placing it down on the kitchen island for Cecelia to admire.

'Oh, Annabelle. This looks fantastic!' Cecelia says, the praise in her voice genuine as her eyes sweep the beautiful miniature garden that her daughter created: its intricate rockery that had been made from painted egg boxes, and rows of bright and colourful flowers that had been made from fixing crumpled pieces of tissue paper to thick green pipe cleaners.

'Sasha let me use her make-up mirror for the duck pond,' Annabelle says, beaming with pride at the finished result, before shooting a huge smile at Sasha.

'And Sasha let me make my own duck from yellow tissue paper. I was allowed to keep it too,' Zachery says, not wanting to be left out. And it's only then that Cecelia spots it. The tiny yellow duck that is sitting next to Zachery's bowl, its head tilted down towards the tiny splodge of milk on the worktop to make it look like the duck is eating his breakfast too.

'Well, I'm super impressed. And wow, is that our tree-house?' Cecelia says, taking a closer look at the garden and grinning when she sees the tree at the very back of the garden, with the little wooden hut made from lollypop sticks halfway up the trunk. A small drawing that has been coloured and cut out, and stuck on the inside, of a woman sitting with a little girl and boy either side of her. 'Ooh, I love the way you've done my hair.'

'That's not you, Mummy! That's Sasha!' Annabelle purses her mouth before rolling her eyes dramatically. 'You're not home, you're at work. Again.'

'Oh, right,' Cecelia starts, stung a little by the cold, dismissive tone her daughter uses.

'We played in the treehouse just before we started making the garden, didn't we, Sasha? It was so fun.' Zachery beams.

'Sasha said it can be our secret den. That we can take our books and blankets out there one evening and have a story in there before we go to bed. She said I can bring my rocket torch. She said we can have hot chocolate too.'

'Oh, that's lovely. Maybe I could join you.'

'Yeah maybe,' Zachery says without any enthusiasm. As if he too was expecting his mother to make another promise to him that she can't keep. Cecelia feels it, the sting of her children's words. How neither of them are hanging from her own any more.

They have Sasha to have fun with now.

Sasha sees it too, the hurt in Cecelia's expression. That she's been excluded.

'Right, kids. We need shoes, coats and book bags please. We are leaving in five minutes,' Sasha says, in a bid to break the growing tension. Glad when the kids do as they are told, getting up from their seats and putting their bowls in the sink, before leaving the room without so much as a single word of an argument.

'I don't know how you do it.' Cecelia shakes her head and smiles now, as if she can't believe what she's seeing. 'You've only been here a couple of days and well, they're like different children. They seem to have really taken a shine to you.'

'Isn't that always the way though. Kids always behave better for everyone else other than their parents. I think it's like, the law or something,' Sasha says with a laugh, hoping to lighten the mood. She can see that Cecelia is impressed with her doing such a great job with the kids, but she can also hear the underlying bitterness there that her children seem happier in Sasha's company than hers.

'Hey, they missed you, you know. They spoke about you non-stop,' Sasha says, and it's not a lie. They had spoken about Cecelia a lot. Though most of it hadn't been favourable. Still, Cecelia didn't need to know that.

'Did they?' Cecelia says, not entirely sure if she can believe that. The children seem indifferent to her somehow. 'God, it's always such a dilemma, isn't it? Juggling everything. Trying to make everything work. It's like one thing excels and everything else around it just turns to chaos and disarray. Why can't I seem to do it all?'

'You're doing a great job!' Sasha says, reassuring Cecelia now. 'They are great kids and that's down to you. God, I can't even imagine how hard it's been, running your own interior design business and making such a success of it, while bringing up two small children. And you're going through a divorce too. None of that can be easy.'

Cecelia takes a slow deep breath.

'You're right. It has been a lot. I don't know, maybe because I'm tired, I'm feeling a bit more sensitive than usual. I just don't want the kids to start resenting me, you know. For being so busy all the time. For "always being at work",' Cecelia says earnestly.

'And I guess the main thing is that the children are happy, and they do seem very happy with you, Sasha. I know that the cover you're providing is just temporary until Jenny is well enough to come back, but actually, I'd really like it if you stayed. What do you think?' Cecelia asks.

'Well, I guess that I could,' Sasha says after a few seconds of hesitation. As she thinks of the house. Of how she hasn't found anything solid here yet, that confirms any of the fractured memories that float around inside of her head, but she still feels that in time, she will.

She can't give up just yet. Besides, she's really enjoying looking after Annabelle and Zachery. The children give her a sense of purpose, they keep her busy, and she needs that. To stop being so much inside of her own head, especially after her mother's passing. They make her feel as if she is very much wanted here too. Sasha likes that. She likes them.

'Okay! I'd love to. Don't worry about the agency, I'll call

them and let them know!' Sasha grins widely, and Cecelia returns it.

'Perfect! Annabelle and Zackery will be thrilled. In fact, I'm going to go and break the news to them, right now!'

Sasha stands against the counter and scans the room. The large open-plan kitchen that had been added to the house after Cecelia and Henry had taken over the property's renovations. A part of the house that hadn't even existed when she'd been here all those years ago.

She needs to concentrate on the older, original part of the house.

The bedrooms upstairs. The bathroom. The garden too.

There are answers here. Even though, so far, she hasn't found herself any closer to getting them, she knows deep down that they are here.

Lingering just underneath the surface, waiting for her to discover them.

She just needs more time.

Time, which Cecelia has just kindly gifted to her.

11

SASHA

Sasha opens her eyes and scans the darkness of her bedroom. Something had woken her?

She's been at the house a week now and yet it still manages to catch her by surprise, when she wakes in complete darkness with a jolt from one of her nightmares, forgetting where she is. Tonight though, it is not another one of her dreams that has woken her.

Someone is here in the room with her.

'Zachery?' Sasha sits up, staring at Zachery as he stands silently at the foot of her bed. His blond mop of hair falling down across his blue eyes, but not enough so that it conceals the puffiness there. Is he crying?

'Zachery? Are you okay, sweetheart?' Sasha glances over at the clock and sees that it's almost 2 a.m. She guesses that Zachery has woken up in the middle of the night looking for his mum, only to find her bed still empty.

Cecelia has worked away a lot lately and Sasha had decided not to make a big deal about it. Not wanting to disrupt the new routine she'd got the children into. She'd figured that as soon as she got them both to sleep, there would be no point in telling them that their mother wouldn't be home again tonight. They'd sleep right through until morning without noticing. Only that clearly hadn't worked.

'Don't be sad, Zachery. Mummy will be home tomorrow. You can see her when you get back from nursery.'

The boy doesn't answer; instead he stands there unmoving, staring at her intently, his eyes boring through her as if he's in a trance.

'Zachery honey? Are you okay?'

He is sleepwalking, she thinks. He doesn't even realise that he is here, standing in her room at the foot of her bed. Getting up, Sasha moves slowly towards him not wanting to startle him. She knows only too well from experience how that feels. She doesn't turn the lamp on and it's too dark to see his features properly, but he looks different in this light.

Not just his face, but there is something about his stance too. Something about his posture.

He seems smaller somehow. His body chunkier.

'Zachery, darling. Can you hear me? You're asleep, sweetie. I'm going to take you back to bed,' Sasha whispers.

And he hears her. He must, because as she nears him, he holds out a small, chubby hand, as if he is aware that she is there, as he wills her to take it. Sasha stretches out her hand to do just that. So that she can guide him back to his bed without waking him, only just as her fingers almost touch his, the little boy disappears.

Gone. Disappearing into thin air.

She is alone again, standing disorientated in the middle of the dark, empty room.

'Zachery?' she says, her gaze sweeping each corner of the room as she searches for signs that he was here, past the pretty, green, wooden dressing table and stool that sit beneath the window. A velour chair in the corner, holding the clothing that she took off last night and threw there.

'Zachery?' she calls out, but the sound is strained from her mouth, forced.

The room feels suddenly hot and stuffy. As if all the air has been sucked from it. Her skin is clammy, dripping with perspiration as her heart hammers inside of her chest. Just like she feels when she wakes from one of her own nightmares.

Was that what just happened? Had she dreamt that she had seen Zachery standing here? Only, she feels as if she's just seen a ghost.

She needs to check on the children, she decides, wrapping a gown around her, before padding quietly out onto the landing. Noting how the door to Cecelia's bedroom is still wide open. The bed still immaculately made and empty as she passes it, making her way to Annabelle's bedroom then, to where she'd left the children snuggled up together earlier in Annabelle's bed.

The little girl's bedroom door is cracked slightly ajar from where they'd insisted upon having a beam of light pour into the room from the hallway, to comfort them.

Sasha had painstakingly stood there closing the door ever so softly, so slowly, checking when the perfect point to stop is. And if she got it wrong and closed it too much, they made her start again.

She had her suspicions that the children were just playing with her, seeing how much they could get her to do for them without complaining. Because she doubted that it was part of their regular routine. Cecelia wouldn't have the patience for that. Not from what Annabelle had told her about the woman.

She stands in the doorway now and peers in through the gap, noting how Annabelle's little body is sprawled out on the bed, the covers down by her legs where she'd kicked them off in a bid to cool down. Zackery is lying next to her. His side of the duvet is pulled up tightly around his chin, his chest rising and falling beneath it. His thumb firmly inside his mouth.

He is sleeping so soundly that she's sure there's no way that he could have moved from his bed just minutes ago. It can't have been him that she saw in her room. But how can that be? Because she was certain that she'd seen him. Hadn't she? Perhaps she'd been dreaming after all.

Perhaps she'd been the one who was sleepwalking?

It wouldn't be the first time that happened and every time it had before it had always felt the same, hadn't it?

Real.

She feels silly as she tiptoes back into her room and closes the door quietly behind her. Anger coming for her then.

She's annoyed with herself that her nightmares can still catch her off guard like this. That they can still sneak up on her like that and make her doubt what is real and what is not. That they can still play tricks on her.

She should know better by now, because she's suffered bad dreams all of her life, ever since she was a small child. Plagued with them, so often back then, that she hadn't known sleep without them. She thought that everyone was the same as her, that they closed their eyes and only saw dark, unsettling visions at night.

For a while her bad dreams had taunted her too much that, like Zachery and Annabelle, she'd been forced to sleep with a night light on, or to not sleep at all. She's older now, her nightmares less frequent. When they come now, these days, they are just the vague, distant merging of shapeless, fuzzy bad dreams, that she can no longer reach after she has woken.

Tonight was different. She had felt it, how her nightmare had played out in vivid, technicolour detail. Had it been Zachery that she'd seen standing there? Only he had looked different. Smaller, his face fatter. It had been his eyes that had haunted her. How they had stared right through her.

His expression empty.

Stop it. Stop freaking yourself out! she chastises herself, knowing that she won't be able to go back to sleep now, even if she wanted to.

She thinks about going downstairs and making a nice, strong cup of tea, but she doesn't want to chance making any noise and disturbing the children. She turns the lamp on instead, and picks up her book, about to get into bed and read for a while, in the hope that it would be enough of a distraction to keep her from overthinking things. Creepy things in this creepy house.

Only something stops her.

The lamp light reflecting on the opposite wall. Casting shadows there which outline the faint rectangle shape etched in the floral wallpaper.

She hadn't noticed it until now. How there is a small cupboard door, concealed with matching wallpaper, blended in almost seamlessly with the rest of the wall. She feels curiosity get the better of her as she makes her way over to it, before she bends down and wedges her fingers into the gap around the door, then yanking it open and peering in.

It's dark inside, but she can see enough to know that the empty crawlspace spans the length of this bedroom. To her disappointment there is nothing of any interest inside. There is nothing inside at all. The cupboard holds no undiscovered clues or secrets for her.

She's about to close the door and go back to bed, to stop encouraging the vivid imagination from getting the better of her once and for all, only she spots something up ahead, hanging from the wall at the back of the cupboard. A small piece of green and gold flocked peeling wallpaper. A flash of familiarity as something clicks inside her mind.

The sound of a child's voice.

Green, Gold. Green, Gold.

The voice repeating the words over and over again, all the while she imagines a tiny, thin finger tracing the raised foil pattern that runs across the wallpaper.

Was it her finger? Her voice? Had she been in here before? Inside this cupboard?

She feels that she might have been. A small jolt of adrenaline surges through her as she wonders if this wallpaper might be part of the original house, that it's the same wallpaper that had been here all those years ago. When she'd been here too.

Finally, she'd found something real that she could relate to. Something that has stirred a curious feeling inside of her.

She needs to look closer.

Pushing the cupboard door wide open, to allow as much light into the crawlspace as possible, still she can't see from here. So, she starts to crawl. Shuffling along the dark narrow space on her hands and knees. The urge to run her fingers over the wallpaper one more time so much stronger than her fear of small, claustrophobic spaces. She doesn't think about that right now. About how the walls feel as if they are closing in on her as she moves.

How it is so dark that she can barely see her own hand in front of her.

That there might be creepy crawlies in here.

Focus!

She keeps her head down and her mouth closed tight. Flinching a few feet in as she feels the silky spider's web breaking against the skin of her cheeks. Another few feet and she is there, at the very back of the cupboard. A bigger patch of wallpaper now directly in front of her. The same as the smaller piece she saw before. She has seen this paper before. Deep green embossed with a shimmering gold. Peeling and torn at the edges, coming away from the wall.

The wallpaper doesn't hold her attention as she'd hoped it would, because now she is here, her eyes are drawn to something else. To the five jagged lines that are etched in the wall directly beneath it.

Claw marks, like small, narrow scratches from someone's fingernails.

A small child's?

Shaking, her heart hammers in her chest as she reaches out her own fingers and traces the gouges in the wall, to check that this isn't her mind playing another trick on her. That she is not seeing things that aren't really there.

She feels them.

Are they hers?

An image flashes in her mind then, of being stuck inside a small dark space just like this. She is crying. She is shouting to be let out. Kicking frantically at the door. Clawing at the walls. Begging and screaming for someone to let her out. The memory is so consuming that before she realises it, Sasha is unable to breathe. Her chest feels tight, the air gone from inside of her as if the oxygen from the crawlspace has evaporated.

She just needs to get out.

Moving backwards, shuffling quickly now, back towards the door, panic inside of her rising rapidly. She no longer cares about spiders or mice. She is almost there.

Almost at the door when a rush of sudden cold air fills the crawlspace, and she is plunged into complete pitch-black darkness.

Someone has shut the cupboard door, she realises to her horror.

Someone has locked her inside.

12

EMILY

The smell wakes me.

Charlotte had mentioned it yesterday. How she thought that something had gone off in the fridge. How she'd thrown some of the food out. The smell had only been faint then. Like a mild whiff of milk that has soured, lingering in the air around us. Now though, the smell is potent. Suddenly it is so much worse. Like something rancid and rotting that's been fermenting in the heat of the room, while I have been sleeping.

It's pungent, like rotten eggs. So acrid, that it makes me feel sick. Saliva fills my cheeks and I think I am going to gag. I'm going to vomit right here on the floor next to my bed. I cover my nose and mouth with my hand and drag myself up from where I lie, making my way to the fridge, convinced that something must have gone bad in there and Charlotte must have missed it. I hesitate, reluctant to open the door, expecting the waft of rot to overpower me. But when I open the door, the smell does not get worse, and as I lift and examine each bottle and packet of food that's stored inside, checking the dates, checking for any signs of discolouration or smell, I realise that the smell isn't coming from the fridge at all.

It is coming from somewhere else inside my flat.

I turn and scan the space, wracking my brain to think of what I last ate. A microwave meal of pasta tonight before bed, the plate washed up and already put away. I'd made myself a cheese sandwich, earlier, for lunch. But I'd eaten it all. It's not like me to leave dirty cups or plates with food on them simply lying around the place to go bad.

Untidiness makes me feel anxious. A clean and tidy flat means a clean and tidy head. That's what I tell myself anyway, because I'm so particular about my living space. Especially now I'm here, in this flat, all of my own. At last. I would never ruin that. I might not have much, but what I do have, I like to keep organised and neat. Everything is washed and cleaned and put away in its rightful place. So what is causing the stench?

I brave it and take one more long, deep breath, trying to decipher what direction it's coming from, only the smell of rot makes me heave. The smell is everywhere now, I think as a fly buzzes above me in the air. A bluebottle. A sinking feeling then inside my stomach, an awful thought inside my head. Bluebottles are not a good sign. And hadn't I seen a couple yesterday too? What if something has got in here? What if an animal has somehow found its way into my room and died somewhere?

I search the room. The corners, under the sofa. Down behind the TV unit. Anxiety bubbling away in the pit of my stomach as I pull the dresser out from the wall. Because I am running out of places. I'll find whatever it is soon. I pull out the bin. Unsure of what I am looking for but look I must. Because this smell isn't going to go away, it's only going to get worse. Soon I have searched everywhere.

Almost everywhere. I stare over at my messy bed. The duvet hanging from where I'd thrown it from me when I'd got up. I'd smelled it over there first, hadn't I? The stench had been stronger there. Worse.

I hesitate for a few seconds and then I move.

Crouching down on my hands and knees, I peer underneath the bed frame, wincing as I do, because sure enough there is something there. Pushed right at the very back by the wall.

Whatever it is, I can't see it properly from here.

What is it?

I'm not prepared to crawl under there to find out; instead I get back up and drag the bed frame out across the carpet, into the middle of the room. Before making my way around to the other side, my eyes wide with fear as I look down. To my horror it is moving.

I scream, convinced that it is a rat. Squeezing my eyes tightly shut for a few seconds in a pathetic attempt to shut it out.

Deal with it. You have dealt with worse.

I open my eyes again, and that's when I realise that the movement isn't an animal at all. The thing I am looking at is not alive. I peer closer, my mouth in a grimace. My heart thudding inside my chest. It's a small plastic tray of what looks like raw chicken breasts. The wrapper has been cut open to expose the green-grey, slimy-looking slabs of meat inside.

Rotten meat.

Writhing with hundreds of wriggling fat maggots.

13

SASHA

The cupboard door doesn't budge, no matter how hard she hits at it with her fists.

She's losing all sanity, all reasoning now. Being locked away in here in the dark, wild panic consumes her, and she no longer cares that it's the middle of the night and the children are in their beds, sleeping soundly. She wants them to hear her. She wants them to come and let her out.

'Annabelle? Zachery?' she screams hysterically as tears cascade down her cheeks. Tears full of shame and embarrassment. Because she does not cry. Ever. She refuses to. But she is crying now. Brought so low, so vulnerable in just a few seconds. Her fear of small tight spaces has always had this kind of a hold on her. From as far back as she could remember. She should never have crawled in here.

'Please, let me out! Let me out!'

Her voice no longer her own. Laced with strangled fear, the terror makes her sound almost unrecognisable even to her own ears. She needs to get out. She needs air. She needs to breathe.

Because she is going to die if she is left in here for a minute longer.

Her heart can't take it, it will simply give out.

She is going to die. She is going to die. She is going to die.

She is back there again.

Trapped in this small, tight space. The door is shut, she can't get out. Her fingers clawing at the walls. Her legs and feet kicking out, slamming against the walls and door in a desperate bid to get out.

Her head is sore, she feels a trickle of something warm running down her forehead and even in the pitch, black darkness, as she wipes it, she knows it's blood.

'Let me out. Let me out,' she screams.

And someone does.

Finally. The door opens and there is a man standing there.

Reaching into the cupboard he pulls her out.

Rush.

The memory dissolves just as Sasha manages to push the door wide open.

A gust of air pours in. Light too.

Sasha doesn't wait. She moves then, frantically. Scrambling to get out. Throwing herself onto the thick bedroom carpet. Sprawled there, she gulps huge greedy bursts of air down into her lungs and closes her eyes tightly, to shut out the memory of what just happened to her.

She is safe. She is out.

Nothing can harm her now.

'Sasha?' Cecelia's voice cuts through the darkness, and it's only then, as Sasha's eyes flicker back open, that she sees Cecelia crouching down next to her. Her coat and boots still on as if she'd only just come through the front door.

'Are you okay?' Cecelia asks, an expression of concern flashing across her face as she crouches at Sasha's side. 'I heard you screaming... Were you inside the crawlspace?'

Cecelia eyes the cupboard door, which is wide open now,

and the sight of Sasha sprawled on the floor in front of it, gasping for breath. 'What were you doing in there?'

Sasha shakes her head, still trying to catch her breath, not wanting to admit that she'd willingly gone in there to look at the small familiar piece of flaking wallpaper on the back wall. Because that would have made her sound mad.

That she'd been creeping inside the crawlspace in the dead of night. How the fear had rapidly spread through her at the sight of the deep scratches gouged inside the cupboard's walls. Scratches that she is convinced she had once made. Because she remembered it then. How she'd been inside that cupboard before. She'd felt it. The memory of the utter terror behind that closed door. The panic she had felt at not being able to get out.

It would make her sound crazy, wouldn't it?

And what about the little boy standing at the foot of her bed, how she'd thought that it had been Zachery standing there, but how he'd disappeared as she'd got close to him. How he'd simply vanished into thin air. Cecelia would think she was unhinged, coming home and hearing all of this.

'I think I was sleepwalking,' Sasha answers. Her voice quiet and small as she plays it down. And it's only a half lie. She might be wide awake now, but she hadn't been awake for all of it, had she? Maybe she had been sleepwalking after all. Maybe she dreamt about the little boy. She could accept that. How he can't have been anything more than a figment of her imagination. Only, being locked in the cupboard had felt so real.

'You were sleepwalking?' Cecelia doesn't look convinced.

Sasha nods before she sits up and tries to compose herself. Mortified at how weird she must look now, at how weak she must have seemed as she lay panting breathlessly on the bedroom floor. She needs to calm down, to compose herself. To disguise the distress that is still surging around her body. Cecelia had only left her alone with the kids for the past twenty-four hours and this was what she'd walked back in to.

Sasha, clearly not coping.

She needs to pull herself together. To show Cecelia that she is capable of being here alone and looking after her kids.

'I do that sometimes, yes. Not often though. Mainly when I was a kid,' Sasha admits, not adding how she's spent a lifetime plagued by nightmares and sleep terrors. Often waking in the middle of the night, to find herself standing in the strangest of places, doing the strangest of things with no memory of how she'd got there.

'I keep meaning to sort out that cupboard door. It always catches and sticks, especially as the weather gets colder. Do you want me to get you anything? A glass of water? You look as if you've had quite a fright.'

'No, honestly, I'm fine. I'm just embarrassed. I thought that I was locked in, and I just panicked. I'm so sorry that you've come home to this. We've been doing just great.'

'Please, don't be embarrassed. Stuff happens.'

'How come you came back early?' Sasha asks, remembering how Cecelia had told her she wouldn't be back until tomorrow afternoon at the earliest. That she'd see her and the children, once they'd finished school.

'I made the deal. Downed the obligatory glass of champagne and jumped on the last train home. I just wanted my own bed! I've got an early start again tomorrow, but at least I'll get to spend five minutes with the kids,' Cecelia explained before adding, 'Are you sure you're okay?'

Sasha nods.

'Well, if you need anything, give me a shout. Good night,' Cecelia says, excusing herself.

And Sasha knows that the woman is being kind, that she is giving her some space and privacy to recover. She needs that. Alone once more, Sasha takes a long, deep breath. Cecelia had been more than understanding but she'd seen the expression of uncertainty on the woman's face that had matched her tone.

The woman wasn't convinced that Sasha was all right at all, but she was giving her the benefit of the doubt. Sasha couldn't afford to let something like this happen again. Because Cecelia might start to question if Sasha is stable. If she is up for this job of looking after her children while she is away. Sasha is so close now to finding the answers that she came here for, she is sure of it.

She just needs more time.

Her heartbeat finally slows back down to normal, and Sasha starts to feel calmer again. More in control.

Forcing herself to go back to inspect the cupboard door, she runs her finger down the doorway and rests on the small, narrow white bolt. Had the lock caught like Cecelia had told her, or had someone physically pulled it across and locked her in? Because it had felt as if someone had locked her in. She thinks about the little boy then, standing at the end of her bed. He had been a figment of her imagination, hadn't he?

14

EMILY

I heave loudly. My throat raw, I retch violently as I throw the tray of maggot-infested chicken breasts into a bin bag and double bag it, before tying it tightly and taking it down the two flights of stairs to the back door. Outside, I dump it in one of the communal bins, but I can still smell it. The strong stench of sulphur floating up the stairwell with me, in every hallway.

It's still here in my flat when I return. For a while I think it's on me. That the pungent scent is engrained in my hair, my clothes, my skin. I need to shower, I need to wash my clothes and scrub at my hair and my skin, but first I need to clean the flat. It takes me hours. Cleaning everything properly, scrubbing everything thoroughly. The smell gradually fades beneath the overpowering smell of bleach. And white vinegar. And baking soda.

I have tried all the cleaning hacks, yet when I'm done, the smell of rotten meat still lingers.

I need air. Wrenching open the windows as wide as they will go, I savour the burst of cool air that rushes in and sweeps around the room. Soon, it's freezing, and I want nothing more than to shut them again and keep the cool air out. Only the bleach I've poured all over the carpet is so strong, it's burning my eyes and my throat and it's making my head throb. In my angst, I used too much. Pouring the liquid all over the carpet beneath my bed until it was saturated. I've soaked the edge of the skirting that lines that wall too, just in case any of the maggots have somehow found their way into the tiny gap beneath it.

It's done. Nothing remains of the rotten meat now. But the overwhelming feeling of something dark lingers. I stand with my arms wrapped tightly around myself, as if to stop the feeling of crawling beneath my flesh. I scratch at my arms, clawing at my skin as if to relieve the itch there, as if the maggots have found their way in. I need a shower.

'Oh, are you having a spring clean, Emily?' Louise's voice startles me.

I'd been so preoccupied with dragging my furniture back now that I'd disinfected the room, with the uneasy feeling inside of me, that I hadn't heard her come in. I am not ready for her. I see her, staring around the room, her nose wrinkling at the smell, a strange expression on her face. I see it. How her mouth is twisted. How she looks as if she is trying her hardest not to smirk.

Oh my God, it was her.

She doesn't have to say it, I just know.

She is the one who did this to me.

Now, she is waiting for my reaction. Standing just inside the doorway, waiting for me to tell her about the decayed, maggot-infested meat that 'someone' had shoved underneath my bed. She wants me to show my disgust. My upset. Any kind of emotion at all. When I do, she will take great satisfaction in downplaying it. She will humour me or worse, gaslight me into blaming myself. Planting her seeds that will leave me wondering if, somehow, I had been the one who had dropped the meat down there. She'll try and make me believe that this was all my doing.

You've only just moved in, she'll say. *You're still finding your feet.*

This is all so new to you. Living here on your own.

These things happen.

She says that one a lot. As if they simply need no other explanation than that. As if she is only *confirming* her views that she thinks that I am not ready yet for this. To live here, alone. To be rehabilitated back into the community. Well, I'm not going to give that bitch the satisfaction.

'I just thought I'd give the place a good go-over. My mum used to spring clean our house once a month. "A clean home is a happy home", she'd say!' I keep my back to her. Because I can't look her in the eye right now.

I hate her. I hate her so much that I'm worried I'll say it. That my hatred for her will pour out of my mouth and I won't be able to control myself or the level of anger there. I'm not stupid, I know the rules. I know my place in this game. I know that no matter what, she won't let me win. It will be my word against theirs. Against hers.

I have put up with these kinds of twisted, provoking games by these bullies. I've learned to accept them now.

How the support workers and healthcare assistants, who despise me for what I did, like to treat me.

How some think that I need to be punished more. For longer.

That I don't deserve this second chance.

And maybe I don't.

But I've been given one. Another chance at this half-life, scraped together from the ashes of the life I'd destroyed before. Finally, I am ready to take it. I am going to grab it with both hands. Even if it means that I have to pretend that Louise isn't trying to make my life harder. That she hasn't got it in for me, when I know that she has.

Even if I have to do everything in my power to ignore the sound of the crying girl, to make out that it isn't happening. So that I don't react.

Because everyone deserves a second chance.

Including me.

15

SASHA

She has overslept. After lying awake for hours in the middle of the night, riddled with anxiety about the cupboard in her room and how she ended up locked inside, she must have passed out from exhaustion. She doesn't even remember turning the alarm off this morning when it rang out. That's how tired she must have been.

Now, she is late. The one morning that she knows Cecelia has to be up and out of the house early. Hadn't she told her last night that she had an early start? That she'd only have a few minutes with the children this morning.

Urgh! Sasha will end up being asked to leave if she isn't careful; already she has made herself look as if she can't cope.

Getting dressed as quickly as she can, she takes the stairs, hearing Cecelia's voice ringing out as the woman moves noisily around the kitchen. Breakfast bowls clanging loudly as they are placed on the breakfast bar. The sound of cereal being poured out. The children arguing animatedly.

'She's got more than me.'

'He just took my spoon.'

'That's enough!' Cecelia says, and Sasha can hear it. The

tension in her voice. How she is trying her hardest to hold in her temper.

'Sasha!' The children scream excitedly in union as Sasha walks into the kitchen, before they jump down from their stools and wrap their arms around her. Sasha is grateful for that. That the children's display of affection towards her will prove to Cecelia that she is good enough to be here. That she's doing a great job really.

'Wow, anyone would have thought it was you who had worked away the past few days, not me,' Cecelia quips, a look of what Sasha assumes is irritation on her face.

Or is it exhaustion? Because Cecelia has black, puffy circles under her eyes and Sasha knows that's on her.

'I'm so sorry that I didn't hear the alarm go off. Or maybe I did, but I was just so tired that I don't remember switching it off,' Sasha stutters apologetically, still feeling a pang of embarrassment at how Cecelia had found her when she'd returned home late last night.

'You don't remember switching it off, because you didn't. I did. I figured you could do with an extra hour in bed,' Cecelia says, her back to Sasha as she busies herself pouring out two cups of tea before she places one down in front of her. 'Strong, one sugar, boiling hot, right? You seem to have the magic touch! They haven't stop bickering since they woke up,' Cecelia adds, nodding to where the children had got back on their seats at Sasha's instruction and were now quickly and quietly spooning mouthfuls of cereal into their mouths. Both wanting to impress Sasha with who would finish their breakfast first.

'They are good kids...' Sasha says, just as the children start arguing again.

Sasha recalled that Annabelle had confided how Cecelia always seemed short-tempered with them. How she was always telling them off. Sasha had wondered about that, because from what she'd seen so far, the children were incredibly well-behaved. At least they were until they were in Cecelia's company.

'Mummy! Zachery just dipped his hand in my cereal!' Annabelle's squeals fill the room and she hits out at her brother.

'Ouch! You're not allowed to hit me!' Zachery pouts, tears forming in his eyes at the sting of the slap that his older sister just gave him.

'And you're not allowed to eat like a pig,' Annabelle counters, her words sounding as if they'd just left her mother's mouth not hers, before she deliberately begins to wind her brother up, making snorting noises.

'Stop it, Annabelle. I'm not a pig. Tell her, Mummy, I'm not a pig. I'M NOT!'

'Ouch! Don't kick!' Annabelle screeches as Zachery takes it upon himself to kick his older sister.

'Enough, Annabelle!'

Zachery loses his temper, swiping the bowl of cereal across the breakfast bar and sending milk and sugary cereal hoops across the floor and up the nearby wall.

'I SAID THAT'S ENOUGH!' It was Cecelia's turn to scream as she stares in horror at the trail of milk dripping down the wall and onto her laptop bag that she'd stupidly placed beneath it. 'If you two are not going to eat properly, then you're not eating at all. You can both go hungry.' Cecelia's temper finally getting the better of her, she moves between them, pulling their chairs out. 'Go on, go up to your rooms until it's time for Sasha to take you to school. Go on...'

'I'm glad that Sasha is taking us and not you. You are a mean Mummy!' Annabelle huffs.

Zachery nods his head in agreement, his eyes red-rimmed and tear-filled at the thought that he is the one who caused all of this. He is the one who threw the milk over his mother's bag and made her so angry in the first place. He runs from the room then too, leaving Cecelia to crumple. Bending over and resting her head on top of her arms on the breakfast bar counter. Her shoulders shaking with each exaggerated sob. 'God! Why am I so useless at this? They act as if they hate me!'

'They don't hate you! They're just kids. They are lashing out, saying things that they don't really mean,' Sasha says, stepping forward and placing a hand on Cecelia's arm to offer her some comfort.

'I can feel myself losing it, Sasha. I've got so much I need to do. I'm the one left here to do everything all by myself. To run this bloody house, to look after the kids. How am I supposed to run a business too? I can't do it.' Cecelia continues to cry.

'What about your husband? Henry? Can't you speak with him, see if he can help a bit more?' Sasha asks, curious about Cecelia's husband.

He'd left, Cecelia had said. They were getting a divorce. She hadn't enlightened Sasha with anything more than that about the man. But the children had spoken fondly of him.

'Henry? He can barely look after himself,' Cecelia spits bitterly. 'He's too busy with whatever new PA he's shagging. Who knew the love of my life would turn into a walking, talking cliché? And here I am left to pick up all the pieces. Only I can't do it, I'm a bad mother—'

'You are not a bad mother, things just got a bit heated, that's all. It happens! And you're right, you can't do this all on your own. You do need some help. Which is why I'm here,' Sasha says, hoping her words of comfort might console the woman. 'Only I haven't been much help this morning, have I? Not after last night. I'm so sorry.' Sasha feels her cheeks redden at the admission. 'I should have been down here getting the kids ready and none of this would have happened.'

Cecelia has stopped crying and is wiping her tears, her erratic breathing steadying now. 'But I shouldn't need to depend on you, Sasha. They are my kids. My head's all over the place. The phone's always ringing, there's always a long list of emails that are awaiting replies and the kids, well, they need my attention too, of course they do.' Cecelia shakes her head at her own words as she gains some clarity. 'Something has to give, and at the moment it's them. That makes me feel awful. I just never thought I'd have to choose. I've been so caught up in the dizzy heights of the excitement of having my name out there, printed in all the fancy glossy interior design magazines, that I've taken my eye off the ball at home, haven't I?' she asks, admitting to Sasha that she has been rather absent of late. That her mind has been elsewhere. When her energy should be here, with her two children.

'Maybe I should just cancel my client today and stay home? I can't bear another night away from home. That's why I came back so late last night. After seeing Annabelle's homework she'd done with you the other day, I felt left out. I just wanted to be here when they woke up, but now I've gone and ruined it, haven't I, by shouting. Maybe I could take them to school and do the pickup today instead. I could take them to that little dessert restaurant on the high street afterwards, and get them some ice cream and pancakes. They'd like that, wouldn't they?'

'You can't cancel your client. You need to go! Get your work done, and then come home and spend some time with the children, once you're done. It's only one more night away. You'll be back before you know it. I can take them to the ice-cream place if you like. I'll tell them that you wanted to treat them, that it was all your idea. You're right, they would love that.'

Cecelia nods her head. Seemingly much calmer now. 'Yes, you're right. I can't just cancel on my clients at the last minute, that will do the business more damage than good. It's been a stressful morning, but I guess none of this was ever meant to be easy, huh!'

'The kids are who you are doing it all for at the end of the day! That doesn't make you a bad mother at all,' Sasha reasons.

Though as she speaks, she thinks about how her own mother had pushed her away by doing the very opposite.

Sasha never had the opportunity to complain about how her mother never made time for her. Or how busy she was with work or all her social commitments. Because Sasha had been the woman's whole life. Her mother always told her that there was nothing and no one more important that required her attention than her own daughter.

But in doing all of that, Sasha had always felt as if her mother was too much.

Sasha never had any space.

Even so, she gets it.

She sees it in Cecelia's children, how they feel their mother's neglect. That Cecelia is pushing them aside. That's why they are acting up whenever she is home. They are vying for their mother's attention.

Though Sasha doesn't say any of that to Cecelia right now, as she knows that it's not the right time. Cecelia has enough on her plate right now. She is already aware of what she is doing; she already knows what she needs to do to put it right.

Sasha just hopes that it isn't already too late for Cecelia. Because sometimes once the damage is done, it is irreversible.

Sasha should know.

16

EMILY

My journal has gone.

I have looked everywhere. But it has gone. I am certain.

I have ripped my room apart, rummaging around inside my bedside drawer, where I know I left it last, tucked away carefully at the bottom. A pile of my things placed on top, to conceal it in case Louise ever had a sneaky look inside.

I've pulled everything out; I've placed my pile of belongings down on the carpet.

It's not here.

I check the pile twice.

Unless... maybe the journal has fallen down the back of the unit?

I am hopeful, scrambling to my knees. Peering inside, running my hand around the edges, in case the notepad has slid down and got wedged in a gap in the wood. But it's not there and I sink to the floor, my head in my hands, my fingers covering my ears to block out the never-ending crying.

The crying has been relentless today.

I need her to stop.

That's why I wanted my journal. So that I could write it all down; so that I could get all of these horrible thoughts out of my head. Only someone has taken it.

Louise!

She came here earlier to gloat. Watching me as I dragged my furniture around the room, the place stinking of bleach, the windows wide open, letting in what felt like an arctic gale. I hadn't let on that I'd discovered the meat she'd hidden. I hadn't wanted to give her the satisfaction. I am good at pretending. I've been doing it so much lately; it comes naturally to me now. I've trained myself well, to not look over at the wall when she is here, and the child is crying.

Only the crying is wearing me down, and I think I must have slipped a few times because she's becoming suspicious. Turning up at different times of the day as if to somehow catch me out, watching my every move while she's here. I've seen the way she looks at me, when she thinks that I'm not paying any attention. The way that her eyes bore into the side of my face, as she drinks in my expressions. How they follow me as I move around the room.

She must have gone through my things when I'd been busy showering. I wanted her to leave, and I had needed to get that wretched stench of rotten meat from my skin, but she insisted on staying. I'd been quick, though. As quick as I could be, rinsing the soap off my body before quickly drying myself in record time, so that I could get back out there again. Because I'd been convinced that I could hear her moving around the room. That is the kind of thing she does, given half the chance.

Snoops.

Going through all my things.

She'd love that, wouldn't she? To thumb the pages of all my innermost private thoughts. To read about the shock and horror of finding that meat stashed under my bed where I sleep. Of how I almost threw up at the sight of the maggots crawling along the decaying chicken's flesh.

Well, she'll be disappointed now, I think to myself, because I hadn't written in there about the meat yet. I was going to, but I'd been too busy cleaning.

But I had mentioned the child.

She'd see that. She'd know then.

Shit! Shit! Shit!

I shove all of my things back into the drawer of my bedside cabinet and slam it shut. How dare she?! How dare she come into my home and take my things from me? It's not fair. It's not right. I should report her, I think. But who would I report her to? Because who would listen to someone like me?

It will be my word against hers.

Me, the crazy woman that hears the voices, against her, a supposed professional.

Louise will no doubt lie.

I can hear her now, with her singsong, patronising tone.

She will say that I must be mistaken, that maybe I simply misplaced my journal, that maybe I'd put it somewhere so safe, that even I can't find it now. She'd laugh. And only I would hear the spitefulness there.

She might even add insult to injury and offer to help me look for it. Or perhaps she'll do none of that. She'll simply hide behind another one of her smirks whilst suggesting that maybe I put it in the bin. That I mistook it for rubbish. A subtle dig, because that's what she really thinks about the thoughts inside my head.

That they were all rubbish. That they deserved to be tossed away just like the rotten maggot-infested meat. That they weren't worth the paper they were written on.

I block my ears.

The little girl's crying seems to be growing worse. The sound is so loud now that I can't keep it out.

I must. I must keep her out.

I rush about the flat, like a woman with a purpose. Turning

thoughts and drags her out of her head and back into the present.

She's not sure how long she has stood in this spot at the window, but the mug of tea she is holding in her hand is no longer hot.

'SASHA?' Annabelle calls again.

This time, there is urgency. The sound of distress as the little girl calls out to her. The children! *Shit!* She'd left them alone in the bath. Sasha rushes, ignoring the trail of water that has seeped out from the bathroom door, making its way across the floorboards in the hallway.

'I'm sorry. I'm here...' she says as she pushes the door fully open and does a double take.

FLASH.

Sasha feels startled for a second, disorientated. As if she has crossed over into some other warped time.

Gone is the beautifully renovated bathroom with the rolltop bath and double basin sinks that Cecelia had painstakingly installed. In its place is a damp, tired-looking room that smells as stagnant and as rotten as it looks. The sides of the bath look scummy, as if it's never been cleaned. And there is black mould stretching out across the tiles. The room seems darker now too, as if the bright morning light that has been streaming through the window from outside has been somehow dimmed.

She sees it straight away.

Him.

The small body floating in the murky-looking bath water.

'ZACHERY?' she screams, realising that he is not playing.

He is not giggling. He is not making a noise. He is not moving.

He is not holding his nose and seeing how long he can keep his head underneath the surface.

She is there then.

Plunging her arms into the freezing cold bath water.

Frantic now as she grabs at his lifeless body, desperate to pull him out, to save him.

But her arms can't seem to reach him.

He is gone. It is just water.

'Sasha?'

A voice behind her pulls her back.

'The water went cold. So, we got out.'

Sasha turns to see Annabelle standing in the doorway, with Zackery standing close beside her. They are wrapped in towels. Trails of wet hair dripping down their skin. Expressions on their faces that say that they think she is quite mad. And maybe she is. Only right now, she doesn't care about any of that.

'Oh, Thank God! Thank God,' she cries out with relief, pulling herself back up onto her feet, aware of how deranged she must seem as she rushes over to the children, pulling them in and hugging them to her tightly.

'Uh, you're soaking wet!' Annabelle squeals, wiggling free.

A look of puzzlement on her face.

'I am! Aren't I!' Sasha is laughing now. The involuntary sound spilling out of her as if it's beyond her control.

The children are safe. Zackery is safe.

But she has finally seen a flash of something real. Something from before.

A broken, fragmented memory from her past.

It was real this time.

She knows it.

18

EMILY

When I wake, there is only silence.

The noise has stopped, that's my very first thought. It has stopped finally. Thank God. Thank God. I open my eyes, the fog starting to lift inside my head too. Though my thoughts still feel fuzzy. I'm in my bed.

Hadn't I been on the floor? I don't remember how I got into my bed.

'Here she is!'

A voice in the room startles me. Then a face. Louise. Her lined forehead wrinkling as she smiles down at me, exposing her tobacco-stained teeth from where she'd smoked too many cigarettes over the years.

'You gave us a bit of a fright last night. How are you feeling now? Better?' Her voice is thick with a warmth that doesn't suit her, and as I pull myself up into a seated position I see why.

We are not alone.

'You remember Doctor Mead, don't you?'

I nod.

Scared then, wondering why the doctor from the facility I've just been discharged from is standing in my room. An uneasy sense of dread washes over me, at the thought of these people standing over me whilst I slept, of them being in my flat. How long have I been asleep, I wonder? Because it's not morning yet. The lights are on, so it must be dark outside, I realise as my eyes go to the clock. Almost 2 a.m.

I've lost the whole evening.

Had I blanked out?

A small pocket of time has disappeared from my mind completely.

'I found you on the bedroom floor, Emily. Do you remember?' Louise asks.

Again, I shake my head. As if hoping to shake the bewilderment that lingers there. I remember being on the floor. The loud noise in my flat blaring as I fought so long to drown out the crying girl, but it hadn't worked, she'd just become louder. I'd started screaming. Covering my ears with my hands, I'd opened my mouth and screamed at the top of my voice.

I don't remember anything after that.

That's how Louise must have found me. She must have helped me back to bed. She must have called out the doctor.

Why can't I remember?

'You were holding your ears, Emily. You said that the noise had got inside of them. That you couldn't make it stop,' Louise continues, though she speaks with caution now as she reads the confused look on my face. Aware of the doctor's presence and the obvious distress I'm in at having no memory of how I ended up here, in my bed. I'd tried to drown her out, hadn't I? The crying girl. I'd tried to make my own noise, but it wouldn't stop.

She has stopped now, I realise. I can't hear her.

Why can't I hear her?

It's only then that I see it, the empty needle that the doctor has placed on the side.

'What is that? What have you given me?'

'Louise found you in a state of extreme distress. You claimed you could hear noises? Can you still hear them now?'

I feel the pinkness creep up my cheeks, wondering what else Louise has told him. What else had I confessed to her? My hands automatically go to my ears at the memory of the noise. How loud it had sounded. How it had felt as if it had found a way inside of my head. It had been all too much for me to bear. The weight of it all. The constant pretending that I couldn't hear it, when all it did was follow me around.

I'd collapsed to the floor in agony.

That is my last thought, my last recollection. I have no memory after that.

'No. I can't hear the noises. It's quiet now.'

'How are you feeling?'

How am I feeling?

Disorientated. As if I'm outside of my body, floating in mid-air. There are huge gaping gaps in my memory, and I don't remember getting into bed. I don't remember Louise arriving.

I want to say all of that, but I daren't. I want to tell him that there are parts of my mind that only see the murky shades of grey between some of my memories. That there are blank spaces I can't possibly fill. But I stay quiet, I keep all of that to myself. Otherwise, I know that I'll end up back there again. Locked away in that room.

'Can you tell the doctor what you've been hearing?' Louise says, placing a hand on my arm as if to offer me some comfort. I stare down at her long, bony fingers. The way the woman's hand is wrapped around my wrist like a claw.

She knows what the noises are, I think, because she took my journal. That is why she came back tonight, to check on me, no doubt. That's what all of this is about. She wants the doctor to see it too, that I am going mad again. That I don't deserve to be here, in this flat. That I don't deserve a second chance.

'I don't really remember the noise as such,' I lie. Though I know it's a beat too late. I see the look that they exchange. How already they don't believe me.

Try harder. Be more convincing.

'It was more of a pain. Hot and stabby.'

That isn't a complete lie either. I had been in pain. I remembered that. The feeling of an explosion going off inside my ear canals. The shrill sound tunnelling its way through to my brain.

'You can check them. My ears. But they really do feel better now,' I say, hoping that she can appease the doctor.

'Well, we can start there. Why not!' he says, moving closer to the bed as I remain sitting, obedient. Wanting to show him that I am calm now, that I am complying. Because I've learned from the past that the panic that sometimes erupts inside me only makes things worse.

It makes me reactive and when I'm like that, I start to make no sense.

'It's going to feel a bit cold.'

I flinch as he places a cold instrument in my ear before shining a small torch and peering inside. He does the same to the next one.

'Well, they look just fine,' he says. And there is something about his tone. Something that tells me that he is pretending, just as I am. That all of this, is just him humouring me.

We both know this isn't about an earache.

The voices are back. Something has triggered them, but I don't know what. And that bothers me more than anything, because I've been so much better lately. I've started to feel like myself again. Myself, before. Before that house. Before the children.

'Louise says that you've been hearing the girl crying again?'

'She's lying.' The words shoot out of my mouth before I can stop them, and Louise buts in.

'Emily, the doctor just wants to check that you are okay. That you're not starting to spiral again, that's all.' She speaks softly in a voice that isn't really hers. She's acting too. 'That's what we all want. To make sure that you're okay, darling.'

'Darling?' I spit.

LIAR. LIAR. LIAR. I shuffle backwards on the bed, defensive, before shooting an angry glance towards Louise for her betrayal. 'I know what you did,' I snap. 'You hid rotten meat underneath my bed, and you took my journal. Now you're trying to use it against me. This has been your plan all along, hasn't it?' My voice shakes with anger as I call her out. Is she the one that has triggered the madness to go off again inside of me? Is she the one causing me to doubt myself?

I bet she thought she'd hit the jackpot when she'd walked in and found me on the floor earlier. I'd stupidly played right into her mean, clammy hands, only I didn't have any choice. The noise was too much, it felt as if it was breaking me. But I am not broken now, am I? I am still here.

I am stronger than she thinks.

'Rotten meat? Emily, what on earth are you talking about?' Louise shakes her head as if I am speaking in a foreign language that she doesn't understand.

Oh, she is good! I'll give her that.

It is stupid of me to think that I can win. To believe that they'll listen.

They won't.

I backtrack.

'Nothing. Forget it. I am okay. I just want to be left alone,' I say, shrugging my arm away from Louise's grasp. My voice sounding higher pitched than normal as I protest too much; even I catch the desperation in my tone.

'I think we should reassess your medication, Emily,' the doctor intervenes, and I shake my head.

'For my ears? Do you think it might be an ear infection maybe?' I say, determined now. Because I know what's coming. They are going to put me back on that stuff they had me on before. The strong meds that made me feel so spaced out that I barely even knew my own name.

'We can up the dose of diazepam just for a little while and see if that helps. And perhaps some stronger sleeping tablets to help her get some regular rest. Did she have any side effects last time?' This time the doctor isn't directing his conversation at me. He is talking to Louise. Speaking about me now as if I'm not even in the room. As if I'm completely invisible. As if I am irrelevant.

As if I'm not capable of making important decisions about my own state of health.

'No side effects,' Louise confirms.

Liar. Liar. Liar.

The medication that they'd given me had felt like poison as it had been pushed around my veins. The heaviness it bestowed upon me. The darkness that I had felt. Until quickly it had stopped me from feeling and thinking at all. Until I was just going through the motions and barely existing.

I had lost hours to that stuff. Whole days in fact. And even after they'd weaned me off it, I hadn't felt myself for months afterwards.

Louise wants me kept sick.

She must.

Because at the first chance she gets she wants me back on these meds.

Why isn't she telling him how good I have been, how far I've come along the past few months? About me living here these past few weeks. How I have my own routine. How I like to watch my favourite TV shows and write in my journal. How I keep myself to myself. How the thought of a simple, quiet life makes me feel sane.

Why doesn't she tell him that I've been better. I've been good.

I watch the doctor write something down on my notes, and

then he takes out a small bottle from his leather satchel. A brown jar of tiny white pills, which he hands to Louise.

'Two pills, three times a day with food.'

'That sounds good, doesn't it, Emily? And that's all we want to do. Help you get better.' Louise holds my gaze, her eyes fixed, unwavering. Just like the power she holds over me.

I nod. Because we both know that I must do as I'm told. If I refuse to take the pills, there'll only be one alternative. They'll force me to take them; they might even send me back to the mental health facility.

It's two against one.

I need to play it smart and let her think that she is winning.

For now, I have no other choice but to keep quiet and comply and do as she says.

19

SASHA

'Mummy look at the paintings we did with Sasha today!' Annabelle says excitedly, strutting into the kitchen and holding up the brightly painted artwork for her mother to see.

'Sorry, I was putting them to bed, but they heard you come in and they've been dying to see you all day and show you what they made,' Sasha says, following closely behind, with Zachery running next to her.

But Sasha can see that Cecelia is distracted. Perched at the kitchen table, her laptop on and a glass of wine next to it.

'Sorry, I didn't realise that you were still working...' She throws an apologetic look at the woman, before Zachery interrupts.

'No, Mummy. Look! My one is better, isn't it? It's a space rocket like the one in my room.' Vying for her attention, pushing his way past Annabelle who stands by her mother's stool at the breakfast bar.

'Wait your turn!' Annabelle huffs, pushing Zachery back so that her mother can admire her picture first. Only Zachery pushes her back. Causing Annabelle's head to jolt forward, hitting the wine glass that Cecelia had just poured herself and sending it flying across the kitchen counter. Annabelle starts crying as Cecelia turns red and shoots out of her chair.

'Oh for Christ's sake!' Cecelia shouts. She had been so engrossed in her work that she had paid no attention to the kids until it was too late, and the glass had already toppled. The dark red liquid pouring out across the breakfast bar like a river of red, soaking the keyboard of her laptop, before dripping down onto the kitchen floor.

'NO!' she cries as the screen starts to merge into a mass of coloured lines criss-crossing the black background. 'You have to be kidding me!' Picking up the laptop she runs to the sink, tipping the remnants of wine that swim on the keypad down it, before dabbing at it with a clean tea towel; but Sasha can see that it's already too late.

The keys have become sticky, stuck down to the pad.

The screen goes black.

The laptop is destroyed.

Cecelia turns to the children and roars. 'That was my work! Very important work that needs to be done tonight. Why do you always have to ruin everything? Why can't you just behave!'

'Hey! It was an accident! They didn't mean...' Sasha says, feeling defensive as she sees the children stand still like statues, rendered silent. Both wounded at their mother's harsh words and the way she is shouting at them. Zachery's bottom lip trembles. The colour has drained from Annabelle's face.

'They only wanted to see you. To show you their pictures—'

'It's bloody ruined!' Cecelia cuts her off. Shaking her head in despair, before slamming down the laptop on the kitchen side. 'It's way past their bedtime. Perhaps if you'd put them to bed properly this wouldn't have happened,' she snipes. Her anger aimed at Sasha, as if it was somehow her fault that the children had accidentally knocked her drink over.

'They missed you...' Sasha starts, but she knows her words

are wasted on Cecelia. The woman is furious now as she mops up the drink dramatically.

'The picture is of you, Mummy... you look pretty,' Annabelle says half-heartedly as she points at the smiling woman with bright yellow hair in the middle of the page.

Sasha gives the girl a small smile, recognising that while she is only six years old, she is trying to defuse the situation and make her mummy stop shouting. Only Cecelia doesn't even bother to turn and acknowledge her.

'Stupid paintings. We shouldn't have done them,' Annabelle cries and runs from the room, and Sasha feels furious. How dare Cecelia make Annabelle feel so small? So useless. How dare she simply ignore her? About to say just that, Sasha is stopped in her tracks as the shrill of Cecelia's mobile phone sounds out across the kitchen. Striding across the room, Cecelia picks it up. Rolling her eyes up when she sees the caller's ID.

'Great timing, Henry,' she mutters to herself, before nodding her head in the direction of where Zachery is still standing. 'Can you put them to bed?'

Sasha watches as Zachery does as he is told and sulks out of the kitchen, his head down, his shoulders sagging with disappointment. Sasha follows, leaving Cecelia to speak with Henry alone, in the hope that maybe she'll calm down by the time the children are settled in bed.

She'll speak to her then.

'Come on, you two,' she says with false frivolity as she reaches the top of the stairs. 'How about you both jump into Annabelle's bed and snuggle up again, and I'll read you both another story? Any one you like. You pick!'

'Can we have two stories? That way we can pick one each?' Zachery says between breathless sobs.

'Of course, you can!' Sasha says as they reach the bedroom, and the children climb underneath the duvet.

Sasha tucks them in and picks up two of the story books that the children both point to from Annabelle's bookshelf. Only, no amount of silly voices or being loud could drown out the sound of their mother, downstairs. Her voice carrying up the stairs as she argues with the children's father.

'It's not fair, Henry. Why am I the one left to deal with everything? Why do I have to do it all on my own? They are your kids too.'

'Doesn't Mummy want us any more?' Zachery asks quietly, catching the last part of his mother's sentence.

'Oh of course she does, silly. She just wants your daddy to help out a bit more too. That's all,' Sasha says, putting down the book.

'Is that why she's always so mad, because of Daddy?'

'She's not mad at you guys... and I don't think she's really mad at Daddy either. I think she's just finding everything a bit overwhelming right now. She's trying to do her best,' Sasha says as she soothes down the front of Annabelle's fringe with the flat of her palm, before kissing Zachery on the forehead. An unfamiliar feeling swelling inside her.

A protectiveness. A want to make things better for them. Because nothing about this divorce is fair on them.

Cecelia shouldn't speak like this to Henry when the children are in the house. She shouldn't speak to the kids the way she does either. She might be finding it hard, but she shouldn't take it out on them. They were the innocents in all of this. None of this was their fault.

This is what they'd been born into.

She thinks of the apple tree again, the vague memory of standing beneath it invading her head once more. A voice, condemning her.

BAD GIRL. BAD GIRL.

A woman grabbing her by her arm. Wrenching her to her feet.

BAD GIRL. BAD GIRL.

Not her mother's voice. Her mother never spoke to her like that. She thinks about the last words her mother had written. The words she had used in that letter.

How she'd saved her.

Then she thinks about the cupboard. How she felt as if she'd been inside of there before.

Trapped. Clawing at the walls. Kicking at the door.

'Sasha! You're bleeding.' Annabelle's voice breaks her train of thought then and she jumps at the feel of the girl's light touch, as Annabelle places a hand gently on her arm. 'Look. You've scratched yourself.'

Sasha follows Annabelle's horrified gaze and realises that Annabelle is right. She'd been sitting hugging herself, her arms wrapped so tightly around herself, her fingernails digging into her flesh. Scratching anxiously at her skin at just the thought of being back there again. Inside that cupboard. Of the door being shut. Of not being able to get out. The blood trickles down her arm and drops onto the carpet.

One tiny red splodge, sinking into the thin grey fibres.

That will stain.

Blood on the carpet.

Another flash of something familiar.

Blood on the bathroom floor.

A woman on her knees mopping it up, wringing out a cloth into a bucket of water. Only the water is red. Red with blood.

The image is gone again, and Sasha stares down at the red gouges in her arms.

'I'm okay. It looks worse than it is,' she says finally, pulling at her cardigan sleeves, in a bid to hide the damage she's done there. 'Right, I kept my promise and read you both a story, now you need to keep your promise and stay in bed. Okay?' Sasha speaks firmly, smiling at them as she does, so that they know they aren't being told off again.

They've had enough of that from their mother.

'Do you want to stay in here, Zachery? Is that okay with you, Annabelle? You can stay snuggled up!'

The two children nod their heads, looking happier as Sasha lifts the corner of Annabelle's covers and makes sure that they are properly tucked in.

'Night night!' she says as she gently closes the door to, before making her way back down the stairs to Cecelia.

20

EMILY

The room is dark, and I can hear voices. I'm in my bed, I realise. I am awake but my eyelids feel too heavy and weighted for me to open. So, I stay still and listen instead.

It's not the crying girl this time. The voices that I can hear now are older than that.

Women. Two of them.

Talking in hushed whispers as they stand close by, next to my bed.

Crisis teams and assessment units and anti-psychotic medication.

Those are the words that I manage to catch every now and then, amongst the jumbled snippets that I don't.

I hear my name then and realise that they are talking about me. Only I can't quite grasp their entire conversation. Just the odd muttered word or half a sentence sometimes, if I'm lucky. If I concentrate hard enough. I can just about catch them as they teeter and creep nearby, close enough for me to grasp every now and then.

'What have you given her?' It's Charlotte's voice. Softly spoken, almost gentle. As if she is tiptoeing around what is being asked because she doesn't approve. 'She doesn't look herself.'

There's a swell of something inside of me then. I can hear the shock and concern etched in her voice at the difference in me. She sees it too. How this poison they've enforced on me has affected me. How it has made me worse not better. I am just lying here, in this bed, like a zombie. Every part of my body feels heavy and weighted, but at the same time I feel as if I am made from air and floating around the room.

How can that be? How can I be both of those things at once?

'Doctor Mead increased her meds.' It's Louise's voice now, her tone as cold and hard as steel. Matching her personality. There's a matter-of-factness to her statement, as if she had no say in the matter, when I know that she was the one who orchestrated it. She is the one that wants me left like this.

There's a flippancy about the way she talks about me, too, as if I'm not even in the room. As if I simply just don't matter. And to her, I know that I don't.

'He upped the dosage of the anti-psychotics because of the auditory hallucinations that she's been having.'

'I thought she was getting better?' Charlotte asks. 'Isn't that why you moved her here? She stopped hearing the voices?'

I could kiss Charlotte for that. Because I know that I can trust her now. She could have told Louise; she could have confessed what I had told her about how I hear the crying girl. Only she kept my secret for me.

'She was better, but it seems as though, unfortunately, something has triggered her. I suspect that it's the move from the unit to here. It's a big step. It can be overwhelming. I knew she wasn't herself. I caught her a few times, playing her music loudly, and leaving the taps constantly running. The TV has been blaring loud too on more than one occasion. She used to do that a lot, in a bid to drown out the noise. Then the other night I found her dousing the flat in bleach. That's a new one! She'd spent the entire night scrubbing the walls and the carpet in the stuff, so much so that the carpet was saturated. God only knows why.'

Bitch! Lying fucking bitch! I want to jump up from my bed then and scream the words in her face. I want to claw her beady, spiteful eyes out. She knows why I scrubbed my flat.

Because of her. Because of what she did.

Because of that rotten meat that she planted underneath my bed.

Because of the rancid maggots and the flies.

She did that to me and now she is using my behaviour against me. She is making out to Charlotte that I am mad. That I am the one who is acting crazy. This was her plan all along. She never wanted me to have a second chance at life, to be rehabilitated back into the community, and she is doing everything she can now to stop me. 'She thinks that I stole her journal and she's accused me of hiding rotten meat under her bed. Has she mentioned any of that to you?'

'Rotten meat? No. That's the first I've heard of it.' There is a moment of silence before Charlotte finally speaks. A slight delay as uncertainty festers.

She is piecing it all together. Recalling how convinced I'd been when I'd confided in her that Louise doesn't like me. She is smart enough to see through Louise's malicious ways. She knows that these are not wild allegations. There is truth here.

'Will she have to go back to the unit?' Charlotte asks and I brace myself for Louise's answer.

Because that is Louise's end game, isn't it? That is what she really wants for me. To go back there and continue the punishment that I am owed.

To never get out. To never be free.

I wait for her to finally say it.

'Hopefully not. It will be a shame if she does, after getting this far. Let's see how we get on with the meds first.'

The scream inside me has nowhere to go. It is a hard round lump in my stomach and my throat. Oh! She is good. She is so bloody good at this.

The conniving bitch. The actress.

Making out that this is all out of her control and that it's down to me.

Me, who has no control at all.

Me, who has been forced on these drugs that make me feel as if I am floating.

Am I floating? I lift my arms up into the air, reaching up to the ceiling, to see if I can touch it. I think I can. I am probably capable of touching the sky. Of scraping my fingertips through the clouds. I move my fingers then finally I open my eyes, my gaze fixated on the abstract shadowy shapes they make, that are cast from the lamplight as it shines upwards onto the ceiling above me.

A rabbit with two ears and a pointy nose.

A spider with eight gangly legs.

A sound finally escapes my lips as I let out a burst of laughter, louder than I meant to, because both the women immediately stop talking and stare over to where I lie in the bed.

Ahh, so I am real. You can see me. You do know I'm here.

'The medication makes her like that?' There is distress in Charlotte's voice now. I hear it. How she doesn't agree with how vacant and spaced out the medications made me.

YES. I want to shout.

The medication has done this to me.

Make it stop. Make it stop.

Only I can't focus. I can't think. I can't move. Right now, I can only just open my eyes.

'Yes. It's an extreme measure, but we are hoping that it will stop the hallucinations and minimalise her psychosis. If we can just stop her from hearing the crying child she claims to hear, it will be a start.'

'Has she spoken about who the child is?' Charlotte asks.

I bristle at the bluntness of her question. At the curiosity there. She has asked me this too, only I hadn't wanted to give her any answers for fear that I couldn't trust her. A mistake on my part, I think now. Because now she'll get Louise's version of events instead of the truth.

'Is it the little boy...' she continues, purposely stopping her sentence there as if she is unable to say the words that follow. The words that I know that they are both thinking.

Is it the little boy that she killed?

MURDERER. MONSTER.

It pains me that Charlotte knows why I'm here. She knows what I have been through. She knows what I did. But there have been times where I have wondered if, perhaps, she didn't. Because she doesn't seem to hold any judgement towards me.

She is still kind to me.

I've started to look forward to our little chats. I look forward to seeing her, because unlike Louise, she talks to me like I'm a real person, not some monster that the media made me out to be.

'It's not the boy.' I hear Louise's voice now. How she pauses and takes a long, dramatic breath before she speaks again. 'After they found him—' She stops abruptly. As if her voice has become caught inside her throat. Entangled there due to the heaviness of her words which are laced in sadness. For him. It's genuine too, I think.

Because I feel it too.

A huge ball of grief that swells inside me as I picture his sweet little face. That mop of blond hair. I feel sick and dizzy and hot all at once.

Stop talking about him.

Stop talking about him.

'They found the little girl too. She was alive, but she was badly injured. Emily refused to talk about her. She refused to speak about her full stop. It's like she just cut her out. But I think it's her that she hears.'

I zone out. Because Louise knows nothing of my life back then, she was no part of it. She only knows what she's been told. And I refuse to listen to her version of events.

I can't think about the girl.

I won't think about her.

'So, if the medication helps blocks out the trauma? If it blocks out the noises she hears, does it make her forget other things too?'

'It can, yes,' Louise confirms, and I feel fury at how vague she sounds in her answer. She knows that the medication they've given me leaves me empty. How I become little more than a shell of a person. How all my thoughts become blurred into one. My head feels so fuzzy.

I can't think straight. I keep losing my train of thought.

She has stopped, I realise.

I've been so distracted by the conversation going on around me that I've only just noticed the little girl isn't crying any more. Other than the two women's voices, the room is silent.

I should feel happy about that.

I should feel relieved that the girl is no longer taunting me.

Only there's a sinking feeling of despair in my stomach, an ache in my gut that tells me that even though the sound of the crying child has stopped for now, it's not over.

She'll be back.

She always finds her way back to me in the end.

21

SASHA

Reaching the bottom step, Sasha can hear that Cecelia is still on the phone. The shrill of her tone venomous, her voice louder as it travels through the house as she continues to argue with Henry.

'Well, maybe you should come and take care of the kids sometime, then maybe you'll realise how hard it is to raise two children on your own. Like you've left me to do. I mean it, Henry, I've had e-bloody-nough!'

Sasha glances up the stairs, praying that the kids can't hear their mother talking in this way. She knows how it will hurt them. Screaming at their father like this. About them.

The slam of something loud a few seconds later makes her hurry into the kitchen, to check that Cecelia is okay. As she reaches the kitchen door, she can see that she is. Her mobile phone, however, having been launched at the wall, is broken into several pieces. A black mark denting the middle of the wall just above where it has landed.

'Shit!' Cecelia says, running her shaking hands through her hair, as if she has only just realised how much she lost it.

'Are they in bed?' she asks then, taking a deep breath and

trying to compose herself, as if she has only just remembered that the kids are in the house.

'Yes, they are, but they're not asleep yet,' Sasha says, hoping that Cecelia will take the hint that the children can hear her.

She does. Crossing the kitchen, Cecelia opens a fresh bottle of wine and pours herself another glass, before drinking it back in one.

Sasha picks up her mobile phone, what's left of it, and places it on the kitchen table. She waits then. Purposely. For the inevitable to happen, for the alcohol to hit Cecelia's bloodstream and calm her down. Before she finally feels brave enough to speak. This isn't going to be an easy conversation, but she feels that she needs to say it. For Annabelle's and Zachery's sakes.

'They could hear you down here, you know. They could hear you shouting,' Sasha starts. Unsure how to say her piece without offending Cecelia, because regardless of what she thinks of her, she is her employer. If Cecelia didn't like what she was hearing, if she thought Sasha was crossing the line, she could throw her out. She could banish her from her house.

And Sasha doesn't want that. Not now she's started to finally remember being back here. Little snippets of memories, but memories still.

'They were upset.'

Cecelia laughs. Though the cackling sound that leaves her mouth is full of bitterness and contempt. The wine is strong and drank that quickly, would no doubt start to take effect in calming Cecelia down. Though instead, it seemed to have the opposite effect and was making her more and more angry.

'And do you not think that I'm upset too? I've lost hours of work tonight, not to mention the fact that I'll need a new laptop now too. It's bloody ruined. And a new phone. And then I've got Henry in my ear with all his patronising, condescending advice on parenting. Though in reality, he's nowhere to be seen.

The absent bloody father.' Cecelia shuts her eyes and raises her hand in the air, catching herself mid-rant just as her temper starts to get the better of her once more.

'I'm sorry. I'm sorry,' she says finally. 'You're right. I shouldn't have lost my temper with the children like that. And I know I shouldn't have just shouted at Henry like that either. But God, he just makes me so bloody mad. And I certainly shouldn't be taking it out on you. You're the only one around here actually helping me. And the kids adore you.' She sighs then and shakes her head before taking a deep breath and trying to justify her actions. 'Henry just knows how to press my buttons. I'm finding it so hard. Being here on my own with the kids. In this house.' She spits the last words out of her mouth as if they left a bad taste. As if she is full of contempt.

Sasha sees it then for the very first time. Cecelia doesn't like it here. In this house. It hasn't been a labour of love for her like Sasha had thought.

'But you love the house? And you've done such an amazing job...' Sasha starts, but Cecelia shakes her head.

'This house was Henry's dream, not mine.' Cecelia pours herself another glass of wine. Her face is screwed up and her lips are pursed together as if she is struggling to keep her thoughts inside. There is a look of something on her face that Sasha can't read. A strange, pained expression.

Cecelia finally speaks. 'It looks nice, doesn't it?' she starts. 'And it is nice. It's more than that. It's a thousand times better than when we bought it. But I don't know... there is just so much history here. Henry knew it too. That if I knew what had happened here, I would never have gone along with buying it. But, typical, good old Henry, huh! Once he has his eye on something he wants, he'll do anything to get it.'

Cecelia picks up her glass and takes another big mouthful. She is on a roll now. Venting about everything that has clearly been building up inside of her. Sasha doesn't mind. She wants

Cecelia to confide in her. She wants to know more about this house; except, she isn't sure if Cecelia is talking about the house any more, or if she's veered off on a tangent and is talking about her failed marriage. Not wanting to break the spell, now that Cecelia seems willing to talk, Sasha waits patiently for Cecelia to continue.

'He was always cunning and manipulative. I just didn't ever think he'd be like that to me.' Cecelia laughs bitterly. 'I thought that I was untouchable. Because he *loved* me. He knew the history of this place and he kept it from me, purposely, until after we'd already signed the mortgage deeds and it was too late to back out of it.' She shakes her head sadly.

'What history? What happened here?' Sasha asks, hoping she sounds casual, as she braces herself to hear another version of what she already knows. She'd spent hours scouring the internet and reading old newspaper articles, after her mother died and left her that final, gut-wrenching letter. Trying so desperately to piece together the fragments of her life that she had no memory of living.

Cecelia stares at her. Her teeth digging into the flesh of her bottom lip as if she is contemplating how to word it. The horror that had once unfolded within these walls.

Looking as if she is about to say it, until eventually she shakes her head. 'I can't,' she says finally. As if even saying the words out loud were too much. But then Cecelia adds sheepishly, 'Do you believe in ghosts, Sasha?'

'Ghosts?' Sasha doesn't mean for her voice to come out in such high-pitched, exaggerated surprise. But that had been the very last question she'd been expecting to hear from Cecelia's mouth. The expression on her face must have told the woman that too, because Cecelia laughs. Shrugging off her embarrassment as if she had just purposely made a joke.

'Not ghosts, really. More like, I don't know. An energy? I've often wondered about it. In my line of work. You know, working in so many of my clients' homes,' she adds quickly. 'Do you think that a house can be disturbed? Or, I don't know, permanently scarred by a tragedy that once occurred there?'

Sasha shakes her head as if she doesn't understand, because Cecelia is being so vague now and Sasha needs more.

'Like here, in this house. We tore up the carpets and wooden floorboards. We stripped the walls of paper. We even knocked some walls down. Yet, it still feels as if something lingers. More like a heaviness. A sadness. I probably sound crazy, don't I?' Cecelia concludes.

Sasha shakes her head. Wondering if she can get Cecelia to tell her more.

'It's an old house. It's bound to have a lot of history.'

'It just feels like there's a bad energy here sometimes And I don't know. Me and Henry used to be so happy. But now look at us. And the kids. They don't seem very happy lately either.'

'And what about you? You're not happy?'

Cecelia shakes her head.

'And what, you think that it's because of this house? That it is cursed or something? Because of whatever happened here, before?'

'It sounds stupid when I say it out loud.' Cecelia laughs again, in the hope of lightening the mood. But she sounds nervous. And Sasha sees the genuine sadness in her eyes as she continues. 'This is just not the life I wanted for myself. Or for the kids either. It's like ever since we moved into this house, our lives just fell apart. Sometimes I feel like I've got too much going on. I wasn't expecting my career to take off like this, the minute that Henry upped and left me for another woman. And the kids are so full on. Sometimes I wonder if I can do it all. Or if it's all too much. If something, eventually, is going to give. What if it's me, or worse, them? The kids.'

Sasha watches as Cecelia puts down the empty glass and holds on to the kitchen counter, as if suddenly it's the only thing holding her up as she makes her final admission. 'I feel like such a bad mum.'

'You are doing your best,' Sasha says in reply, though her conviction is weak.

And it's as if Cecelia can see straight through her; it's as if she can read her thoughts.

'But my best simply isn't good enough, right?' Cecelia offers a tiny laugh then when Sasha doesn't answer.

'I didn't mean that...' Sasha starts to explain. Wanting to reassure Cecelia that she and the children would be okay, but Sasha wasn't sure she believed that herself. Annabelle had already confided in her how unhappy she was at her mother always working, and how when she was home her mind was always elsewhere and she was always losing her temper. Maybe it was a good thing that Cecelia was finally acknowledging it.

'Don't worry. You don't have to say anything. I know it's not good enough. I've got another early start tomorrow. I'm going to go and get a shower and get into bed,' Cecelia says finally. Before placing her glass next to the sink and leaving the room.

22

EMILY

When I wake again, it's only Charlotte who is here. There is no sign of Louise. I am glad of that.

'Here, let me help you to sit up,' Charlotte says as she sees me struggling to pull myself upright in the bed.

And I do need help. I feel so drowsy. The medicine that Louise had given me earlier must be so much stronger than the pills I'd had before. Because these ones have knocked me for six. It's dark outside. Which means that I must have slept away the majority of the day, yet still I don't feel rested. If anything, I feel even more exhausted than ever. I feel as if I could close my eyes and continue to sleep well into the night.

I see the tray on the side.

The pot of tea. My next set of pills.

More pills.

I bristle and Charlotte catches it, the way my body pushes away from them. From her. And for a brief second something invisible passes between us. There is a fleeting look of compassion there, of sympathy in her eyes. Sympathy for me.

She sees it. How I can't take more. Not now. Not yet.

'Thought you'd like a nice cup of tea when you woke up,'

she says, picking a napkin up and placing it over my medication, as if to make a point. She is not going to make me take them.

Not yet anyway.

She can see how bad they have made me, how I lose myself in them. The medication only makes me worse. She is going to give me a break. I am so grateful for that.

'Here, let me help.' She hands me the cup and saucer, and I take a sip.

It's scalding hot, and strong, just the way that I like it.

'Why don't you judge me like the others have? Why are you nice to me?'

'Why wouldn't I be nice to you?' Charlotte says simply, without giving my question so much as a second thought.

I can feel my eyes brim with tears at her answer, and I want to believe her. I want to desperately believe her, only I don't know what to believe any more. This is how low Louise has managed to bring me. She's dragged me down to such depths that I am beginning to question everything. I don't know who I can trust any more. I'm not even sure that I can trust myself.

What if this is just an act? What if Charlotte goes back and reports everything I say right back to Louise? What if she is a spy and they are both in this together? Can I trust her?

What am I doing? I think, wincing. My eyes tightly closed at the realisation that I am acting paranoid.

'Because of what I did.'

I watch her face. Looking at her properly then. Waiting for the look of disgust to flash across it. Only she keeps her expression neutral.

'I'm not here to judge. I'm here to help you get better. To support you.'

I go to speak again, but my hands are shaking now and the cup that I'm holding slips from my grasp. I wince, closing my eyes, anticipating the scalding heat of the water to seep through my bedspread and burn my stomach and legs. Only I feel nothing.

Am I completely numb to the scalding heat? Have the tablets done that too? Stopped me from feeling anything at all?

I start to cry.

'Hey, it's okay. I'd say there's no use crying over spilt tea.' Charlotte laughs. 'Only your cup's empty. Hey, you've drank it all, Emily. Don't worry there's no harm done. Here, shall I pour you another?'

I look down at the covers and realise that Charlotte is right. There is nothing on my covers. The tea didn't spill from the cup? I'd drunk it already. Though I have no memory of finishing it.

I start to sob even more then.

I am so very, very scared.

The pills are too strong, they are stealing pockets of time from me, making chunks of my life disappear. I'm losing my memory. I am losing my mind.

'Hey, don't cry. It's okay. You're going to be okay.'

Handing me a fresh cup, I sink back into my pillows and try and calm myself down. The tea helps. I drink it back. Savouring the sweet, syrupy taste as I feel a rush of calm spread over me then, a stillness.

'I can't do this any more.'

Charlotte raises an eye, questioningly.

'She's mean to me.'

The words leave my mouth like a whisper. As if I'm scared that Louise will somehow hear me. They come out without any thought or warning. Because I can't think straight. I can't think at all. Going by the shocked look on her face at my sudden admission, Charlotte must think that too. That I'm not making much sense.

'Who is mean to you?'

'Louise. She is nasty to me,' I continue. 'She's been snooping through my things. She took my journal. She had no right.' I know that I sound like a petulant child when I say the words. But there, I've said it now. The words are out there now, there's no taking them back.

'Louise is nasty to you? No! She is just worried about you,' Charlotte starts.

I shake my head. 'That's what she wants you to think. She's manipulative. She's good at it too. I know how she can appear on the outside to be so nice. So caring. But she's really anything but that. You don't know her like I do. You don't know what she is capable of. The lengths that she will go to, to get what she wants.'

'And what is it that she wants?' Charlotte asks, and I can see by her face that she is still not convinced.

'She wants to send me back there. To the secure unit. She told the doctor that I'm not settling in very well. That I am getting worse. But that's not true. I like it here. It's her that doesn't want me here. She is the one who is making me worse.'

'What do you mean? Why would she do that? That doesn't make sense. Has she actually said that to you?'

I shake my head. 'She doesn't have to. I can see it in her eyes. The way she looks at me. The way they've all looked at me. The staff in the secure unit, the police, social workers. Like I'm a monster. Like I don't deserve to breathe the same oxygen as them.'

'I'm sure that's not the case,' Charlotte continues, a horrified look on her face. I see the way she fidgets now, on her chair. This conversation is making her uncomfortable.

But I need her to listen, I need her to believe me.

'I don't need to be on this medication. I am better,' I say with more conviction than I feel as I stare at Charlotte, eyes fixed on hers as I plead and beg. 'Can you speak with the doctor. Without Louise knowing? Can you tell him, can you explain?'

It feels like it's my only chance.

'Well, I guess it can't hurt to have the conversation,' Charlotte says eventually, but I hear the uncertainty there. We both know, deep down, that the doctor won't listen to her over Louise. Charlotte is only a Support Assistant; she isn't a qualified Health Care Assistant like Louise.

She doesn't hold the same authority or experience.

'Look, I don't want to say anything out of line here, Emily, but I think that we can be honest with each other. I can say things to you, and you won't be offended, because you know that I only want to help you, right?'

I nod. I think I do believe that she wants to help me.

'Why don't you talk to me about what happened? Louise says that you've always refused to talk about it. That you've never spoken a word about what happened. But maybe you should try, because if anything, it might help you get it all out of your head,' Charlotte says softly. 'It might stop the noises permanently if you deal with it. Then you'll be able to show that you really *are* better, that you really don't need these meds.'

Charlotte nods down to the tray again. To the tablets that she has concealed there, the tablets that she had no intention of giving me just yet. She's done me a favour. She's trying to help. Maybe she is right about this too.

'What's the point in talking? No one would listen now,' I say finally. My words coming out slow, laced with caution. 'They'd already made their judgements on me. They don't want to hear my version of what happened. They just want to see me suffer. To be punished forever.'

'I don't want to see you suffer, Emily,' Charlotte says eventually. 'I want to listen. Tell me about the house, Emily. Tell me about what happened to the children.'

'The children...' My lips barely move as I try to find their names in my mouth.

Only they are too painful to say out loud, so I hold them there on the tip of my tongue instead.

'He was playing in the bath,' I say finally. Narrowing my eyes as the memory I summon fills my head. The pain that starts to build inside of me feels immense. Just as raw as it had felt that very night. The tears come too. For all that I lost. For all I regret.

'I loved him,' I say then and look Charlotte dead in the eye. 'They can all say what they want about me. And they have. Child-murderer. Child-killer. Monster. Witch. I've been called every name under the sun, and I don't care. They are only names. What really hurts is that they don't ever say that. That I loved him.'

I can't speak. The rock-hard lump that swells in my throat burns raw as the tears stream down my face.

'What about her. The little girl? Is she the one you hear crying through the wall?'

I nod my head. A rare image of the girl filling my head then. The last image I have of her. Blood trickling down her forehead. A look of hatred in her eyes.

BREATHE!

'I can't. I won't. I won't talk about her,' I whimper, shaking my head as the panic inside me starts to build. Swirling now. Twisting within me, causing the room to spin violently round and around.

'Hey, it's okay. You're okay. You are safe here, Emily,' Charlotte says gently as she passes me one last cup of tea.

I drink it back in one. Hot and sweet and... laced with something bitter. It is only then, when I stare back down at the tray, I realise the napkin has been moved. The tablets have gone.

'I'm sorry, Emily. I know you don't want to take them, but you must. Louise will know otherwise. She'll know that I didn't give them to you, and I will lose my job. You don't want that, do you? For me not to be able to come here any more?' Charlotte is talking fast now.

She is trying to make me understand that she didn't have any other choice.

'I will speak with the doctor. I promise. I will keep an eye on Louise. But in the meantime, we must act normal. And that means you need to keep taking your medication. For now, at least.'

Charlotte's words start to blur and warp and mute, until they are gone completely, and I give in to the darkness of my dreams.

My nightmares.

Now that I have dared to speak of him, they are all about him.

Back at the house. Playing in the bath. Splashing water, having fun.

Squealing with delight.

Until he wasn't.

His body lifeless in the water. Face down, his hair splayed out around his head like a halo floating on the surface.

That feeling of waking up from a trance and not understanding why there was blood on my hands. Blood all up the walls. Blood all over the floor.

The manic scream that had left my mouth.

God almighty, what have I done? What have I done?

23

SASHA

'Okay, so let's see, we've got blankets. *Check*. The story books. *Check*. My rocket torch. *Check*,' Zachery says as he snuggles into the corner of the treehouse, leaving enough space next to him for Annabelle and Sasha to sit down too.

'Hang on, you forgot: annoying little brother! *Check!*' Annabelle grins, nudging Zachery playfully as he rolls his eyes, laughing too despite himself.

'This is so cosy. Can we sleep out here, Sasha? Pretty please?'

'Well, It's a bit cold, Zachery. I think sleepovers in the tree-house will be better for some time in the summer.'

They've only been out here for a few minutes and already she is regretting suggesting it, as the cold air whips all around the treehouse. The leaves above them on the branches dancing wildly in time with it.

'Yeah, like when we have a heatwave!' Annabelle chimes in, her teeth chattering despite wearing a big coat and having a blanket around her. Sasha couldn't help but laugh. The children were still upset about yesterday and Sasha just wanted to cheer them up. Hopeful that when Cecelia comes home later tonight, they can all put last night's argument behind them all.

That was the plan, at least.

'I didn't realise that it was going to be so cold tonight. Hopefully our hot chocolate will warm us up a bit,' Sasha says, pulling out the flask from her bag that she has made for the children especially, before pouring the drinks into the three cups. To her surprise, it seems to do the trick. Zachery seems content with that. Taking the cup gratefully, he cradles it in his hands. Annabelle does the same.

'Okay, everyone comfortable?' Sasha asks as the children nod in agreement. Sasha starts reading.

'"Right at the bottom of the ocean, inside a giant oyster shell, a mermaid sleeps"...'

The children were enchanted. Snuggled together under the blankets, their hands wrapped around the warmth of their mugs as the gentle soothing torchlight illuminated the inside of the treehouse. Mesmerised, they hung on Sasha's every word, as she knew they would. The children had become obsessed with mermaids and mermen. So Sasha had taken a trip to the library while they were at school and got them a selection of books on both, which she knew would please Zachery no end. Proof that men could be mermen too.

'"As she swims her long seaweed hair floats all around her. Her top made of magnificent pearls and tiny shells. Ariel grabs Finbarr's hand and they both swim back down to their secret cave. Happy to be back home again. Back where they both belong. The end."'

'Ahh, can we have one more? That was such a short one,' Zachery says, eyeing the small pile of books. 'We don't want to go back inside yet. Do we, Annabelle?'

'No, not yet. This is so fun.'

'Okay!' Sasha laughs, glad the children are enjoying themselves and knowing that she'd never hear the end of it if she said no. Zachery wouldn't give in. 'But this time, Annabelle, I think you should read one for us. We can say it was part of your school homework,' Sasha says, knowing that she'd let the children off doing their homework again tonight. They were at school for so much of the day and she didn't think it was fair that they'd be made to sit at the table for an hour every night working too, when they could be doing other things, better things, like this.

'Okay! Which one shall I read?' Annabelle asks Zachery, accepting the challenge just as Sasha knew she would.

'This one. This one.' Zachery hands Annabelle the merman story and Sasha gives Zachery the torch to hold.

Annabelle begins. Slowly at first, each word pronounced clearly, concisely. The child's voice soothing, hypnotic almost. As the shadows from the torchlight dance across the wooden planks of the room, Sasha is daydreaming. Lost in her thoughts as she wonders how much use the children actually got from this treehouse. Because they weren't allowed up here unless they were supervised. It was too high. And Cecelia always seemed so busy, Sasha can't imagine that Annabelle and Zachery were up here much at all.

Sasha stares out of the small window watching the branches as they sway in the wind. Tiny droplets of rain falling. An image popping into her mind. *Red wellington boots sinking in the mud.* She is standing at the foot of a tree and looking up. Then she's climbing. The rain pouring down on her as she lifts her foot and places it on a tyre swing. Her hand reaching up for the rope.

Above her is a big red juicy-looking apple.

If she tiptoes, she can just about reach it. Just a few more inches.

Her fingers scrape at the flesh of the apple.

Then she is falling fast.

THUD!

Pain in her head explodes as she hits the ground.

She lies there, startled. Staring up at the darkened night's sky as the grey clouds, illuminated only by the moon, dance above her.

Her hair and clothes caked in mud. Her face is wet from crying.

She can't get up. Winded now, the air expelled from her body.

Everything hurts, but her head is banging.

Reaching up she touches her scalp before pulling her hand away and seeing the blood on her fingertips.

A woman nearby is shouting.

Her voice angry and hysterical.

BAD GIRL. BAD GIRL.

She is grabbing at her arm, pulling her up. Forcing her back on to her feet.

The woman's fingers pinch hard at her skin, digging into her flesh as if she purposely wants to hurt her.

'Sasha?'

Annabelle's voice cuts through Sasha's thoughts, making the memory immediately disappear.

'We finished the book,' Annabelle says, a disappointed look on her face that Sasha hadn't been paying attention.

'It was very, very good,' Sasha lies. 'Top marks in your homework book for you, missy!'

That seems to do the trick, as the hard look on Annabelle's face softens.

It is raining harder now, and the wind has picked up. Sasha needs to get the children inside.

'Come on, let's run you both a bath to warm you up properly before bed.'

The children do as they are told, gathering their things and passing them to Sasha as she stands at the bottom of the tree-house ladder, guiding them carefully down. As she looks up at the apple tree, she wonders if the memory she'd just had, had been real.

She thinks that it might be.

What kind of a woman could chastise a small child while they lay there bleeding and hurt on the floor? What kind of a woman stands there shouting instead of caring for her, instead of picking her back up and placing a kiss upon her head and checking that she was okay?

Instead, she is screamed at. Dragged up by her arms back onto her feet and shouted at.

Bad girl. Bad girl.

Sasha feels the anger swell inside of her then.

What kind of a woman could do that to a child?

24

EMILY

'How are you feeling, Emily?' Louise's voice fills my ears as soon as I wake.

How am I feeling? Is that a joke? I feel like a zombie. There's a dull pounding ache banging against the inside of my skull. As I try and sit up, my limbs feel heavy and awkward. My mouth is dry, and my lips feel cracked.

'I thought Charlotte was here,' I say, confused. Because she'd been sitting by the bed a while ago. We'd both been drinking tea.

'What time is it?' I ask, though part of me isn't even sure what day it is. I've completely lost track.

'It's dinner time. I'm just heating something up for you in the microwave.'

I nod. Wishing it was still Charlotte here instead. I was only supposed to get one visit a day, but this new medication has put paid to that.

They take turns to come and see me. Dividing the three visits a day between them, so that they can ensure I'm taking my meds at regular intervals. Charlotte mainly does the lunchtime shift, sometimes the odd evening. She can't do the mornings because she has other commitments. Louise's only commitment, it seems, is me. Because she is the one who is here the most. Which means I have to be on my guard constantly now that I know she has got a personal vendetta against me, but it's so hard to focus because all I want to do is sleep.

'You were having a bad dream. You were talking in your sleep,' Louise informs me. There is a smugness gleaming from her eyes as she speaks. Like she's aware that she has some power over me, that she knows things about me that I do not.

I hate that.

That I have no control over what's coming out of my mouth when I sleep and no memory of what I've said when I wake afterwards.

'What was I saying?' I ask, feeling anxiety bubble then, as Louise looks right through me.

'You were talking about living in another house. An old house with an apple tree in the garden. Do you remember?'

I shrug, shaking my head as I look down. Breaking eye contact with her, because she always sees straight through me. Did I talk in my sleep? I'm not sure. I think that maybe she is playing more games with me. She knows all about that house and what happened there. She knows about the apple tree too. Of course she does.

Is this just another way of her taunting me again?

I think back to the conversation I had with Charlotte last night. How she'd asked me about the children. She'd asked me to tell her about what had happened to them.

The children.

They had been my last thoughts before the drugs had taken me and I had closed my eyes and given in to darkness. I had dreamt about them.

I had dreamt that I was back there with them both, inside that godforsaken house.

The crying girl? I still can't hear her, I realise, as I glance around my room. The humming vibration from the microwave the only real sound.

She's not crying any more.

That's the only small mercy that these tablets have given me. That they are strong enough to shut her up. To shut her out. I guess I should be grateful for that if nothing else.

PING.

The microwave makes a sudden sound to alert us that the food is ready, and Louise brings it to me on a tray. My stomach growls with hunger as the smell of something delicious floats around the room.

'Chicken stew, yum,' she says as she places the tray down on my lap. Her steely gaze unwavering as she holds mine.

I glance down at the steaming bowl and fight the urge to be sick as I see the large clumps of white meat swimming in brown, watery juice. My mind is straight back there, engrained with the image of the maggots that crawled across the grey, slimy flesh of the rotten chicken breasts that Louise had deliberately hidden underneath my bed.

She is doing this on purpose, isn't she?

This is all part of it, another game of hers. She is enjoying it too.

'What's up, Emily? You like chicken stew, it's one of your favourites.' Her expression gives nothing away, but I know that it is in there. The malicious intent behind her words as she taunts me now, as I try my hardest not to gag.

'I'm not really hungry,' I lie.

'You have to eat something, Emily. You need to keep up your strength.'

I swirl the spoon in the slop that swims in the bowl, biding my time as she watches me. Willing me to take my first bite. She won't leave until I've eaten it. I know this. Because it's only then that she can give me my next lot of medication. I am stubborn but she is too, and we will play this game all night if I don't give in and do as she asks. I bring the spoon to my lips and swallow down a mouthful without bothering to chew first, all the while I am trying not to think about the contents as they slip down my throat. But it is there. Lingering. The memory of the stinking, foul, rotten stench of chicken that had lingered in my flat for days, makes me gag.

I feel the bile rise in the back of my throat and I instinctively swallow that back down.

BREATHE EMILY, I tell myself.

Don't give her the satisfaction of seeing you suffering.

I take another mouthful. And another. And soon the bowl is empty. I lie back against my pillow and wonder how she does it. How she manages to keep such a straight face, when behind her expression is so much hatred for me.

'I picked up a couple of books from the charity shop in the high street. They're good ones. I'll leave them here on the table for you,' Louise says, as if we are friends that belong to the same book club. As if we regularly sit in a packed room with other book-loving women, sharing recommendations whilst sipping on cold glasses of cheap white wine.

'Charlotte left you some too?' Louise says, eyeing the small pile on the kitchen table, before placing hers on top. I nod. Then mouth the words *thank you*. Because I don't want to seem ungrateful. Books are probably one of the only things that me and Louise do actually have in common, though sometimes I wonder if she has any real friends of her own, or if that's why she shares her books with me. Maybe she doesn't have anyone else to talk to about the plots and the characters after we're both done.

'Right, time for your meds.' She is back, standing next to my bed, holding out a glass of water and two tiny white pills. Tiny but lethal. These two white pills are capable of taking so much from me.

She sees me hesitate.

'I know you don't like them, but trust me, they are for your own good.'

I bite my lip.

For my own good. She uses that one a lot. It's one of her favourite forms of manipulation. She watches as I place the pills on my tongue and then bring the glass to my mouth. Her eyes scrutinising me as I swallow the cool liquid back.

'Good girl.' The words are patronising and condescending, as intended, and she takes the glass. She doesn't know that I have managed to slip the two pills underneath my tongue. That I pressed down hard as I gulped at the water, so that they wouldn't move.

I wait now, until she has turned her back, before I spit the pills back out into the tissue that I've concealed inside the sleeve of my pyjama top. I screw it into a ball and shove it quickly, underneath my pillow.

I can't do this any more. I can't keep slipping back to that dark place. I won't allow her to keep making me feel sick again. To start questioning my reality, my dreams. To fear what I am saying out loud in my sleep.

Finally, satisfied that she has done everything she came here to do, she leaves.

I run towards the bathroom. Unsteady on my feet, I stumble. The force of my body slamming hard into the kitchen table, sending the pile of books flying. I quickly pick them up and arrange them neatly again, before staring at the front door.

I'm worried she'll come back at any second and catch me in the act of disposing of the tablets.

There is no sign of her.

I need to be quick.

I run to the toilet and throw the tissue holding the tablets into the water. Then I flush the chain. Watching as the whirlpool of water gathers momentum, spinning in circles before sucking the pills down the drain along with it. They are gone. I did it.

I need to fight now, for myself.

Louise makes out that she is trying to help.

That this is all for my own good. But I know that it's not.

I am the only one who can save me.

25

SASHA

Sasha can't shake the image from her mind that she'd seen when she was in the treehouse. It had felt like it was real, like a memory of something that had actually happened once. To her.

Or is she just imagining it? Because her mind does that a lot to her, doesn't it? Plays tricks on her. She thinks about the letter then.

Her mother's final, parting gift.

How she'd finally told her the truth in a bid to set her free.

Sasha is unable to suppress the bitterness in the laugh that escapes her now. Because this is almost comical, isn't it? How had it been three months since she'd set eyes upon it for the very first time? Three months since her whole entire life had come crashing down all around her.

'Saved.'

That was the word that her mother had used, wasn't it?

Saved by her.

Sasha wants to laugh at that. She grips on to the bath's edge, squeezing the porcelain so tightly with her fists that the pinks of her knuckles turn a bright white. The word *saved* makes her think of being rescued. Rescued like a mangy, stray, unloved dog that has been dumped out on the street once its owners have grown bored of it.

Saved was what happened to vulnerable, fragile people. Sasha wasn't any of those things. Her mother had used other words that Sasha hadn't liked, in her letter too. Words that had left her feeling blindsided and numb.

Like 'adopted'.

Because you would know something like that about yourself, wouldn't you? Deep down, somewhere in your subconscious, you would feel that, wouldn't you? That you didn't really belong. How the woman that raised you wasn't really your biological mother. How Sasha hadn't been born from her.

She wasn't a Hammond and never had been. The family that had brought her up were not bound by the same strong hold of blood that held some families firmly together like glue. Her father, the man she had a long time ago grieved for, hadn't been hers either.

Only Sasha had no idea, because it had been cruel of her mother to allow her to grieve for something that had never really been hers to mourn. That revelation had pained her greatly.

Igniting something so deep in her soul that even she couldn't reach inside and touch it. But she had felt it burning there since. A slow building anger, bubbling and simmering away just underneath the surface, at the injustice of it all.

Not ever being told her own truth until now, and even now she still only knew the bare minimum. How she had several missing years of her life that she had no recollection of ever living. Several missing years of her life. The girl she was before. Her life was destroyed now; her whole world had violently imploded since then. Crashing down all around her, leaving nothing but chaos and destruction in its wake.

She had questions now. So many questions.

Only the harder she tried to seek out the answers, the further away she seemed to get from them.

'SASHA!'

A high-pitched voice swims around inside her head. For a second it feels as if she is imagining it. As if the screams that echo off the walls are dimmed before they reach her ears. Muted, as if it is coming from somewhere way off in the distance.

Not right here in this room where she sits.

Where is she?

Because she feels as if she is sinking inside of herself, caught with the dark thoughts inside her head.

Is she asleep?

'Get off him. GET OFF HIM.'

The high-pitched voice comes again. Louder this time. Filled with terror.

'SASHA! Sasha. Get off him!'

Annabelle?

Sasha feels it then. The scrape of something sharp clawing at the skin of her arms. Pinching and hitting her.

'GET OFF HIM!' The little girl's voice roars through her.

There's an almighty pain then, the feeling of sharpness sinking into her flesh followed by a burning agony that radiates down to her very core.

FLASH.

Sasha is back in the room, out of her trance.

Staring down at her arm. To where Annabelle's mouth is locked on to her skin.

The child is biting down, frenzied, like a wild animal.

'Annabelle?' Sasha shouts, pulling her arm away in a bid to break free. Sending the girl flying across the bathroom floor and landing in a heap.

'Oh my God, Annabelle, I'm sorry,' she starts, distracted by the pain that radiates from her arm which is searing now. She stares down at the circular teeth marks that have been sunk deep into her flesh, realising the damage that Annabelle has done. Watching in horror as a thin trickle of blood trails down her arm, towards her wrist.

'What the hell? Annabelle?'

Sasha doesn't understand what has happened. Only minutes ago, they were all playing. The children splashing wildly around in the water, enthralled in making a mess. All of them laughing. Now, Annabelle is crying. Sobbing loudly as she drags herself up from the floor where she landed and hurries back towards the bath. She reaches down into the water and drags her distraught younger brother out by his arms.

'Zachery?' Sasha says. Seeing how red and puffy his face looks as he coughs and splutters and pants for breath.

Why is he coughing like that?

Like he has been struggling to breathe.

Like he's been submerged under the water? Had he been playing mermen again while Sasha had become distracted?

'Zachery, darling. Are you okay?'

Sasha searches his eyes, but Zachery stares back at her with contempt. There is fear there too. Wide-eyed and filled with terror as he spits out mouthfuls of water that has seeped inside his mouth. Filling his throat, his lungs, his stomach. He retches, emptying the contents of his stomach all over the bathroom floor, until there is nothing left inside of him.

'My God! Zachery? What happened?' Sasha says, but her voice is small now. Pricked with fear as she anticipates his reply, the air around her turning icy. How long had she been daydreaming? How long had he been under the water? Too long, she thinks, seeing how his lips are tinged blue, his skin ashen as he fights to steady his breath. How had she not realised what was happening?

'Annabelle?' Sasha's voice is almost a whisper. The little girl's mouth is fixed in a fierce, straight line. A furious expression on her face. Furious with her?

'Annabelle? What happened?'

Annabelle doesn't answer. Instead, she quickly ushers her younger brother back to his feet, wrapping a towel around his trembling body before leading him quickly from the room. It's only then that she realises she is wet too. The sleeves of her sweater gathered at the crook of her arms are soaked.

Saturated as if they too had been submerged in that bath water.

Oh my God! She realises with horror then.

She'd been holding Zachery down underneath the water.

Shaking in shock and disgust at her actions, a chill of terror runs through her.

She'd lost control completely.

She'd almost drowned him.

26

SASHA

'Annabelle? Zachery?' Sasha's shouts are frantic now as she desperately searches the children's bedrooms, looking for them to no avail. Both children are upset, and rightfully so.

Sasha feels frightened too.

She has no memory of holding Zachery down under the water, no memory of her actions at all. It was as if something had got inside of her and made her do it. She thinks of what Cecelia had said to her about believing in ghosts. About the bad energy that she felt lingering inside of these walls.

Sasha can feel it here too. It was as if something had possessed her. What on earth was going on inside of this house?

Cecelia will be home soon, and the last thing Sasha needs is her walking into this chaos. The children will tell Cecelia what happened. They will tell her that she had tried to hurt Zachery, that she had held him underneath the water and almost drowned him.

Cecelia would call the police.

She needs to find them.

Throwing herself down on the floor Sasha scans underneath Annabelle's bed, before getting up and checking the only place she hasn't looked yet. Inside the wardrobe. Pulling the door open, she pushes back the rail of clothing, checking that the two children are not cowering there in the darkened corners at the very back.

They are not in there.

The wardrobe is empty, the bedrooms are too.

Taking the stairs, Sasha runs from room to room as she continues to call out the children's names.

'Annabelle. Zachery. I know you're scared right now. But I want you to know that I didn't mean for what happened. It was an accident and I'm very, very sorry.'

No one responds to her pleas.

The house is silent, her voice carrying through the empty space and echoing off the walls as if she is the only one in here now. She feels sick. Anxiety pools in the pit of her stomach. Her head starts to throb.

All she wants is a chance to explain, to make it right. To tell the children that she hadn't meant to harm Zachery. That she'd been in some kind of a trance. She'd had no control of what she was doing. Though even to her own ears, her reasoning doesn't make any sense.

She sounds like a crazy person.

Is she crazy?

Because ever since she arrived at this house last week, she has felt as if she might be.

It's like a darkness from within these walls has taken hold inside of her.

She can feel it, how something sinister has seeped underneath her skin and wound its way around the deepest recesses of her mind.

As if it has shaken awake all of the bad thoughts inside of her.

It feels as if the house is trying to communicate with her in some way, as if it's trying to tell her something. Or trying to remind her.

The nightmares and visions that she has been plagued with for her entire life have become worse here.

The little boy standing at the end of her bed, then he was gone. Just like that.

The horrific sight of the boy's body floating lifelessly in the bloodied bath water.

Were they fragments of the awful events that went on inside this house back then or was her memory slowly coming back to her?

Or worse, what if they were premonitions of what was still to come?

'Annabelle, Zachery. Please listen to me. You need to come out. Stop hiding. This is silly. You know me. I would never hurt you.'

Her voice is firmer now. Full of authority. Determined to show that she is still in control, that she is the adult here. She is the one in charge. The children need to listen to her. They need to do as they are told. She is met by only silence still. Reaching the front door, Sasha sees that the door is slightly ajar. The catch is up high, but Annabelle is tall enough and more than capable of reaching it and getting them both out of the house. Sasha grabs her shoes and shoves her feet inside of them.

A glow of yellow streetlamps and streams of light pouring out through other residents' windows illuminate an otherwise dark and empty street. There is no sign of them. Though she is certain that they couldn't have got far in the short time they'd been gone. They'd be freezing if they were out here. Sasha eyes the curtains of nearby properties looking for signs of people peering out from within. Watching for her.

Would Annabelle and Zachery have made it that far? Would any of the do-gooder, nosy neighbours believe two little children if they turned up at their front door telling stories?

They might do, if the children seemed distressed. And it wouldn't help that neither of them were dressed. That they were still wet from their bath and covered only in towels.

It had been cold enough when they'd been out here earlier, having stories in the treehouse.

The treehouse.

It was an obvious place. Even though the children had left via the front door, it would have only taken them seconds to slip around the back of the property. Maybe that is where they are hiding out as they wait for their mother to return. Sasha hurries, making her way the length of the garden, and clambering up the wet wooden steps.

'Annabelle? Zachery?' Sasha says as she reaches the top, and she sees the dark, huddled silhouette crouched down at the very back of the treehouse.

Zachery starts crying loudly then, the incident in the bathroom has clearly left him terrified of what Sasha will do to him. Annabelle is the one to push herself forward, shielding Zachery behind her now as if she is his protector. They are both shivering uncontrollably from a mixture of shock and fear, no doubt, Sasha thinks.

'Please, come inside. It's freezing out here. You'll both catch colds.'

'Leave us alone,' Annabelle shouts assertively, but as the words come out of her mouth, her bottom lip trembles giving her fear away.

'I didn't mean it. You have to believe me. I can't explain what happened. I was daydreaming. I was in a trance. But it wasn't me. You know me,' Sasha says, stepping close to the children, her arms stretched out, palms up, an open gesture. Of telling the truth. She wants them to believe her. She needs them to believe her.

'Please, Zachery. I'm sorry. You believe me, don't you? I would never hurt you,' Sasha asks again. Closer now. Her hand reaches out and ruffles his mop of hair. He winces, flinching backwards at her touch, as if she is on fire and her touch has just burned his skin.

'I want my mummy!' Zachery cries in his small, singsong voice. 'I want my mummy. I want my mummy.'

Annabelle joins in. The two children chant together, a united front. After all Sasha has done for them, they aren't even prepared to listen. They aren't even prepared to give her the benefit of the doubt.

'You want your mummy?' Sasha says sadly, nodding her head. 'Look at my arm, Annabelle. What do you think your mummy will say when she sees that you made me bleed from biting me? And what about the water that's all over the bathroom floor, Zachery? Do you think Mummy will be cross about all the mess you've both made?' Sasha says, watching as the children exchange a nervous look.

'You've seen how angry Mummy gets when you don't do as you're told. But that's okay, I understand. I just hope she doesn't shout at you both again, like she did when you threw your breakfast bowl, Zachery. And when you accidentally knocked over Mummy's wine glass, Annabelle.'

The children falter. Sasha sees it in their faces, how they are not so certain now that telling their mummy what Sasha had done tonight was the best idea. How they might get in trouble too. If they tell Mummy about tonight she might get mad again. Because she was mad a lot lately. Both children had told her that.

'Look, I didn't mean what happened in the bathroom, you have to believe me. I'm sorry. I really am,' Sasha tries again, now their anger has subsided. 'Come on, let's go back inside and snuggle up warm in bed?' Sasha gently holds out her hand and guides each child towards the ladder of the treehouse.

'You'll catch your death out here.'

27

EMILY

I can read. For the first time in what feels like forever I can actually concentrate on reading almost an entire book, cover to cover. I've managed to miss three doses of my meds now without Louise noticing me spitting out my tablets. That's almost a whole day and night without them. The paralysing concoction is finally out of my system.

I know this, because the crying girl is back with a vengeance.

Her loud cries radiating through the walls.

When I first heard her, I had actually laughed out loud. A proper belly laugh. Partly relieved in a way, that I was no longer numb to my surroundings, that despite the constant torment she brings me, she is the indisputable sign that I am back in control of my mind and my body. Even though she is loud, somehow, I can think more clearly now that I am back in control of myself.

I have been thinking a lot today. About how if I can keep spitting my meds out, unnoticed. How if I just try and block the girl out completely, if I just pretend with everything that I have inside of me that I can't hear her, even when I'm here all by myself, I might just be able to do this. To prove to Louise and the doctor that despite their concerns, I am really better.

That I do deserve to be here.

They can't send me back to the unit if I'm not causing any drama, can they?

I can't go back there. Back to where the nurses press their face against your bedroom window at fifteen-minute intervals, so you never feel as if you have any privacy. Back to where there are always a pair of beady eyes watching you.

It's noisier there too. Even without the girl crying. The constant loud shrill of alarms going off. Numerous residents punching and hitting at their doors in desperation to be let out. The constant awful thud of the woman opposite my room as she repeatedly smacks her head off the wall.

No. I won't go back there.

Pulling my blanket back, I hold my thumb inside the pages of the book that I am reading, so that I don't lose my place, and make my way to the kitchen to boil the kettle. I have at least another hour until Louise or Charlotte come. I pray that it will be Charlotte this time, because if it is her, I won't have to pretend that I'm not taking my meds. She already knows why I don't want to take them.

If Louise comes, she'll see straight away. She'll know that I am functioning, when I should be anything but. I'll have to act my innocence out, get back into bed and pretend that I'm still enslaved to the medication. Looking disorientated when she wakes me and pretend that I haven't been reading at all.

The reading would be a giveaway. She'll know I don't have that amount of concentration. Is that why she left the books? To taunt me with them.

I pour myself a pot of tea and sit down at the kitchen table. Satisfied that the pot will cool, and I can rinse it out so that no one will be any the wiser. As the tea brews, I keep reading.

Thumbing my fingers through the pages, drinking in the words. Lost in a world of make-believe.

When I turn the next page, something falls from the book. At first, I think a page has come loose, or that it is a long-forgotten bookmark pressed between the pages. I bend to pick it up, recognising the thick, bold print to be a newspaper headline. The edge of the cutting is jagged, as if it's been roughly torn from the newspaper page.

I see the image of the face below and it makes me falter.

I knew that woman once.

A long, long time ago.

Blonde hair hanging down and covering one side of my face, as if I'm trying to shield myself from the crowd of reporters. Only they caught me anyway. Piercing blue eyes, wide with fear and something else. Shame.

My eyes fix on the headline.

MONSTER DROWNS BOY IN THE BATH.

Monster. Me. I am the monster.

Part of me doesn't want to read on. I've tried so long to block it out. To purposely not think about it. Telling myself how it was another lifetime ago now. A different lifetime altogether. So far from my life now that it almost doesn't feel real.

I am no longer that person.

But it did happen, and I force myself to read it. To acknowledge the words that are emblazoned on the paper in his memory. It's the very least that I can do.

It is thought that she murdered the three-year-old boy, while suffering from undiagnosed psychosis.

I see his name. My eyes can't move from it. There is a tightness in my chest as a raw, burning pain replaces the air that is quickly expelled from my lungs. I don't want to read on, but I must. Even though I know that the reckless pain that will come will consume me. And I deserve that still. I deserve everything that comes my way.

For him.

The little boy's body was discovered in the garden of his family residence next to what is believed to be a partially dug, shallow grave.

The words begin to swim erratically blurry black and white against the page. I can see it then, inside my head.

That house.

That bathroom.

The apple tree in the garden.

His tiny lifeless body lying in the wet mud as rain lashed down all around us.

My fault.

My fault.

Pleaded guilty to manslaughter by reason of diminished responsibility and has been sent for treatment at a psychiatric hospital indefinitely.

My hands shake. My eyes fix on the word 'indefinitely'. That was what this was all about, wasn't it? That's why she has done this. Louise. She has put this clipping inside the book on purpose for me to find it. As a reminder to me about what I did. As if I would ever forget. To remind me that I am not worthy of having another chance at life. Of living here on my own. That I am not worthy.

And maybe she is right, and I am wrong. Maybe I do belong back at the secure unit with all the deranged, crazy people.

Maybe they should lock me up and throw away the key.

But I am not crazy any more. I am not deluded.

Or am I?

Because I can hear her again, can't I? The little girl.

How she keeps on crying.

I had wanted to kill her too.

Murderous thoughts entered my head at least a thousand times.

I wanted her dead.

You're a bad person, Emily!

'Stop it!' I shout. Slamming my hands against my ears. As her crying grows louder as if she knows my thoughts. As if she knows the guilt inside of me is crucifying me.

'Stop it!' I am beating at my head now. Pummelling my fists against my skull. Trying to push her out. My chest heaving as I lose my breath, as my heart hammers inside as I feel the onslaught of a panic attack. My second one in as many weeks. Louise has done this to me. With the rotten meat that she hid underneath my bed, and this newspaper cutting she left inside one of the books. She is trying to break me and it's working.

I can't do this. I can't do this any more.

I can't fight her.

I punch harder. Smacking my ears, my face, my skull.

The pain isn't enough. It's never enough.

'Emily? What are you doing? Stop!'

Charlotte is here. The panic in her voice as she runs in through the door makes me suddenly stop.

'Emily? It's okay. I'm here. I am here.'

I feel as though I am outside of my body, but as she crouches down beside me on the floor and wraps her arms around me tightly, somehow, she manages to pull me back in.

'It's going to be okay, Emily.'

BREATHE.

I don't believe her.

'No! It's not going to be okay. Not really. Not now, not ever,'

I say, trying to find the words to explain, but I don't know where to start. So, I pick up the discarded newspaper clipping from the floor and wave it in front of her. Hysteria taking over.

'She is doing this to me. Louise. She put this here. She wants to put me back in that unit INDEFINITELY.' I manage to splutter the last word in that article that I'd read.

BREATHE.

Charlotte reaches for it. Her eyes scanning the words and, as much as I can barely stand to see her reaction as she processes it, I feel that I must.

'Where did you get this?' she asks, her hand going to her mouth, before she looks at me with tears in her eyes.

'I told you. She stole my journal and read through all my private thoughts. She left rotten meat underneath my bed, and now this.'

Charlotte's expression is unreadable. She is trying to stay professional and give nothing away. But I can see it in her eyes. She believes me.

'She torments me. Every. Single. Day. So that I'll break. And I will break soon. It's inevitable. Then Louise will get her wish and she will send me back there. To the hospital, where they'll lock me up in that room again, and I can't go back there. I don't want to go back there. I am better now. I need you to help me. To stop her.' I sob. 'She is trying to break me, and it is working.'

I search Charlotte's face as I ask the final question. 'You believe me, don't you?'

There is scepticism there. A flicker of doubt. And I start then to doubt myself. Until, finally, Charlotte nods.

She picks up the bottle of pills that have been ready in her hand and slips them into her pocket.

She is taking them away. She's not going to give me any more.

She believes me. Thank God. Thank God!

It's the only lifeline that I need.

28

SASHA

Sasha hovers outside Annabelle's bedroom door. She feels nervous now, full of dread as she leans in and presses her ear to the girl's bedroom door, straining to hear the voices from within. Because they are deliberately speaking in muted whispers, which only confirms to Sasha what she already knows deep down. That Annabelle is confiding in her mother about what happened tonight.

She is telling Cecelia what she did to Zachery.

Shit!

Sasha closes her eyes and bites down hard on her lip. Her jaw is set hard with tension now, and there is a heaviness bearing down in her chest. She'd never meant to hurt or scare Zachery. She'd never hurt either of the children. Not intentionally at least. She scrunches her fists into tight balls at her side, angry that tonight, of all nights, Cecelia has come home early. The last thing she wants is for Cecelia to think she might harm one of the children, to distrust her, to let her go.

She can't leave now, not when she is so close to remembering what happened here, when she'd been a child.

If she'd just had a bit more time with the children so that

she could have convinced them, she could have fixed this. She is sure of it.

She had made a start. Admitting to the children about the funny turns she sometimes had. Sitting on the edge of Annabelle's bed, as she confessed her deepest darkest secrets, in a bid to get them to believe that she really hadn't meant to hurt them. She'd felt at her most vulnerable then, finally telling her truth out loud. Even if it was to a six- and three-year-old. She'd told them about her weird daydreams and terrifying nightmares that had plagued her all of her life. From way back, as early as she could remember. When she'd been a small child, just like them.

She'd told them how sometimes, not often, she acted out the visions that she saw. Not purposely. Never purposely. She didn't have any control over that. It was as if sometimes her body and mind just took over. She'd wake to find herself standing in the freezing cold garden in the complete darkness of night with no idea how she got there. Or worse, like the other night, she'd wake to find herself locked inside the bedroom crawlspace cupboard.

She saw people too. Or at least she thought they were real people. Only now, she wonders if they are ghosts. Glimpses of spirits before they disappear into thin air. Just like that little boy who stood at the end of her bed the other night, who she'd thought was Zachery.

The children had sat, wide-eyed and teary as they'd hung on to her every word. She had started to get through to them too, she was sure of it. She'd seen how they had clung to one another, their little arms locked together tightly as she'd continued to pour her heart out to them. How the sympathy they had for her shone out from their eyes.

Or had she read it all wrong and what she'd really seen looking back at her had been fear? Because she would have sounded crazy, she realises now. Telling them about the strange, creepy episodes she had. How she saw people who weren't really there. How she acted out things in her sleep.

After what they'd just witnessed from her in the bathroom.

They would have been terrified.

Annabelle had screamed for her mother to come upstairs, as soon as the children heard her key turn in the front door, and demanded that Sasha leave the room. Sasha had stood outside, trying to listen in, ever since. As the children's crying turned into hushed whispers.

She is pacing now, marching up and down the narrow hallway as she recites her excuses inside of her head, so that she is ready for Cecelia when she steps out of that room. What she did tonight is inexcusable, and she can't find the words to make any of this right. Cecelia will ask her to leave now that she knows what happened; more than likely, she'll call the police.

They'll find out who she is then. How she shouldn't really be here. She's not who she's pretending to be.

Sasha wonders if she should just leave now, while she still can, but the pull of the house is so strong. The memories of her life here feel as if they are so close, just hovering nearby almost in her reach.

She stares down at the large, angry purple welt on her arm. Recalling the look of distress on Zachery's face as Annabelle had finally dragged him free from her hold.

Then she hears a movement in the bedroom. The sound of Cecelia planting soothing kisses on the children's foreheads. A lamp being switched off. Footsteps moving towards the door.

Sasha retreats down the stairs, making her way into the kitchen so that she looks as if she's been down here keeping busy, not up there, listening in. Sasha goes straight to the fridge and pours them both a large glass of wine, because they would both need one, when Cecelia joins her for the inevitable fallout.

'Sasha? What in the hell is going on?' Cecelia demands, walking into the kitchen, a thunderous look on her face as if she is still trying to digest what she's just been told. 'Annabelle and Zachery are beside themselves up there. They told me that there was an incident tonight in the bath?' Cecelia emphasises the word *incident* as if she can't bring herself to say the words that Sasha knows she's been told.

That Sasha tried to drown Zachery in the bath.

'Well?'

Sasha falters, because Cecelia is not throwing her out of the house. She is not screaming accusations at her, or worse, launching herself at Sasha. Attacking the woman in a vicious attempt to protect her babies at all costs. Because that's what any mother would do, wasn't it? If she really thought someone tried to intentionally harm her child.

She'd fight to the death to protect them. But Cecelia isn't doing any of that.

She doesn't believe them, Sasha thinks, relieved then, as Cecelia searches her face for answers.

If she stays calm, if she acts normal, Cecelia might just take her word over the children's. Because if Sasha had done something so heinous as trying to drown one of Cecelia's children, she wouldn't be standing in Cecelia's kitchen right now, offering the woman a glass of wine. She holds the glass out, and to her amazement Cecelia takes it, as she hoped she would. Drinking a large gulp down as she waits for Sasha to tell her what has been going on here tonight.

She is giving her a chance to explain.

Sasha takes it.

'Annabelle bit me,' Sasha says, playing the only trump card she has to use against the child, as she holds up her arm. The two U-shaped arches of teeth marks gouged in her skin, which has turned a deep, mottled shade of purple now. There is blood too.

'I told her it was time to get out of the bath and she bit my arm, hard. She said that I didn't let her have any fun. That I was mean and horrible, "just like Mummy"!' Sasha's words are purposely loaded, because she knows the guilt that Cecelia holds. How the children have been so upset with her lately. How this would hurt.

Cecelia falters.

Sasha sounds so convincing. Even she can hear it, the conviction behind every word she is saying. She just needs Cecelia to believe it too.

'Annabelle told me that she bit you in a bid to get you off Zachery. She said that you were holding him down under the water?' Cecelia's voice shakes as she speaks. With anger mainly but there is an uncertainty there too. An undertone of doubt creeping in. That Sasha would be capable of doing such a thing.

She sees it then, how the woman just can't seem to process the children's claims as true. She can't quite believe that Sasha is capable of doing something so horrific. This is all Sasha needs, a tiny flicker of doubt that she can use to her advantage.

'Annabelle says a lot of things,' Sasha says carefully, pausing then, as if she is unsure whether or not to elaborate further. Though she knows that she must. 'Look, I didn't want to say anything to you earlier, because I know how much you've already got on your plate, but...' Sasha says carefully. As if she doesn't know how to broach such a sensitive subject. 'I've seen this type of behaviour before. The storytelling, the cries for attention. I think your divorce has affected the children more than you realise.'

'The divorce? You think Annabelle is making up stories about you trying to drown Zachery in the bath because me and Henry are getting a *divorce*?' Cecelia spits the word, as if she is unwilling to accept that she and Henry are the real problem here.

Sasha doesn't give her an answer, instead she sips at her own glass of wine. Watching as Cecelia follows suit. Tipping hers back and draining the glass. Pleased that she's clearly hit a nerve, just as she intended.

'I know that this is hard for you to hear, Cecelia, and to be honest with you, I didn't want to say anything, as I know how stressful things have been for you lately. But Annabelle's behaviour has been a real concern to me. I thought maybe you were just ignoring it. But you have seen it too, right? All the times she has lashed out at poor Zachery. I think that she is doing it on purpose, that she is taking out all her anger and insecurities on her brother by mimicking your behaviour.'

'Mimicking my behaviour?' Cecelia almost shouts then at the audacity of Sasha's unfair observation.

'Don't you see it?' Sasha asks, narrowing her eyes. 'How she calls him names and is always arguing with him. Just like you do on the phone with Henry.'

'What?' Cecelia's voice is incredulous. High-pitched with indignation. 'That is not the same thing at all. I am trying to deal with my husband and our breakup.'

Sasha sighs loudly and raises her hands. 'I'm not blaming you, please don't think that. I am just trying to tell you what has been going on,' Sasha says, before adding purposely, 'right under your nose.'

'Are you actually kidding me!? What are you implying here? That my daughter is having behavioural problems only I've been too busy to notice it?' Cecelia is defensive now.

Sasha knows her triggers. She lowers her voice as she continues. 'Tonight, in the bath, the children had been playing mermaids. You know how they are obsessed with that game?'

It's another dig. Cecelia has no idea of the children's latest obsession with mermaid stories before bed, at how they act out their favourite scenes each evening in the bath. That's Sasha's thing with them. Cecelia doesn't have a clue, and Sasha is using it against her for that very reason. To prove her point. That Cecelia is so preoccupied with her work and messy divorce, that she is missing everything that is going on around her.

She is missing out on her kids.

'Tonight, Annabelle had been playing a little too rough. She was too forceful when she pushed Zachery underneath the water. And I'm not proud of myself but I shouted at her. I am sorry for that, but I was so shocked at the venom behind her actions. At how she could have really hurt, Zachery. Or worse...' Sasha leaves that last statement to sit with Cecelia for a few seconds before she continues. 'I told her that I'd be telling you when you got home from work, and that's when she bit me. She wanted to get to you tonight first, so that she could tell you her version of the story, only she is telling lies. And bless her, she doesn't really mean it. I know that. She is only a little girl. She's hurting—'

'What do you mean she's hurting?'

Sasha can see how the cogs are turning inside Cecelia's head as she starts to try and piece together what she is being told. She too has noticed a change in both of the children. How they are shutting her out, preferring to spend time with Sasha instead of her. How Annabelle and Zachery have been arguing more than usual. They constantly vie for her attention too. But it's not enough.

'Annabelle wouldn't lie about something like this though,' Cecelia concludes adamantly.

Sasha raises her brow questioningly.

'I know my daughter,' Cecelia continues, faltering as she sees Sasha shaking her head.

'Do you know that Annabelle told me that she thinks you don't love her any more. That you're going to send her away, just like you did to her daddy.'

'What?' Cecelia's anger gets the better of her, and she is more defensive. 'I didn't send her daddy away. Henry cheated on me. I couldn't have him here after that. Why is he getting off scot-free in all of this and I'm the one left here to pick up the pieces and getting treated like the bad guy all of a sudden?'

The shock of her daughter's revelation tonight, replaced now with an overbearing feeling of guilt, that somehow, she is to blame. Sasha felt it the minute she arrived here at the house. Cecelia is so close to breaking point. The pressure is building. How she is so consumed with work, and running this house on her own, that she has neglected her children.

And she knows it too.

'She feels neglected.' Sasha keeps her face neutral as she fires the word at the woman like a bullet. Knowing that it would hit her where it hurt. Right in the heart. She expects tears at least. She expects to see Cecelia's expression fall, for her lip to tremble; but Cecelia doesn't do any of those things. Instead, she gets even more defensive.

'Maybe I have dropped the ball a bit lately. Maybe I do need to prioritise the children more. But my intentions are only good. Everything I do, I am doing for them.'

There is something there in Cecelia's expression. A glint of something that Sasha hasn't seen before. A fierce protectiveness of her family.

'And maybe the divorce has affected the children more than I wanted to admit, but I know my daughter and Annabelle doesn't tell lies,' she says finally. As if she has pieced together both the stories she's been told tonight. As if she knows in her gut who is telling her the truth and who is lying. Cecelia might be scatty and chaotic, but the woman is not easily fooled, much to Sasha's dismay. Her gut instincts are kicking in.

She believes the children.

Cecelia sees it now, how she has been so careless to leave her two most prized possessions in the hands of a perfect stranger. Suddenly she feels it, that while Sasha is here, none of them is safe. There is something not quite right about her.

Sasha sees Cecelia's eyes flicker to the kitchen counter in

search of the replacement mobile phone she'd bought earlier this morning.

It's gone, no longer sitting next to her empty wine glass.

The confusion on her face warps into despair as she realises, she is not mistaken, she had left it there.

Sasha has taken it.

Because she knows that Cecelia doesn't believe her.

Cecelia knows that Sasha is lying. Not that any of that matters any more.

'Where's my phone?' Cecelia starts, but suddenly she is breathless; her speech is slow and heavy. Sasha watches with morbid fascination as Cecelia tries her hardest to continue what she is saying. Her words coming out in an inaudible slur.

'Sasha, please? I don't know what is going on here. They are just children...'

Cecelia's last words sound more like a desperate plea, but Sasha doesn't hear the end of the sentence, because the woman doesn't get to finish it. A brief look of panic flashes across Cecelia's face as if something sinister has only just dawned on her.

She is falling.

Her body slumping down from the kitchen counter where she'd stood with a loud thump. Her body motionless. Splayed out on the floor at Sasha's feet.

Sasha brings her glass to her lips and finishes her wine.

29

EMILY

Louise is here this morning.

The sound of her stomping loudly around my flat wakes me up.

She is doing it on purpose, making no effort to hide her noise as she busies herself, letting the water rush from the tap loudly, clanging the china cups together as she rinses them out in my kitchen sink. She's tidying up. Louise never cleans up. She always leaves that for me.

Lecturing me, she likes me to know that she has enough to do as it is. That if I'm capable of being given a lovely flat like this, all of my own, another one of her digs, then the least I can do to show my appreciation is to keep it clean. Not satisfied that she's got her point across, that she doesn't think I deserve any of this. That I shouldn't have things like this handed to me, she'll then throw in another bitchy comment about how cleaning might keep me out of mischief.

I always fight to hold my tongue then, so as not to react. Because I know she wants me to. As she allows the comment to hang awkwardly in the air between us. Like a red flag to a raging bull. I want to bite back. To say something that will truly shock her. Something worthy of her disdain for me.

'Yeah, because washing out cups and putting them away in the cupboard is enough of a distraction to keep me from killing any more kids, Louise.'

I don't say that though. Of course, I don't. I am not brave enough or brash enough to pull off that kind of dark humour. It would come out wrong and then she would memorise it and use it against me. She would tell my doctor that my words were loaded. That I'm not showing any remorse for what I did. That I am evil to my core.

That I am not to be trusted.

'Not your thing?' Louise asks as I sit up in bed, just as she reaches into the wastepaper bin and retrieves a book that I have dumped there.

'I couldn't get into it,' I mutter. Not willing to give her the satisfaction of a reaction to finding the newspaper cutting she'd planted inside for me. She'd love that. Knowing that she was getting to me. That's exactly why she is doing all these things to me.

'So, you just threw it in the bin?'

Her eyes narrow and a suspicious look flashes across her face. She doesn't believe me, and I silently curse myself then for giving such a weak excuse of why I've thrown the book away. That's what she is thinking too, isn't it? She is a true bookworm just like me, and it was sacrilege, wasn't it, to throw a book away just because you don't like it.

Only her next sentence tells me that she wasn't thinking that at all.

'Nice to know you've got your focus back and you can read again.'

Her tone is clipped.

Shit!

She has caught me out. She knows that if I've been able to read a book, that means that I have my concentration back. Which means that I can't have been taking my meds.

Because the meds make me unable to function, to think straight, to think at all.

Let alone read.

I've been so focused on not letting her get the better of me. I am not acting disorientated like I usually would when Louise comes to see me. I look normal this morning. Without the tablets, I feel like my old self again.

'Did Charlotte give you your medication last night?' Louise asks, her eyes boring in to mine as she waits for my answer.

'Yes, just after dinner. Just like she always does.' I'm lying. The words coming out in a jumbled nervous stutter, and I know that Louise isn't buying it.

'Where did she put them?' She has her back to me now as she moves again around the room, suddenly distracted. Her focus gone from me as she continues to make her way around my flat, picking things up and placing them back down as if she is searching for something. My meds, I realise as I stare at the cabinet in the kitchen and see that it is unlocked; the door has been left wide open and the pills are gone from where Louise keeps them inside.

Charlotte didn't put them back last night.

She took them. I saw her slip them into her cardigan pocket so that I wouldn't have to take any more. She was getting rid of them for me, because she could see the damage they were doing. She could see how they were making me worse not better.

'I can't remember. I wasn't paying attention,' I offer vaguely, and I feel my cheeks burn red hot as I speak.

She sees it too. The guilty look of a liar written all over my face. She shakes her head as if she is disappointed in me. Pausing then, as if she is about to say something else, only she decided otherwise. Before finally she adds. 'Have you found your journal yet?'

My embarrassment turns to anger at her blatant torment. She is taunting me once more. Trying to prove a point, that she holds all the power over me. She wants a reaction, but I will not give one to her.

'No, but I expect it will turn up eventually. Just like the tablets will too.' I smile, knowing how much my sickly sweet sarcasm won't go unnoticed. How it will wind her up. Good, I want it to.

'I can ask Charlotte about the tablets when she gets here later,' I say. And I will. I'll tell her that she needs to put them back. That she shouldn't say anything to Louise right now, because the last thing I want is for Charlotte to get into trouble.

'She won't be coming later. She called in sick.'

Louise is lying. I can always tell, because I've seen her do it a thousand times before. It's textbook too. How she diverts her eyes to the floor when she is talking, instead of looking directly at me. I think about the conversation I had with Charlotte last night. Wondering if somehow Louise has found out.

'What's the matter with her?' I ask, 'because she seemed okay last night.'

'Hmm, who knows. Some kind of a bug I expect.' Louise pauses thoughtfully, before she continues. 'What were you talking about? You and Charlotte.' She is trying to sound casual now, as if she is just making polite conversation, but I pick up on the undercurrent there. She is digging for information.

Alarm bells ring inside my head then, alerting me that something's not right. I think about the tea that Charlotte makes me. How she always makes such an effort to make it hot and sweet and strong, just the way I like it. I think about our last conversations then too. I'd confessed about how my journal had gone missing, and about the rotten meat, and newspaper clipping that Louise had planted.

'Sometimes we talk about the weather, or what I'm watching on TV.' I shrug off my lie.

'You talk about the weather?' Louise repeats the words with a straight face though her eyes look as if they are mocking me.

Does she know? Has Charlotte already confronted Louise about what I told her last night? Is that why she is here, making her way around my flat, searching for the medication? Does she know that Charlotte agrees with me? That I shouldn't be on them.

Does she know that Charlotte has taken them deliberately, to stop her? Louise wouldn't have been happy with that. With Charlotte poking her nose in where it wasn't wanted. With me finally having a friend to look out for me. To have my back, an ally of sorts. That would have firmly put the woman's nose out of joint.

Louise would have wanted her gone then, she would have got rid of her, sacked her. Is that what has happened here? What if Charlotte isn't really sick? What if she has lost her job because of me?

Oh, God! What have I done?

I never should have said anything. I should have kept my mouth shut. I knew how dangerous it would be, when I'd made those accusations. How they could come back on me.

'Charlotte didn't give you your meds last night, did she?' Louise says, and I start to nod my head, to try and convince her that, of course, she had, because I don't want to get Charlotte in even more trouble.

'I'm not stupid, Emily. You wouldn't be able to read a book if you had taken them.' Louise isn't in the mood to entertain my lies and she sees straight through me as I hang my head. 'I bloody knew it. It's not up to Charlotte to make those kinds of decisions.' She is furious now, barely able to control the high pitch of her voice.

Yet somehow, she manages to force her fury back down.

Taking a deep breath then, she holds up a small bag triumphantly.

'Never mind. The doctor gave me a spare bottle of pills just in case.'

Louise pours me a small glass of orange juice, before she passes me the two tablets. I do my thing. Drinking back the juice as I pretend to swallow them down, before holding the glass out for her to take. But immediately I know that something is very wrong, because Louise doesn't take it from me like she usually does. She doesn't get up from the chair and move towards the sink. Instead, she remains perched next to my bed, staring at me. Her beady eyes drinking me in, staring right through me, as if she can see straight inside my mind.

She knows.

I can see it in her face, the way her expression is set hard, and her eyes are fixed on me.

'Open your mouth,' she says. Her voice is stern, she has run out of patience with me.

I twist my tongue inside my mouth desperately trying to dislodge the pills from where they are pressed down against the floor of my mouth. I suck up some saliva. It's not enough to try and wash them down, but I need to try.

'Open your mouth.' This time it is an order. She is not going to wait. I fear that if I don't do as I am told, she might prise my mouth open. I open wide.

'Wider. Lift your tongue.'

I do as I'm told and raise my tongue, revealing the tablets that I so carefully concealed there.

'Drink!' She nods down at the glass in my hand.

I take a big gulp of the orange and swish it inside my mouth, feeling the liquid taking the tablets. Then I spit them in Louise's direction. With more force than I mean to use. The tablets flying across the room, the orange juice runs down Louise's angry, shocked face.

'Emily!' she shouts, jumping up from where she sits and grabbing a towel to dry her face. 'Don't you want to get better?' There's a look on her face that shows confusion and I wonder what part of it she doesn't seem to get.

The tablets won't help me. They only mask over the problems I have. They are not the solution. They just quieten me for a while. They quieten the crying girl too.

She is only ever gone for a little while, but she'll be back.

She always comes back to me in the end.

'Emily, we can either do this the easy way or the hard way, that's up to you,' Louise says, relentless. Determined not to give up.

'WHY? Why are you doing all of this to me? Haven't I suffered enough already? Haven't I paid the price for what I did? Don't I deserve another chance?'

I am off the bed, wild fury burning inside of me. My fists clenched at my side. As Louise steps towards me, I wonder if I am brave enough, or stupid enough to use them.

'I know what you've been doing to me. I know you took my journal, and I know you left that rotten meat under my bed. I know you put the newspaper cutting in the book for me to find too. About the children.' My voice catches deep down in my throat. 'About what I did back then.'

'What are you talking about? I have done no such thing,' Louise says; but I'm not falling for her virtuous act.

I know what she's done as much as she does.

'I told Charlotte everything. She is going to help me. She is going to tell everyone what you've been doing. She is going to make you pay—'

I am stopped mid-sentence as Louise grabs her opportunity while I'm momentarily distracted. She is prepared, she must have been half expecting my reaction. Because she grabs at the flesh of my arm and pinches me hard. The sharp scrape of a needle stabbed into my skin with one swift painful movement.

I scream out in pain, in shock, as I look into Louise's face and recognise the steely look of satisfaction there, as the liquid she has just pumped into my veins takes over my body and I feel myself sag.

Wilting to nothing, I give in to it, and lie down on the bed.

30

SASHA

Annabelle and Zachery aren't eating.

Sasha has done her utmost to try and win them over by bringing them here to the pancake parlour, a place that they have both spent the best part of this week begging her to take them to. Only, now that they are here, not even fluffy, hot pancakes smothered in Nutella are going to help her make this right with them.

The children hate her.

Ever since they woke up this morning to find their mother gone and Sasha still in the house, neither of them can barely bring themselves to look at her. She is surprised about that. She had seen the anger that Annabelle holds towards her mother, and it had resonated with Sasha. Sasha's relationship with her own mother had been the opposite. Unlike Cecelia, her mother had been overbearing. Too clingy. The woman had loved her so fiercely, that she'd made her feel claustrophobic. Except, she hadn't loved her, not really, all she had wanted was a little clone of herself to dress up and parade around. A ready-made, forced best friend.

Sasha had felt it, growing up. A disconnect between them.

The feeling that something wasn't quite right. Her mother had always tried just that little bit too hard to make their forced bond feel genuine. The tighter her mother had clung to her, the more Sasha had pushed her away. She'd begun to hate her for it.

Sasha now knew why her mother had been so suffocating. She'd lived in fear. Fear that one day Sasha would find out the truth about herself and that she'd lose her. Only she must have known that in her death, she would lose her anyway.

Sasha was damaged goods. That was the truth.

It made sense now, how she'd spent much of her childhood refusing to cry because to Sasha, crying was a sign of weakness, and weakness was not her way.

She has always preferred anger to sorrow.

She has always chosen to burn with fury rather than shrivel away with self-pity.

She thinks of how many hours she'd wasted sitting in rooms with strangers over the years, as they tried to help her pick apart the mass of tangled emotions inside of her. To dissect where her burning anger was coming from. How her mother had purposely sent her to those countless counselling sessions unarmed with the truth. Because she was scared if Sasha knew the truth back then, she would lose her for good.

It turns out that Sasha had been right to feel angry.

She'd been right to be absolutely furious.

She had thought that Annabelle felt that way too.

That the child would be happy now that her mother wasn't around to shout at her any more. To tell her that she was too busy working every time that Annabelle wanted the slightest bit of attention. Except, both children seem distraught. As if they are completely bereft and lost without Cecelia. Sasha can't understand that.

'If you don't like them, you can order something else. They do waffles. And milkshakes too.' Sasha smiles at the children. Doing her very best to pretend that she hasn't noticed how they are pushing their food around their plates. Or the way that they've barely spoken so much as a word to her since they woke up this morning.

She is good at pretending. Hadn't she spent a lifetime practising?

'How about a day off school?' she had announced as the children had both declined the breakfast cereal she'd poured out for them this morning, worried that if she sent them to school, they would tell their teachers about what happened to Zachery in the bath. They might not understand that it had been an accident. That Sasha hadn't meant for it to happen.

The school might then try and contact Cecelia. Sasha couldn't have that.

She needed to make things right with them again. To get Annabelle and Zachery back on side.

'Come on, let's have some fun today instead!'

The children hadn't seemed very excited by her suggestion at all, but Sasha was sure that once they were here, they would soon cheer up. Only so far, the children look thoroughly miserable and teary-eyed as they huddle together on the opposite side of the booth. They haven't said very much since they sat down, and Sasha sees it, how they glance at each other every so often, sharing that same knowing look.

A look about her.

They are both scared of her.

They have seen it with their very own eyes. The badness that is inside of her. She is sorry for that.

Sorry that she can't undo what has been done and that nothing she says or does will make any of this better now either. She has unwittingly ruined everything and that pains her greatly, because she has tried so hard to push it back down, to hide it, but the darkness always finds a way to shine through eventually.

She has no control over it.

It's always there, festering. Waiting patiently until it's time to rear its ugly head.

'When is Mummy coming home?' Annabelle's voice cuts through the awkward silence. Her words coming out in barely a whisper, but the directness of her question makes Sasha physically squirm in her seat. She isn't ready for it.

'I'm not sure, sweetie. She is busy working. She might be away for a few days this time,' Sasha says, wondering if Annabelle is testing her. Does the little girl know what she has done? because Annabelle can't look her in the eye now as Sasha answers her. Instead, she looks down at her hands that are resting loosely in her lap as if she doesn't know what to do with them. What to do with herself. She is trying to disguise the lone tear that escapes her eye, without success. Sasha sees it. As it rolls down the little girl's cheek and lands on the table between her and Zachery's plate.

Zachery sees it too.

The sight of his sister's distress is too much for him then, and Zachery begins to bawl loudly. Each huge wracking sob making his whole body shake.

'Zachery!' Sasha says, and she doesn't mean to sound so stern. But people in the restaurant are looking at them. Turning their heads to see where the noise is coming from. They are staring at Sasha. Wondering why the children that she has brought here are so upset. Why they are both crying loudly as their food sits there untouched. She shouldn't have brought the children out in public, she realises now. How stupid she has been.

All it would take is one wrong question from an interfering stranger, one random comment and the children will fall apart. They would take their one and only chance and cry out to them for help. Because like their mother, they aren't stupid.

They know that something is very wrong.

They are right to trust their intuition.

'Hey, don't cry, Zachery!' Sasha quickly softens, thinking fast then. In a desperate bid to make the children stop crying. To show the busybodies she knows are watching that she has everything under control. That there is no problem here.

'Tell you what, how about we go home and you can call Mummy? Would you both like that? Then she can tell you herself when she is going to be back.'

Their sobs fall silent as she knew that they would.

'Come on then. Let's get you back home so you can call her,' Sasha says, forcing yet another smile, as she guides them from their seats in the booth and out of the restaurant. She is amazed how naive children can be sometimes, how quick they are to comply and be obedient.

She has fed them a lie, and they know it. Wanting to believe so badly, that if they just be good and do as she asks, they can speak to their mother, and everything will be all right again. That's all it takes for them to believe her.

They cling to it as if their lives depend on it, that tiny bit of hope.

31

EMILY

My eyes are clamped shut, but I can feel it.

The presence of someone standing right here, next to my bed. Is it her, Louise? Is still she here, watching me in this catatonic state, getting her kicks from how helpless I am as I sleep?

But I am not asleep now, if I can sense her.

Or maybe I am. Maybe I am still dreaming, and this is me just imagining the pair of eyes that burn through the darkness.

The medication has always done that to me, distorted my imagination, played tricks on me.

Open your eyes. Look!

I force them open.

They flicker in disbelief as the dark shadowy figure, dressed all in black, looms over me. A hood pulled tightly over their face so that I can't see any features.

Is this real? I'm not sure.

My head is foggy and my heart pounds loudly inside my chest.

Whatever it was that Louise had injected in me earlier was so much stronger than the tablets.

It has taken hold on me.

Worse than hearing things, I am seeing things that aren't real now too.

I close my eyes and pray silently to myself that this time, when I open them again, the disturbing vision will be gone.

It's just a figment of my drug-fuelled, overactive imagination.

Only when I open my eyes again, the woman is standing so close to me, that if I wanted to, if I so much as dared, I could reach out and touch her.

But I do not dare.

A cloudy thought comes into my head then, sending a jolt of terror pulsating right through me. This could be the modern-day grim reaper. Standing right there, next to my pillow.

Here to take me.

For my sins.

A shrill scream leaves my mouth as the figure moves towards me. Causing me to scurry backwards on the bed. Desperate to get away from this person. From this thing.

'Emily! It's okay, it's me,' the figure whispers.

I shake my head as if I'm not certain that the noise in my ears is real. Am I hearing things again too? Familiarity renders me silent once more, because I know that voice.

'Charlotte?' My voice cracks with uncertainty, because it isn't rational, to think that Charlotte could be standing right here next to my bed, in the dead of night. That she would come here dressed like she is, purposely hiding her face.

None of it makes sense.

'What has Louise given you?' Charlotte asks, her voice laced with concern as I try to answer. Only I can't find my voice.

I see the look in her eyes. How she sees how confused and incoherent I am. How I am barely able to work out where I am, let alone why she is here too.

'She couldn't find the pills; she knows that you took them. She knows you are going to help me. That you're going to tell on her.' My words come out in a slur. 'She injected me this time. It was as if she'd planned it. I hadn't realised she was even holding a needle until it was too late, and she'd already plunged it deep into my arm.'

I am crying now. Feeling sorry for myself. Feeling pathetic. Louise has taken it too far this time.

What will she do next?

'She said that you were sick.'

'She's lying to you.' Charlotte shakes her head. 'I confronted her about the things you told me. I'm sorry but I was just so angry, that I couldn't not. She denied it all, of course, before declaring that my services here were no longer required. She sacked me.' Charlotte pauses. 'You were right about her, Emily. You can't stay here. I need to get you out of here.' Charlotte's voice comes out in a whisper, but her tone is commanding as she holds my coat towards me. 'God knows what she'll do to you next.' I hear the anger in her voice at what Louise has done to me.

'Where are we going?' I ask, struggling to sit up, still dazed from whatever drugs are making their way around my system. Unsure if I have the energy to even get up out of the bed, let alone walk.

'I'm getting you out of here. Away from her.'

There is an urgency in Charlotte's voice, and I am suddenly full of emotion. Grateful that for the first time in a very long time I finally have someone on my side.

Someone to help me.

Charlotte believes me, that is why she has come back, she can see through all the things that Louise has been doing to me. She knows now that Louise doesn't want what's best for me at all. No matter how much she pretends. She wants to keep me sick. To keep me locked away for good. Back at the secure unit. She doesn't believe that I am owed a second chance.

But Charlotte believes the things that I have told her about what Louise has been doing to me. She believes that if I stay here, I'll be in danger. And now she sees it for herself.

'We need to be quick.' She slips her arm around my waist and lets me hold on to her as she drapes my coat around my shoulders. 'Don't worry about shoes. You won't need them. We're getting a cab.' She places my slippers down in front of my feet and I slide them on.

'She'll find me.' My voice is full of panic, full of despair. 'You know that, don't you? She'll find out where I am.'

'And when she does, there will be an investigation into why I felt I should intervene. They'll find out what she has been doing to you. If you stay here, she'll lock you away,' Charlotte warns me. 'You know she will. Look at you now. Look at what she has managed to reduce you to in just a few short weeks.'

Charlotte is right.

That is Louise's endgame, isn't it? She doesn't believe that I deserve a second chance at a normal life. So, she is doing her best to take it from me. She is trying to sabotage all the good that has been done.

Years of good behaviour. Of complying, of following the rules. Of living this monotonous, boring, routine life.

'Come on.' I see the way that Charlotte keeps glancing at the front door. And I realise that she is scared too, that any second now Louise could come bursting through it.

Louise has access to the security cameras that cover the main door and the entrance hall to the building. That's why Charlotte is dressed as she is, with a hood concealing her face. There are cameras outside in the carpark too. She knows the same as I do, that all Louise will have to do is check the security cameras and she'll know that someone is here.

She might already be watching.

She might already be on her way.

'You trust me, don't you?' Charlotte says.

I do trust her, I think, but still I hesitate. Because I don't want Charlotte to get into trouble. I don't want her to lose her entire career in a spontaneous rushed attempt to help me.

'What about you?' I say, because I don't want to drag Charlotte deeper into this mess. My mess. 'You'll get struck off; you could end up losing your entire career.'

'I won't let it come to that.'

I shake my head.

Charlotte might be wrong about that.

'You don't know her like I do though, Charlotte. Louise is manipulative. She has a way of making people believe her. And they will. The always believe her over me.'

'They won't this time,' Charlotte says with such conviction that I almost want to believe her. 'You are not alone any more. We are in this together; this time, it will be the two of us against her. I said I'd help you and I meant it. We'll both tell them what she's been doing to you. I'll back you up, they'll believe us, I promise. But whatever we are doing, we need to do it now.'

I think about the alternative. How if I don't go and Charlotte leaves without me, she is right. Louise won't stop until I end up back in the secure unit again.

I will be left here alone, to lie in this bed and fend for myself. Waiting for tomorrow to come. For Louise to come back and pump me full of more potent drugs.

The torment will continue, it will get worse.

Worse than maggot-infested, rotten meat. Worse than reading that old newspaper cutting and being reminded of what I did.

Of the children.

I can't do it any more.

This is my one chance at escape, and I need to take it.

'Okay!' I nod finally and I am up then, off the bed. My stomach is in knots at what we are about to do as Charlotte takes my arm and guides me swiftly from the flat.

She is right: if I am going to escape tonight, I need to move quickly. I need to do it now.

32

EMILY

When we arrive at Charlotte's house in the taxi, it's still dark outside. I am glad of that. That as we step out onto the street and sneak along the pathway towards her house, we are shielded beneath a cloak of darkness. Unseen by prying eyes, not that any of the neighbours will be awake at this time of the night.

I am unsteady on my feet. The drugs have lingered so much longer this time, they are swimming through my veins. Causing my head to pound inside my skull and my thoughts to feel fuzzy. But even in the midst of my drug-fuelled haze I can't help but stare up at the grandeur of Charlotte's house and admire the beauty there. Staring up at the yellow hue of lights beaming out from the huge arched sash windows at the top of the house. Their warm glow shining down, illuminating the pretty stone brickwork of the walls. The house is uniform. A row of tall, elegant homes, situated in an affluent street.

I wonder if perhaps Charlotte lives here with her parents. Or if she's come into some money, because the house is far grander than I had imagined someone of Charlotte's age to own. Charlotte turns the key in the lock and opens the front door, and I allow myself to relax a little once she's guided me safely inside.

'Wow! This place is stunning,' I say as I stare at the impeccable decor in awe. This house looks as if it has just been pulled straight from the pages of a fancy interior design magazine. There is a scent of warm vanilla from an expensive smelling candle floating in the air around us. Immediately the place feels warm and homely, and I feel safe here.

'Let me take your coat,' Charlotte says, taking it from me before I can answer and hanging it on the hook by the front door. 'Come on, let's get you nice and comfy. You can snuggle up in my bed. You must be exhausted.'

I must. I am struggling to stay upright. Gripping the banister tightly as we take the stairs.

Charlotte sees me struggling and looks distraught.

'What in the world has she done to you!' There is fury and disgust in her voice as she protectively wraps her arm around my waist in order to keep me upright, to keep my weak legs from crumpling beneath me as she leads me into the bedroom, where I am greeted by the sight of the huge king-size bed.

'Here, wrap up.' She lifts the thick duvet back and nods for me to get underneath it. I am grateful that I am still in my nightdress.

'You're shivering.' She pats the duvet down tightly around me, to keep me warm, and it's only then that I realise how violently I am trembling. But it isn't only from the cold, as Charlotte thinks. It's from adrenaline too.

I am scared. Terrified in the face of what Louise will do when she realises that I am gone. It's only a matter of time before she comes looking for me, and when she comes, she'll find Charlotte too. I feel awful for dragging Charlotte into this mess, for involving her, when all she has ever done is show me kindness.

She has so much to lose.

But not as much as me.

'Are you okay?' Charlotte is staring at me, reading the distressed expression on my face.

I smile and nod, but I have no energy to make it look convincing, and while I know she doesn't believe me, she is kind enough not to push me further.

'Tell you what, how about I go and make you a nice cuppa. That will warm you up, won't it?'

I smile again. And this time it's more genuine. Happy now, she leaves the room. I lean my head back and sink into the pillows behind me. Closing my eyes just for a few minutes. I won't go to sleep. Even though tiredness is fighting me. My body is trying to give in to it, but my mind is racing, in overdrive. Playing out endless scenarios of what will happen when Louise finds me gone.

I imagine how she'll call the police first. It won't take long for them to examine the security footage and trace me here to Charlotte's house. They will come then, with blue flashing lights. Placing me in the back of a patrol car and escorting me back to the unit.

They'll lock me away again.

'Right, here we are. I don't have a teapot, I'm afraid. A mug is as good as it gets. Strong and sweet and hot, just as the doctor ordered.' Charlotte is back. Handing me the piping hot mug of tea, she pauses, before shooting me a smile. 'Sorry! That's probably not the best choice of words, is it!'

I can't help but laugh, about to drink the tea back in one, only Charlotte stops me. 'Don't drink it all down at once. Savour it. Drink it slowly so that it warms you up properly.'

She is right.

The heat that spreads through me is soothing, instantly warming me up and making me feel calmer.

Safe.

Wrapped up in the thick duvet, with Charlotte sitting in the chair beside me. If the police come, when they come, Charlotte will tell them how she found me. She'll tell them what Louise has been doing to me. She won't let anything happen to me.

I am safe now.

I take another sip and close my eyes, listening to the sound of Charlotte's soothing voice.

She is telling me that I should talk about it. What happened all those years ago. About the children.

But I don't want to talk about the children.

Not now. Not ever. I don't tell her that though, as I don't want to speak and break the spell, because the sound of her voice is so soothing.

My eyelids are growing heavy, and I think Charlotte is telling me to wake up. That I shouldn't go to sleep just yet.

That we should talk.

But I don't want to talk. I just want to lie here, cocooned in this bed. The soothing sound of her voice floating inside of my head.

'Sasha?'

At first I think I'm imagining it. That name, whispered across the room in my direction.

Someone else's voice.

I think perhaps I have dozed off and dreamt it, only it comes again.

'Sasha?' It's still spoken in a whisper, but it's clearer now. Louder, more vivid.

Finally, I am startled wide awake. I stare over towards the bedroom door, to where the sound is coming from, as my blood runs to ice inside of my veins at the sight of her.

The little girl looming just inside the bedroom doorway, staring straight at me.

It's her.

The same neat bobbed, dark brown hair. Those steely eyes. Her skin is so pale, she looks almost translucent.

It is not a dream, she is really here.

'It's her, she's here. The crying girl.'

My hand shakes violently as I point at the child. My heart pounds inside my chest.

'No. It can't be. It can't be!' I squeeze my eyes shut tightly in a bid to make her disappear.

Whatever Louise injected me with earlier has made me so much worse.

It's brought on the onset of madness.

It's making me see things that aren't really here.

Because when I open them again, expecting her to be gone, she is still there.

She hasn't moved.

'No!' I say as I shake my head as if to free the vision from my mind. 'It can't be you!'

I recoil, pushing myself backwards in a bid to get away. Towards the headboard, towards the back bedroom wall. Even though the logical part of my brain knows that this can't be real. 'Get her away. Get her away from me. She's not real. She is not real.' I am screeching now, manically, and Charlotte is up on her feet as the chaotic scene unravels all around her.

'Get her away! Get her away.'

I repeat the sentence like a mantra as Charlotte makes her way towards the bedroom door.

'Go and get into your bed and I'll be in to check on you shortly.' She speaks and it takes me a few seconds to realise that she isn't talking to me. She is talking to the child.

'You can see her?' I gasp, alarmed now that the child is not a ghost, that she is real. 'She's really there?' I start, only my words stop dead as they leave my mouth, as if suddenly they are suspended in mid-air as I notice the little boy.

How he cowers just behind the girl, silently, as if finding comfort in her shadow.

I freeze at the sight of him.

My heart almost stopping in my chest.

'Sam?' My voice cracks with emotion as I finally say his name out loud for the first time in what feels like forever. Almost as if I'm too scared to speak it, too scared to make a sound in case I break the spell and he disappears again. 'Sam, darling? Is that really you?'

I am unable to tear my eyes away from the magnificent sight of him. That same yellow mop of hair. That spray of freckles that cover his tiny button nose.

It's him. I am sure of it. Certain almost. Even though every part of me is telling me that it's impossible. That it can't be.

'We want Mummy!' The girl is whimpering, and a stream of hot tears runs down my face, the physical ache of her plea ripping my heart in two as I feel her agony.

My heart feels as if it will explode inside my chest, so painful now, I fear it will end me.

They want their mummy.

They want their mummy.

'I'm here!' I get up from the bed.

To go to them.

Wanting nothing more than to wrap my arms around them both and never let them go.

But as I go to them, a voice inside me screams to me how this can't be right.

I falter.

'You can't be here? You're dead? You can't be here?' I am mumbling. My words coming out of my mouth so fast that my brain can't seem to catch up with them.

'Get back into bed, Emily. You'll catch your death.'

I'm not sure if I imagine it but Charlotte's voice sounds different now. She sounds sterner. Preoccupied, as she ushers the distressed children from the room.

Away from me.

'Come on, Annabelle and Zachery, let's get you back to bed.'

Annabelle and Zachery? They are not these children's names?

These children are different children, I realise.

They don't belong to me.

I am so horribly confused.

My head pounds and I feel as if I'm going to be sick. I can taste the hot bile, burning as it shoots up the back of my throat.

The room spins violently my vision blurs, my sight replaced with bright white speckles of tiny dots that swim before my eyes.

A dull ringing starts in my ears and soon it is roaring, louder and louder still.

It is all too much for me.

Coming here. Seeing the children.

Not my children.

My children are gone.

Sam is dead.

My hand grasps for the duvet; clawing at it, I pull it from the bed as my legs give way from beneath me.

And I am falling.

Falling into darkness.

33

SASHA

'Who is that lady in our mummy's room?' Annabelle asks through her sobs as Sasha holds both children firmly by their arms and guides them back to Annabelle's bed.

When Sasha doesn't answer, Annabelle gets louder. 'Where is our mummy? We want our mummy!'

'I've already told you, Mummy is at work. That lady is someone that I'm helping...' Sasha says, trying her hardest to stay calm. To not upset the children any more than they already are.

She needs to get back to Emily, to check that she is all right. She fell hard when she landed. Though no real harm was done, Sasha was sure. It wouldn't hurt her to stay where she was for now. Lying on the bedroom floor.

Sasha would focus on getting the children settled and out of the way.

Then she'd deal with Emily.

'Ow! You are hurting me!' Annabelle's squeals don't deter her.

Sasha only grasps the little girl tighter, in a bid to stop her as she tries to wriggle free from her hold. Sasha nods down at the bed as they reach it and orders the children to both get in. Annabelle might be stubborn, but Sasha is too, and the six-year-old girl is no match for her.

'Lie down, Zachery!' Sasha orders as the boy, picking up on his sister's distress, begins to cry too. 'I told you both to stay in your room,' Sasha says through gritted teeth. Annoyed that the children had come out and Emily had seen them. They were supposed to be asleep. Knocked out for the rest of the night by the concoction she'd given them earlier.

'I woke up. I heard voices. I thought that Mummy was back.'

Sasha looks over at the drinking bottles, and sees that they are still in the same place, on the chest of drawers where she'd left them. That they were still untouched.

The children hadn't drunk them.

Shit!

She'd stupidly assumed that they'd finished their drinks when she'd checked on them earlier. But they must have just nodded off. Sasha had been so distracted thinking about going to get Emily tonight that she hadn't checked and made certain.

A costly mistake for her.

It had worked so well on the other nights, when she'd depended on them both being unconscious, so that she was able to sneak out and do the odd night visit to Emily. Sasha had taken her time on those nights, reading the children their stories until the sleeping tablets had taken full effect. Ensuring that they wouldn't wake up and find her gone.

'Well, she's not. My friend came over instead. And she's not feeling very well. That's why I said she could lie down in your mummy's bed. She'll be gone in the morning.'

'What if Mummy comes back tonight? Where will she sleep if someone else is in her bed?' Annabelle glares at Sasha, testing her.

Somehow, she knows that Sasha is lying. The little girl's gut reaction is to distrust her. She no longer hangs on to her every word. Which is a shame, because it made Sasha's life so much easier not to have to deal with Annabelle's dramatics.

'She can sleep on the sofa. Or in Zachery's bed. Anyway, I don't think she'll be back tonight. She's busy, like I already told you. She's working.'

'We heard you go out. You think we don't know, but we do know. We always hear you go out at night after you've read us our stories. I didn't tell because I thought Mummy would get cross with you. Because adults are not allowed to leave children on their own,' Annabelle says pointedly now. Her tone matter-of-fact.

'Yeah, in case there is an asstident,' Zachery adds, educating Sasha whilst pronouncing the word accident wrong.

'Is that so?' Sasha tries her hardest not to roll her eyes. The children are really starting to grate on her nerves.

'Well, maybe... you are just hearing things! Maybe you think you've heard me going out,' Sasha shoots back, her patience on a knife's edge. She's about to argue her point, to try and convince the girl that she is wrong, when she realises that it doesn't matter now anyway. So what if Annabelle calls her out on it. It's not as if they can tell their mother about it now.

Cecelia is the very least of Sasha's problems.

'You said earlier that we could call Mummy! But you lied to us. We want to call her right now.'

'I told you, your mother is working. She's busy. You can call her tomorrow. Now, I need you to stay in your room. Do you understand?'

She sees the defiance in Annabelle's eyes as she glares back at her. How she refuses to play along. She doesn't trust Sasha any more, she knows that something is wrong.

Sasha no longer cares about that now, she is done with the child's melodramatics, Annabelle needs to do as she is told. The children need bigger consequences to ensure they do as they are told and stay in this room tonight.

'That woman out there is not a good woman.' Sasha makes her way to the chest of drawers at the end of Annabelle's bed. Standing with her back to the children, she picks up the drink bottles and gives them both a shake.

Before handing them to the children to drink.

'I didn't want to worry you but... she has hurt children like you before. Do you hear me? She is a very sick, dangerous lady. That's why you must stay here in your beds where it is safe. I don't want anything bad to happen to you.'

It's a threat. A warning and by the look of terror that flashes across Zachery's face, it has worked. The child's bottom lip trembles and he shifts closer to Annabelle. No longer arguing back with her, Annabelle is silent too.

Sasha hands them their drinks and watches as Zachery places it to his lips and drinks it back, as if to soothe himself. She waits for Annabelle to do the same, only when the child doesn't, Sasha starts to feel impatient again.

'Drink up, Annabelle,' Sasha instructs, but Annabelle remains defiant.

'Can we have one more story?' Zachery asks. And Sasha senses that she might have scared him so much, that now he doesn't want to be left alone. Maybe a story will be what it takes to help them both relax again. Maybe then, she'll win their trust a little and they'll drink their juice.

The tablets that she took from Emily are strong enough to knock the woman out in seconds, so they'll work even quicker on the children. They'll be unconscious in just minutes. Then she can get back to Emily and deal with her.

Sasha had wanted to talk to Emily properly tonight. At least, that had been the plan. That was why she had brought her back here. She'd thought that being back in this house might jog Emily's memory. That now that Emily trusted her, she might finally open up and confide in her about what really happened here.

The chances were now that Emily wouldn't make much sense, even if she did happen to regain consciousness again tonight. Perhaps she wouldn't remember seeing the children, and if she did, Sasha was sure that she could convince her that she must have dreamt it. She'd tell her that she'd fallen out of the bed whilst having a nightmare and that she had banged her head. That she must have concussion and be imagining that she saw them. She could go back to her original plan once the woman was coherent.

She could start over again, knowing that this time the children wouldn't be disturbing them.

'One story. Five minutes. But then I need to check on the lady,' Sasha says, eyeing the water bottle that Annabelle is holding whilst silently praying that the child hurries up and drinks it so she can stop with this charade.

She just wants them to go to sleep.

'If she is so bad, why are you letting her sleep in Mummy's bed? Why do you need to check on her?' Annabelle asks.

Sasha falters, she doesn't have the answers and Annabelle knows it. The girl is too clever for her own good.

'Which book are we reading tonight, Zachery?' Sasha asks, deliberately changing the subject, to distract the children, as Zachery excitedly points to one of his favourite stories, the one about pirates.

Sasha settles down in the chair and begins reading the story out loud, glancing at each of the children every time she turns the pages; the whole time she is silently willing them to both drink from their bottles. But neither child does, and Sasha knows not to push it. Not to make it too obvious that she wants them to finish their drinks.

Because children can be awkward like that; once they pick

up on a vibe of something that you want them to do, it makes them purposely want to not do it.

Only Sasha didn't have time on her side tonight. She needs the kids to drink the medicine.

'Right, the story has finished so come on now, drink up. I'm going to turn the light out and you two are going to get some sleep.'

And they are about to drink up, she thinks. Only they are all rendered silent by a noise outside the bedroom. A thump. The sound of movement.

'I think maybe the lady is okay now?' Zachery whispers. Placing his bottle back down in his lap. 'Is that her? The bad lady. Is she coming to hurt us?' There is a stricken expression on his face. He is scared now and rightfully so after what Sasha had told them.

'No. Of course not. Just stay in your beds, okay?' Sasha says, getting up and making her way to the door. She had heard it too. The sound of footfall out in the hallway, someone moving past the children's bedroom door. Moving away from them, towards the stairs.

'I mean it. Stay in bed. Do not come out of this room.' Her tone urgent. She needs them to heed her warning.

As she makes her way out of the room, all she can do now is pray that her words instilled enough fear into the children so that they do as they are told. She'll deal with the children later.

First things first, she needs to deal with Emily.

34

EMILY

I drag myself up from where I've landed on the floor and rub my throbbing head. It's pounding, the pain radiating through my skull, and when I move my hand back down, I can see the smear of blood on my fingers.

I've been sick too. A pool of bright green vomit spreads out on the floor where I'd just been lying. Charlotte laced my tea with the pills that she took from Louise.

I recognise the familiar effects of the poison as it starts to take hold, as it works its way around my veins. But my reaction to it this time feels more severe, because it's mixed with whatever potent injection Louise had administered to me earlier this evening.

Even so, the sickly feeling inside me remains. Lingering, but not as intensely now that I've emptied the dismal, scarce contents of my stomach all over the bedroom floor.

Why would she give me those pills if she is trying to help me?

She knows how they make me feel. I stand, feeling dizzy, and as I hold onto the windowsill, in a bid to hold myself up, my gaze rests on the silver photo frame displayed in the centre. I hadn't noticed it until now.

The blonde woman standing in the centre, her arms outstretched lovingly to the children that sit at her sides. It's the children that had been in this room.

They are real. They are not ghosts.

I saw them.

They belong to the woman in this photo.

They do not belong to Charlotte, and the children are not mine.

Sasha?

I had heard that, hadn't I? How the little girl had spoken that name.

I hadn't just imagined that too, had I?

I can't be sure, because I became swept up in it all, the sight of them both standing there in the bedroom doorway. Desperately wanted it to be them with every part of my being. To turn back time.

Or had I allowed my overactive imagination to run away with itself then, just for a few minutes as I pretended that I was back there?

In my life, before.

Because that's how much I wanted it.

Sasha.

She'd said it twice, hadn't she? Louder the next time, clearer. I thought she was saying her own name, but now that I think about it, it had sounded more as if she was calling out for someone.

For Sasha.

Hadn't the little girl's pleas quietened when her gaze had rested on Charlotte? Hadn't she looked at her expectantly? She'd done as she was told, too, when Charlotte had instructed both of the children to go back to their rooms. My head aches as

I try and take it in, decipher the scene again as it plays on repeat in my head.

The little girl called Charlotte Sasha.

But that doesn't make any sense, does it?

There's a feeling of something inside of me that I can't quite capture. A wave of trepidation that ripples through me like a current.

Why, of all the names in all of the world, had the child chosen to call Charlotte that? My mind must be playing tricks on me, because it's too much of a coincidence to be anything else. I hear raised voices then, in the next room. The sound of the girl crying. She sounds just like the girl that I often hear, only this child is clearer. She doesn't just cry, she screams for her mummy.

I wonder who Charlotte is to her. Why she is here in this house.

Perhaps she is the children's auntie, an older sister, a family friend?

Charlotte hadn't mentioned much about herself at all, I realise, thinking back to all the little chats we'd had over our endless pots of tea. It is always me that does the talking.

She mentioned the odd snippet, here and there, when I'd bothered to make a point and ask her. She used to be a nurse. That's pretty much the only thing she's shared with me. How she had only chosen that career path to appease her overbearing mother, but that once she'd passed away, Charlotte had lost interest in the job and decided to give it up.

She'd told me that she wanted to do something different. To make a difference. To change somebody's life completely. Caring for people like me. Why would she choose to leave a job caring for the sick and vulnerable, to care for people like me?

Crazy people.

Murderers.

I shudder as I realise, I know nothing about her.

Yet she always seems so interested in me.

And that's strange in itself, isn't it? How someone can sit with you for hours and listen to you talking about intimate details of your life, of your past, and not give you anything back. I hear her talking in muted whispers, her voice carrying through the wall. Just. Enough that I can gauge what she is saying.

'She is a very sick and dangerous lady. She hurts children like you. I want you to stay in your rooms, where it is safe.'

My heart hammers inside my chest at the sudden sting of her words. I feel as if I've just been punched, the air sucked right out of me. Why is she telling the children that? She knows I'm not dangerous. She knows I would never hurt the children.

I am different now. I am not that same person.

Doesn't she believe that I have changed, and that I deserve a second chance? She wouldn't have brought me here otherwise, would she? Here to this house.

Her house?

Only I am doubting even that now as I stare around the room, taking in the decor and the belongings as if I am looking for some kind of clue as to who Charlotte really is. I eye the make-up bag that is open on the dresser. A large fluffy dressing gown that hangs over the dressing table chair. These are not her things. These belong to the woman staring out at me from the photograph.

I wonder where this woman is.

Silently I pull the bedside drawer out, and check the toiletries that lie in a chaotic heap, as if they'd been thrown in there in a hurry. Bending down I open the cabinet door and notice the small pile of books stacked inside. They are all the same. All identical. Fancy hardback interior design books; the same woman's face in the photo frame on the windowsill is staring out at me from the front cover.

Make Your House a BEAUTIFUL Home by Cecelia Clarke. This is not Charlotte's house at all.

This is Cecelia Clarke's house. This is Cecelia's bedroom. All of the fancy detailing and decor coming from this woman's exquisite taste. Just like the photographs inside of her books.

Where is Cecelia now?

I am about to close the cabinet when I spot the folder underneath. I drag it out and take a look. It's a portfolio of a renovation project. My hands shake as I stare at the old Victorian house with huge arched sash windows and a For Sale sign at the front of the property.

I turn the pages and I am immediately transported back in time as I take in the *before* photos. Dingy rooms with mould patches spanning the walls. The hallway with the mirror cracked. The bathtub stained yellow and caked in dirt.

I know this house.

I've walked inside these photographs. I've made my way through each of the rooms on these pages. I can still smell the stench of stagnant damp that had run beneath the floors, the pungent black mould that had slithered its way up the walls.

How it had felt back then, for the longest of times, that the squalor and the dirt of the place had somehow got inside of me, how it had become part of me. My memory of these very rooms even more vivid and evocative than the photos.

I drop the book and watch as it hits the floor.

I look up at the huge arched window above me, and the wrought iron fireplace on the back wall.

How had I not noticed until now that this is the same house?

The house of my nightmares.

The house, before.

35

CECELIA

She is not in her bed.

That is the first thought that crosses Cecelia's mind when she wakes and her eyes try to adjust against the blanket of pitch-black darkness that feels as if it's closing in all around her.

She's on the floor. Her cheek is pressed to the cold concrete. A pool of spit leaving her open mouth. Something string-like and feathery tickles her lips. A spider web, she realises to her horror, too late, as the residue sticks to her skin. The thought of a thick, eight-legged creature scampering across her flesh makes her skin physically crawl. She goes to wipe it, only as she lifts her hand, she realises that her wrists have been bound together with thick black tape.

'What on earth?'

Instinctively, she lifts both hands and rubs at her face ferociously, before checking her hair, running her fingers through her long locks, hoping there's nothing tangled up in there.

A spider is the least of her worries now, but she is sure she can feel something.

Her hand skims against a sore, prominent bump that

protrudes from the back of her skull. Had she fallen and hit her head on the way down? Had something hit her? Or someone?

Where is she? What has happened to her?

She shivers violently, every instinct inside of her telling her that wherever she is right now, she is in real danger.

Wherever she is, she needs to get out.

She has no idea where she is; the space around her is so small and narrow that she can't even turn around. There are walls either side of her, the ceiling just above her, leaving her no room. She feels air behind her, a slight waft of cool breeze, indicating that there's space that way.

She moves.

Slowly. Inching backwards.

Where the hell is she? And how did she get here?

THINK!

Only when she tries to work it out, her head feels foggy, her thoughts come sporadically. She can't seem to gather her bearings. Her body is feeling it too, her limbs weighted, her movements all in slow motion as she starts to slowly shuffle backwards.

Red wine.

She can still taste the bitter sharpness of it at the back of her throat. She remembers drinking a glass that Sasha had poured her as they'd both stood talking in the kitchen. That was the last thing she manages to hold on to.

She must have drunk too much and blacked out?

What had they been talking about?

'Annabelle has some behavioural problems...' Sasha had said. 'She's been hurting Zachery. She bit me.'

Cecelia recalls the teeth marks embedded in Sasha's arm. The serious look on her face when Sasha had implied that Cecelia was neglecting the children. How she was putting work first and the children were both suffering because of it. That it was all her own fault.

Had Sasha been the one who had done this to her? Had Sasha put her here?

She is about to shout for help, but the sound of Annabelle shouting stops her.

'We want our mummy! We don't want you here!'

Her voice is raised, high-pitched, as if she is in distress. She is crying. Calling out for her. The words carrying through the entire house. She imagines Annabelle in her room and tries to work out her approximate location from where she is.

She is in the crawlspace cupboard in Sasha's bedroom.

Now she recalls she'd seen Sasha in here just a few nights ago. Had she been planning this?

'Annabelle?' Cecelia calls out then, her fist banging hard against the door so that she will hear her. So that she will let her out of here.

'Annabelle, darling? I'm locked in the cupboard in Sasha's room...' Cecelia waits. The crying stops.

The house is silent for a few seconds, suddenly very still.

Too still.

No one is coming for her she realises. Because they can't hear her. They don't know where she is.

'Annabelle?' she shouts again, louder this time.

A light in the bedroom is switched on. A slither of yellow pours in from underneath the gap in the door. She hears the shuffling across the bedroom carpet before she sees the two dark shadows that dance across the front of the doorway.

'Thank God! Thank God,' she whispers silently to herself, full of relief. Unable to fend off the feeling of claustrophobia for a second longer. She needs to get out.

The door doesn't open.

Yet she can hear whoever it is making their way around the room.

'Hello?' she calls again, banging on the door once more in

case they haven't heard her. 'Can you open the door? Can you let me out?'

She wonders then if it's the children who have heard her and come to her rescue. If they are scared of all the banging noises she is making.

'Please, let me out! Can you hear me? Let me out!'

The footfall stops. The shadows just outside the door remain stationary now.

Unmoving.

She waits patiently for whoever it is out there to do the right thing and open the door, but they don't. They don't acknowledge her cries either. Why aren't they helping her?

36

EMILY

I drag the dressing gown that is draped over the chair around my shoulders in a bid to stop shaking. Though it is not the cold that is making me shiver right now.

I am trembling from fear. Why has Charlotte brought me here, back to this house?

Because she has gone to such great lengths to get me here. Befriending me and pretending that I have an ally in her, when I know now that I do not. Our friendship of sorts has all been lies.

She brought me here, to this house, under false pretences.

Now, I don't think that her real motive was ever to get me away from Louise at all. It was always about bringing me back to this house. To where it all started. But why? What does she want from me?

She has sat with me for hours at a time over the past three weeks, patiently trying to coax me into telling her about what had happened back here in this house.

Only I couldn't.

I have never been able to speak about what happened in this house. What happened to my darling boy, Sam. Even now, after all this time, just thinking about him hurts me too much. It's like a hot, searing pain that consumes my whole being. Sometimes when I think about it too much, I feel as if the agony of the memory might swallow me whole. Is that why she has brought me back here, so now I don't have any other choice but to talk about what happened here? So that she can punish me further?

Doesn't she think that I have suffered enough?

She pretended that she cared, that she was different, but now I fear Charlotte is just like Louise.

Or maybe they are both in this together. Maybe this is all part of their plan.

To get me away from the unit.

Anything could happen to me now, away from the safety of the other residents in the flats nearby, and from the cameras. They could lie, couldn't they? If anything bad happened to me, they could say that I had one of my 'funny episodes'. That I'd brought it on all by myself. Was I having a funny episode now?

Stop it.

You're allowing the bad thoughts inside of your head to run away with you now. Breathe.

I am not safe here. I can feel it, a dreaded sense of fore-boding that rises up from the deepest pit of my stomach. I need to get away from her.

I open the bedroom door and listen as Charlotte's voice comes in whispers from inside the children's room. I know I don't have much time, so I step lightly. Making my way along the hallway, moving fast. I am almost at the top of the stairs when my focus turns to the bedroom door opposite.

It sits ajar. And while I know I should go, I should leave, I inadvertently move towards it, not worrying about the consequences as I push it open and step inside. Not thinking at all. I just want to look.

Switching the light on, half of me expects to find myself in some sort of a time warp, the same tatty, threadbare carpet on the floor, the same damp wallpaper peeling in patches from the walls. But the room looks nothing like that any more.

No longer the hostel I once lived in, the space is unrecognisable from the bedroom it was once before.

My bedroom.

Impeccably decorated, it looks luxurious, expensive, in keeping with the rest of the house. The creaky double bed, with the sharp wire springs sticking out, has been replaced with a thick, cosy-looking divan. The plastic clothes airer constantly draped with damp, never-ending loads of washing, has gone from where it stood in the window. A pretty, ornate dressing table stands in its place now.

But I am not looking at that. I am staring at the window. Willing myself to be brave enough to walk over there and look. Transfixed now as I move, because I know what is outside in that garden waiting for me, and I see it straight away.

How could I not?

The apple tree at the very back is huge now. So much taller than it had been back then. The trunk is thicker, almost twice the size. Its full, solid branches adorned with a mass of leaves that have started falling.

FALLING.

I wince as my eyes go to the brightly painted treehouse that sits so proudly in the middle, and the sight of it floors me. How even in the dim hue of moonlight I can make out the cheery yellow colour of the walls, how the roof and windows are painted a bold pillar box red. I imagine the two little children that I'd seen in my room earlier, playing inside together, and my heart breaks in two. How our completely different lives, entwined somehow now together, have brought me back here. An image of him flashes into my mind, an image I have spent so many years trying my hardest to block out.

Now I have no choice, I can't do anything else but to give in to it. To allow it to come to me.

He is on the ground.

His tiny lifeless body lying at the foot of that tree next to where I kneel. The weight of him sinking down into the thick, slushy mud beneath him.

I throw down the shovel.

It's useless.

Every time I manage to scoop a spadeful of dirt out of the ground, it is replaced by a puddle of brown, pooling water.

Instead I drag my fingers through the soil, clawing at the mud as the rain continues to lash down around me.

So heavy now that my eyesight blurs and I have no idea if it's rainwater running down my face, or tears.

I think it's tears. I think I am crying.

I can't be sure, because right at that very moment I can't feel anything at all. Not sadness, not grief, not regret. I am numb to it all.

Maybe that will come. Later. After.

But for now, I must dig.

If I stop, I'll lose my nerve. I won't be able to bury him. To hide his small body away from the world.

'Mummy!'

The sound of her voice, like a violent screech of nails dragging their way down a chalkboard, magnifies inside my head.

I bite down hard on my lip to stop my hate-filled words from spilling out.

She is climbing, dangling above me on the tyre swing. Thinking of only herself as she reaches for an apple from the tree.

Who eats at a time like this, with their dead baby brother sprawled in the mud at their feet? It takes everything I have inside of me not to jump to my feet and drag her down by her hair. To wrench her from that bloody swing.

Thud!

When she falls, I am glad that she bangs her head.

When she cries out for me, I go to her. Grabbing her by her arm and yanking her roughly to her feet, holding her away from me as if she is contagious. As if I can't bear to have her anywhere near me.

Because I can't.

Then I drag her back inside the house and up into our bedroom.

I lock her inside of the crawlspace cupboard.

Away from me for now.

But it isn't enough.

I want her gone for good.

I am back in the room. Turning away from the window, I stare down at the handbag that sits on the floor, next to the bed. Charlotte's yellow woollen jumper has been discarded on top. This is her room I realise. These are her things.

Would it hurt to look?

Because as much as I know that I am running out of time, there's an uneasiness inside of me. A feeling of uncertainty. Something doesn't quite add up. Before I know what I am doing, I tip the contents of her handbag out onto the carpet and sift through the belongings. A lip balm, a hairbrush. A small purse containing a few coins and notes. There is nothing there of any real interest, nothing to tell me why Charlotte is doing this to me.

It is pointless.

Standing up, I step back from the bed and it's only then that I see something poking out from underneath the bed, as if it's been shoved underneath. A bold turquoise colour. I slide my fingers under and pull out my journal, the gold peacock emblazoned upon it.

She is the one who took it from me.

It wasn't Louise.

Charlotte is the one who has read all of the private thoughts that I'd documented inside. I stop turning the pages as I reach the section of the journal with loose pages tucked away inside.

Headed paper from a childminder's agency, another woman's name and photo on it. Was that how Charlotte had managed to worm her way into this family's home? By pretending she has come here to mind the children.

There is another piece of paper underneath that, a scrappy torn edge of a notepad. The address of the secure unit that I was kept in, before I was moved to my flat, and Louise's mobile phone number. I slip it inside of my pocket.

My eyes fixed on the final loose page. My hands trembling now as I recognise the same jagged torn newspaper cutting that I'd found, purposely tucked away inside of my book. The headline is missing. And even though I already know the words written on that page, I force myself to read it again.

An 'exemplary mother' who killed her three-year-old son while suffering from undiagnosed post-natal psychosis has been given an indefinite hospital order. Samuel Pinkett was fatally wounded in the bathroom at his family residence, a hostel for single mothers in north London, on 30 November 2003. A second child, a four-year-old girl, also found at the property, who was said to have endured a number of injuries, has also been removed and placed into care. The children's mother, Emily Pinkett, 26, appeared at the Old Bailey with two nurses by her side, and pleaded guilty to manslaughter by reason of diminished responsibility and has been sent for treatment at a psychiatric hospital indefinitely.

I drop the journal and all the papers float out around it.

The crying girl is back with a vengeance.

My eyes going to where the sound comes from. A shiver running through me as I realise that this is where I had heard her. Right here in this house, in this very room. This is where I'd locked her up, inside the bedroom cupboard that leads to the crawlspace.

I hear her now, banging loudly. Crying. Calling out for me to let her out.

How she beat her small fists against the wood; how she'd screamed until her words had sounded raw, for me to let her out.

'You're not real. You're not real,' I repeat to myself over and over again.

Then I think of the doctor and Louise and the numerous counsellors I've had therapy with over the years. How they've told me that the audio hallucinations that plague me are part of my PTSD. Hadn't one of them said that in order to forgive myself and move on, I should visualise letting her out? The crying girl. I don't need to visualise now, because I am here.

Making my way over to the cupboard door I reach out with trembling fingers and slide the bolt across.

I am about to pull the door open, when I stop myself.

I can't. I won't.

What am I doing?

Get out of your head, Emily.

The crying girl is gone from there now. She's been gone from here for years.

The noise is all just in my imagination.

Charlotte is still in this house though.

And I am not safe.

I need to move.

37

CECELIA

'Please? Whoever you are, you have to help me,' Cecelia cries, her voice quieter, laced with fear, as she wonders who it is lingering on the other side of the cupboard door.

Sasha?

For an awful moment Cecelia wonders if maybe it's her standing the other side of the door. She has come to finish the job she started, that she is here to put Cecelia out of her long-awaited misery. Because letting her live will be too costly for her.

Cecelia closes her eyes and prays. Even though she doesn't believe in God. Or angels. Or any form of higher being. But right now, in this moment, calling out to the universe for help is the only thing she has got. It works.

Her prayers are answered.

The footsteps are retracting, getting smaller as they move away from her. Away from the cupboard. And back out of the bedroom.

It's only then that she feels a wave of despair washing over her, seconds later when the bedroom light is switched off and the door slammed shut. Plunging her back into complete and utter darkness and she realises that she is right back where she started.

Her fear of facing Sasha once more had kept her small and quiet when she should have been fighting. She should have shouted louder. She should have done everything she could to be heard. To get out of this cupboard.

Whoever it had been in here, had ransacked the room. She'd heard them. How they'd gone through all of Sasha's things.

It can't have been Sasha.

It was someone else.

Someone else is here in her house and, whoever they are, they are searching for something.

Though Cecelia has no idea what.

All Cecelia does know for certain is that Sasha is not who she told her she was. She is pretending to be someone she isn't, so that she can gain access to her children. To this house. To her life.

And Cecelia has absolutely no idea why.

She only has herself to blame for all of this, she thinks. For being locked inside the cupboard, while a complete stranger sits somewhere in her house, looking after her kids. Her babies.

Cecelia starts to cry. This is all her fault. She has been so stupid, so reckless. So distracted with her career and the divorce. So stressed and busy trying to juggle everything, that she had taken Sasha at face value. When she'd turned up at the house that day and told her that she was the childminder.

Cecelia purses her lips.

She had told her that, hadn't she? Only Cecelia can't quite remember the words that Sasha had used. Thinking about it now, it felt more like an assumption. Seeing Sasha standing in the doorway with a suitcase at her feet, Cecelia had taken it for granted that she was from the agency and invited her in.

Cecelia closes her eyes, recalling how Sasha had told her that she'd forgotten her paperwork. Though a couple of days later she'd given Cecelia a copy of her CV and references, just as she had promised. The documents were still absently sitting on the desk in her office.

Another job she hadn't managed to get around to yet. She'd just been too busy.

It was the one and only time in her life that Cecelia had been lapse and hadn't checked and it had cost her dearly. It had cost her everything. Because now she is locked away inside the crawlspace cupboard, and her children are out there with some crazy woman.

She needs to get out, now.

She needs to get to her kids.

'Help me!' Cecelia shouts, banging on the wall with her fists.

But the walls are thicker than she realised. She hasn't got much strength. Unsure how long she has been in here for, how long she has gone without food and water, a day or two she guesses. She's so weak.

And it seems so much longer than that. That she has been trapped in here, in the darkness.

Thoughts of Annabelle and Zachery are the only thing getting her through the turmoil that is playing out continuously inside her head like a broken record. This is Cecelia's worst nightmare come true.

Sasha is going to leave her in here to die, all alone.

She can't imagine how else this will end. Sasha drugged her, Cecelia is sure of it now. Certain in fact. She's been thinking about it, and she hadn't drunk enough wine to enable her to pass out. To bang her head and not be aware of it. And when she'd woken, she'd still felt so groggy and strange, for ages after. The thoughts inside her head vague and blurry.

She'd been unable to think straight for hours, unable to focus on anything at all.

Her head is starting to feel clearer now.

She stops shouting and listens.

The room remains silent once more. But then she remembers the click. The sound of the lock sliding in the door.

Whoever had been out there had unlocked the door before they'd retreated.

Cecelia can get out.

38

EMILY

The bathroom door is wide open and even though I know that I should keep going, that I should hurry, that if I move faster towards the stairs, I can be out of this house in just a few more seconds.

I don't.

I feel the pull of it. Even from outside in the hallway, it's as if the energy in that room is calling for me. Pulling me in, like a magnet. More so than the bedroom.

Because he is in my head.

Sam.

This is the last room where I saw his smile. Heard his laugh. The last time he had breathed in air.

I want to go to him. To face my demons at long last. But I'm still not strong enough to do it. Instead, I stand in the doorway and stare at the fancy decor of the bathroom. The chequered black and white tiled floor.

The rolltop bath with the shiny Victorian-style taps is the showpiece.

And it's the bath that holds my full attention. I stare at it until my vision blurs and the rest of the room melts away to nothing. The room becoming dark, and rancid and toxic.

I am back there once more. In the damp bathroom of the hostel.

The old white bathtub with the smears of dirt streaked against the porcelain sides. Thick green mould at the base of the taps. The smell in here makes me feel sick as the feeling of trepidation spreads right through me. Rushing up to my head from my feet.

I will myself to step forward and look.

My legs won't move. I am not brave enough. For I know what I will see in that bath.

Do it, you owe him that at least.

Do it.

I tread carefully, inching forward so slowly that it feels as if I'm not moving at all.

But I must.

Despite the fact that part of me never wants to revisit the image that has for years been ingrained in my brain. Another part of me craves it.

The need deep in my heart and soul to see him just one last time.

To see his hair, his flesh, his tiny little body.

Only when I do I experience exactly the same feelings that I had back then. A mixture of terror and pure disbelief at what I am seeing. The dread and despair as it sinks in. I am back there again. With Sam. Staring down into the bath as if I've just woken from a trance.

My hands are submerged under the water, clutching him tightly as he floats lifelessly, face down in the water. His hair is splayed out all around him. His little body bobbing as if he's been under the water for a while.

It hasn't been a while. It has only been a few minutes at the most.

The anger that surged through me dissolves now and is replaced with something else. Something far more powerful and consuming.

Grief. Regret. Numbness.

I am outside of my body. In shock as I stare at the water that surrounds him.

It's turned red from the blood.

The gash on the back of his head has left a smear of it on the tap, when he'd fallen and cracked his skull against the metal.

PUSHED.

I wrench his tiny lifeless body from the water and lie him on the floor at my feet. I wail loudly. A guttural, animal sound expels from my body. Wishing I could take it all back.

'I'm sorry. I'm sorry. I'm sorry.'

There is a movement behind me. A noise. I turn and see Sasha, standing in the doorway. Her four-year-old eyes searching mine.

My first and only thought is to stand deadly still. To block her view. To protect her from the harrowing sight of her baby brother on the floor.

Dead.

39

SASHA

'Hello, Mother.'

The mad old bitch is here in the bathroom, not on the bedroom floor where she'd left her.

Sasha stands in the doorway, a look of triumph on her face as she takes great pleasure in her revelation that she is Emily's daughter. She feels smug in the knowledge that she has managed to trick Emily for the past three weeks into believing that she was someone else completely. Someone who never even existed.

Charlotte.

She waits for her reaction. Watching the expression on her face, drinking in her body language. She wants to see it, the shock that she knows will resonate when Emily finally realises she's been manipulated into believing that 'Charlotte' would ever, could ever, really care about someone like her.

A monster.

A murderer.

Only Emily has got there first.

'Sasha...' Emily whispers her name as if the word is toxic.

There's no surprise to her tone. She knows who she is. She's already worked it out. Sasha feels disappointed at that. That even now, in this moment, at her grand reveal, her biological mother won't even give her that. This one tiny victory over her.

'Oh, so you're not as stupid as you act!' Sasha sneers, and Emily flinches.

Sasha is glad about that at least. How the fear shines from the woman's eyes, how she finds Sasha's presence unsettling. It's almost as if Emily is only just realising what Sasha is really capable of. Finally, cornered here in this bathroom where it all happened, forced to deal with the wrath of her one and only daughter.

'I'm impressed that you actually used my name for once and didn't refer to me like you usually do. As "the crying girl".' Sasha can't help but smirk at that. She is mocking Emily. She'd guessed it early on, that she is who her mother hears crying through the walls. She is the little girl that torments her. The one that gets inside the woman's head.

And it pleases her.

That she has had some lasting impact on the woman's life after all. That despite all her attempts at trying to shut her out, Emily has never been able to block her out completely.

'Of all the nicknames you could have chosen, the "crying girl" is really pathetic,' Sasha spits. 'I was just four years old. You locked me away in a fucking cupboard. Is it any wonder I was crying?' She shakes her head. 'The newspapers said that when the police officer finally found me, I was hysterical. I was covered in mud and my head was bleeding. I needed ten stitches apparently. My mother – the woman who brought me up, pretending she was my mother, at least – always told me that I fell off a slide in the park and banged my head, but it was you!'

Sasha lifts her hair up at the side and turns to show the woman the scar she conceals there. The scar this woman gave her.

'What were you going to do if the police hadn't got me out of there? Kill me too?'

'Why did you bring me back here?' Emily asks, her eye on the door behind her, as if she senses the danger she is in, as if she is trying to work out if she could make it out. She'd have to get past Sasha first.

Sasha steps forward, blocking her way out as if she can read her thoughts. She won't allow her that.

'Why did I bring you here?' Sasha laughs. Her loud cackle echoing around the bathroom, unable to contain the rage that is building inside of her. 'Is that really the first thing you want to ask your long-lost, darling daughter? Why did I bring you here? Are you not going to run into my arms and tell me that you missed me, Mother? Are you not going to say that you are sorry for what you did? Are you not going to beg me for forgiveness?'

Sasha sneers before shaking her head in disgust before she continues. 'My mother... passed away a few months ago. The letter that she left me was her parting gift. Telling me how I don't belong to her. That I was adopted. How she had "saved" me. From you! I sat in my mother's solicitor's office, and I read her will. Then the solicitor reluctantly held out a second enve-lope addressed to me. Warning me that the details inside were delicate, and that I might not want to read the contents.' Sasha laughs. 'Delicate? That's how he described the newspaper cutting my mother had kept for all these years, detailing you murdering my baby brother. A brother I never even knew I had. Sam.'

She shakes her head. 'I hadn't wanted to believe it. That my real mother was a murderer. That the woman who brought me up, wasn't my own. I refused to, because I have no memory of that life before. Here with you. I have no memory of Sam at all. But every instinct in my body confirmed that it was true. I could feel it. I knew it. I'd felt it all my life, how I was different from the family that brought me up. How I didn't quite fit in. My mother had good intentions, she'd kept the truth from me to protect me. To shield me from the horrific trauma I'd lived through, that had left me so broken. Four painful years of my life that I must have unwittingly blocked out.' Sasha glares at Emily. 'I looked you up on the internet after that, and read all the articles about you. I managed to track you down. The fact that Louise was advertising for a carers job working with you couldn't have just been a coincidence, could it? That I was overqualified too. And coming here... I'd only wanted to see the place I'd grown up in. To see if it opened up any memories for me. Because you wouldn't talk about us. Me and Sam. You wouldn't talk about this house and what happened here. So, I wanted to see it for myself. Only, Cecelia thought I was the childminder and invited me in. Fate led me back to you.'

Sasha sees how Emily averts her eyes now she knows the power that she holds. She is so full of shame and self-loathing that she is crumpling before her; she can't even bear to look at her. Still she refuses to take any accountability for what she has done. Just like always.

'Disassociation. You're so good at that, Mother. At blocking things out. You do it a lot,' Sasha says, knowing how in the three short weeks she has spent masquerading as a carer for the woman, she'd witnessed first-hand how Emily point-blank refuses to talk about what she did.

How she purposely tries to block it all out.

Block the crying girl out.

Pretending she doesn't know who she is, or why she is crying.

Pretending she doesn't hear her at all.

But the sound haunts her still.

'It's common, apparently. For people like you, who commit such despicable, violent crimes. I looked it up. It's like a form of detachment, a method of survival. How murderers purposely separate yourselves from everything and everyone around you. Especially from people.'

Sasha is enjoying this. Tormenting the woman.

Spelling out to her why she has done this.

'It's ironic though, how you've spent so many years locked away from the rest of society. Not trusting anyone. So paranoid about Louise being the one who was out to get you, yet you had no idea it was me. Planting that rotten, maggot-infested meat beneath your bed, stealing your journal. Leaving that newspaper cutting inside one of your books. You made it so easy for me. For "Charlotte".' Sasha smirks. 'I thought you'd at least recognise the house?'

Sasha is still surprised that Emily hadn't even recognised the house she'd once lived inside, when they'd pulled up outside in a taxi, earlier. She'd expected it too. She'd readied herself for it, to reveal to Emily the real reason she'd brought her back here. Only, instead, Emily's face had lit up with pure fascination when she'd walked along the front path towards the door. How she had stared up in awe at the house in all its Victorian Gothic inspired beauty, as if seeing its huge arched windows and the high pitch of the roof for the very first time.

Emily had looked up and done exactly as Sasha had done, she'd mistaken the warm glow of light emitted through the large sash windows for the illusion of warmth. Of safety. Of home.

Only there was a vastness here, running so deep within these walls that it felt like a void. This was a house without a beating heart. Sometimes the darkness lingered, as if the house was clinging on to it, to all the bad things that had once happened here. Like a black hole of nothingness that made Sasha feel claustrophobic at times, as if the walls were closing in around anyone inside. Trapping them there for eternity. So they couldn't get out.

'Don't you remember this house?'

Sasha had thought that Emily would start to remember

more once she stepped inside. That the familiarity of being back here again would finally jolt something awake inside of her and she would recognise the house she'd once lived in.

The house she'd once killed in.

Only Emily's face gave away nothing, and Sasha wondered if Cecelia and Henry's renovation had made the house unrecognisable. Though some of the features hadn't changed. Like the original stairway that twisted itself down the inside wall of the house. How there were cast iron fireplaces in every room. The height of each tall, vast ceiling.

Or was it the drugs that were rushing around Emily's body? Helping her to dull it out. As if the past twenty years that she'd spent purposely blocking it all out wasn't enough.

'You live in denial, Emily! You think because you've put so much time and distance between yourself and the heinous crimes that you committed that somehow, they didn't really happen?' Sasha raises her voice. 'But they did and you're not as good at burying your guilt as you'd like to think. I saw your face when you saw the children. When you thought that they were me and Sam.'

The sight of the children had set something off inside of Emily, so visceral, so manic that it excited Sasha's sadistic pleasure. Finally, there had been some real fear, some real emotion, a reaction at last. It had been there all the while, festering inside of Emily. Bubbling away just under the surface.

Sasha had seen the suffering in Emily's expression. The obvious pain there.

She wanted more of that.

'You were scared, terrified. And so you should be...' Sasha didn't feel an ounce of sympathy for her. It was everything that Emily deserved and more. 'Scared, just like how you made Sam feel too, I bet. Before you bashed his skull in and drowned him in the bath. Scared like I was when you locked me away in that cupboard. We were just kids! We were just children.'

Sasha still can't fathom that. How this woman before her could be capable of such cruelty.

How she has simply blocked them both out as if they were never there at all. As if their lives meant nothing to her. How Emily could simply play down her crime. Rewriting the past and making out that she is the victim now. Believing that Louise was bullying her. All those meltdowns she's had about being tormented by an invisible girl that no one can hear but her.

'Not so clever looking now, are you?'

And she isn't so clever. She's not with it at all. Sasha sees it. How whatever that miserable cow, Louise, had injected Emily with earlier was still in her system. It's potent now, mixed with the extra pills that Sasha had spiked the woman's tea with. Emily is disorientated, disconcerted. Unsure of her surroundings. Unsure of herself.

As she grips tightly to the bath.

Not just through shock or fear, but in a bid to hold herself upright. She is slipping again, on the verge of collapse. The meds have well and truly taken hold.

She's running out of time.

'I've listened to you for weeks, spouting all this virtuous bullshit about being a changed woman! Please! Louise told me how you've always refused to talk about what you did! How you've never shown an ounce of remorse. For killing Sam. You've lived your life in denial; well you don't get to do that any more. I brought you back here, to this house, because I want to hear you say it. What you did. I want to hear the words come out from your mouth. I want you to tell me how sorry you are. I want you to beg for my forgiveness.'

Sasha steps forward.

'Even though, no matter what you say, there won't be any of that tonight.'

40

EMILY

My heart is thumping hard, pulsating erratically as sweat seeps from my pores, covering my skin in a damp, sticky film. Despite having just been sick, I can feel it. The concoction of the medication Sasha has given me mixed with whatever potent injection Louise had administered to me earlier this evening.

It's too much. My body can't cope.

Sasha sees it too.

She must. Because there is panic on her face. She sees how disorientated I've become. How I'm clinging on to the side of the bath for dear life, in a bid to stop myself from falling. Again.

That's why I had fallen in the bedroom, I realise. I hadn't just fainted from the shock of seeing the children.

'Why?' My voice sounds as if it has come from somewhere far off in the distance. Like it's no longer my own. 'Why have you brought me back here?'

'I told you. I want to hear you say it. What you did. I want to hear the words come out from your mouth. I want you to tell me how sorry you are. I want you to beg for my forgiveness.' She spits the last sentence out, and I wonder how I haven't seen it before now, the hatred and contempt she feels for me.

It's terrifying, the ferocity of her anger that pours from her to me.

I am in real danger.

'There's nowhere to run now, Emily. It's time to face what you did!'

Sasha is talking too fast. I hear the desperation in her voice, the look of pure panic on her face as she realises that she's rapidly running out of time. She has gone to such great lengths to orchestrate all of this. Manipulating her way inside of another woman's house by pretending to look after those two small children. Getting a job with Louise so that she could gain access to me. This has been weeks of planning and conspiring. Against me.

She has masterfully lured me back here to this house, where it had all started. To this very room.

And she is right, I am alone now, trapped here with her.

This is all part of her sick, twisted game, so that I can finally confess my sins; only we both know that nothing I say will be enough to appease her. She already knows in great detail what happened back then. She has clearly researched me well. Meticulously, reading up on the articles and headlines online. Working as my carer, she would have gained access to my medical reports. To all the notes that my many counsellors have made about me over the years. She's read my journal too. She knows all my private thoughts.

'He is still here in this house, you know. I see him. My brother, Sam,' Sasha says, smirking, as I am unable to hide the horror that I feel as it creeps across my face.

'What? You don't believe me? *You* think that *I'm* mad?' She laughs then, but the sound is empty and full of malice. 'The woman who hears the "crying girl" through the walls, thinks I'm the one who's crazy! Please!'

She is mocking me again.

'I've seen him. Standing in my bedroom in the middle of the

night. I've seen him here, in this bathroom. His body, face down in the water. Just like it said in the papers. Right here in this room, where you drowned him. Look! Look at the bath!'

Sasha is next to me now, she is putting the plug in the bath and running the water. Ignoring me as I slide down the side of the bath, my body sinking down, collapsing onto the cold tiled floor.

'No! No!'

I shake my head and place my hands over my ears. I cannot hear this. I cannot let these words penetrate my ears.

I will not listen.

'I will not allow thoughts of him like that, back inside my head. Not my Sam, not my baby!' I think the words are just floating aimlessly around inside my head, but I realise that I've said them out loud, and Sasha bristles as I continue.

'He had yellow straw-coloured hair and a cute spray of freckles that ran across his nose. His cheeky laugh could fill a room.'

And my heart. I think to myself. The sound of his laugh would make my heart physically sing. Closing my eyes, I do what I always do when thoughts of him fill my head. I recall only the innocence of him. The pureness. I have a few brief seconds to wallow in that, before it comes at me in waves.

The guilt, the grief, the pain.

How I wish with everything inside of me that I could turn back time and do everything differently.

'My baby. My boy. Sam...'

'What about me?' Sasha bellows. 'What about me? What, because I lived, I don't matter? I am here. Standing right in front of you. Where is my longing? Where is my love?'

I try to shake my head, but it hurts too much. I think of her back then. How small she was. How innocent she looked. That bobbed brown hair. That sickly pale skin. So different to Sam in every way.

'The police officer who found me did an interview. He said when he found me, you were just sitting there, listening to me crying inside the cupboard. That I was screaming to be let out. And you just sat there staring at the cupboard door as if you were in a trance.'

I can hear the water rushing out of the taps as the bath fills up behind me. The sound is soothing even though it roars in my ears. Though it's not loud enough to drown her out.

'I want to know why. Why you killed Sam. Why you did that to me. We were only children. Why?'

She wants an answer, only I can't give her one. My head is pounding so violently that my brain feels as if it is going to implode. My eyelids are heavy, closing involuntarily. I can't keep them open. All I want to do is lie down and give in to sleep. To close my eyes one last time and for this all to be over.

She wants my demise to be slower than that, I think, as she tries to wake me back up. Yanking me up by my arms. Her fingers digging into my flesh as she pushes the weight of me upwards.

Until I am standing.

I wonder if she is going to take me back to the bedroom, so that I can sleep off the drugs.

Only the next thing I know is her hands grabbing at my shoulders. Force as she pushes me backwards.

Suspended in mid-air, everything feels like it's happening in slow motion.

My head smashing against the side of the bath with a thump. My body plunged underneath the water.

I try to scream, but my mouth fills with water that I splutter and gurgle and choke.

The water is still running, there is a sensation of burning heat by my left foot, icy cold by my right, as I kick out. Panic taking over, my lungs are on fire, burning inside of my chest.

I see her blurred form standing over me. Reaching out her hands.

She is going to help me; she is going to pull me out of the water.

Her hands clamp around my throat and she pushes me deeper down and holds me there as I thrash against her.

A heightened rush of terror spreading through me as I realise that I am about to take my last breath here.

Here, in this very room, in this very spot, where Sam died twenty years ago.

Sam.

There's a stillness then, a warmness that washes over me.

A knowing.

That these are going to be my final moments.

I'm finally going to be put out of my misery once and for all.

I want to go to him.

41

CECELIA

Cecelia shuffles across the bedroom floor, pulling her arms up onto the sharp, pointed corner of the green, wooden dressing table, before frantically sawing at the tape that tightly binds her wrists together.

Sasha is shouting. Her loud, furious voice carries through the entire house. A swell of rage washes over Cecelia as she thinks of her children. How terrified they will be right now, having Sasha shouting at them like that.

She needs to get to them.

She needs to make sure they are safe.

To get Sasha away from her kids and out of her house.

Christ knows what Sasha has told them about why Cecelia hasn't been home the past few days. They probably think she's abandoned them, that she has simply left them here with this crazy woman, thinking that their mother doesn't care about them. Cecelia wouldn't put it past Sasha to tell them something like that.

She needs to hurry, but the tape is wrapped in so many layers round and round her wrist, that she can't seem to cut through it. She keeps trying. Aware then that there are only two voices and neither of them belong to either of her children.

Sasha is loud, high-pitched. Deranged almost.

The other voice is unfamiliar, but it is that of another woman's.

Cecelia wonders who the woman is and what she is doing here. Is she the one who was in this bedroom earlier, rooting around in Sasha's things?

She wonders what she has done to make Sasha so furious as the tape around her wrist starts to split and fray. Cecelia can hear Sasha demanding to know what happened to the boy. The boy? Cecelia's heartbeat quickens as the feeling of panic floods through her.

Please God, don't let anything bad have happened to Zachery?

Cecelia would never forgive Sasha that.

She'd kill her, herself. But then, she'd never forgive herself either. Because she had been the one who had stupidly let that woman into her home. She'd allowed her around her children.

They are all in danger now.

The shouting continues, and Cecelia knows she needs to move faster. Sawing her arm faster, backwards and forwards, she winces in agony as the sharp edge cuts through the tape and gouges into her flesh.

Ignoring the blood as it drips down onto the carpet, she doesn't care about any of that, all she cares about is getting to her children. And she is almost there.

The tape is loosening.

All she cares about right now is getting to her children and getting them as far away as possible from Sasha. She can imagine them now, in their bedroom, cowering away from the woman. Hiding underneath the covers of Annabelle's bed. Their limbs wrapped around each other as they hold each other tightly. The pull of them calling for her.

They'll be scared of all the noise, all the bellowed words. Petrified at this madness that is playing out all around them. They'll be wanting her. Wondering where she is. Wondering if she is going to come home and save them.

And she will. If it's the very last thing that she ever does.

She needs to get to them.

She needs to get that wicked woman out of her house.

Sawing hard now with urgency, faster than ever.

SNAP.

The tape finally breaks and Cecelia rubs at the sore red welts on her wrist, as if trying to iron out the deep gouges in her flesh. She peels the tape that is wrapped tightly around her legs then too. Relieved to be free, she can run if she needs to.

And she thinks she might need to.

They all might need to.

Because that woman is deranged.

Cecelia steps out into the hallway and listens, realising now that the shouting has stopped. An eerie silence has descended upon the house which is far more terrifying than all the shouting and screaming. At least with all the noise, Cecelia could hear Sasha's voice, she knew her whereabouts in the house.

Now, Sasha could be lurking anywhere.

Cecelia scans the hallway for something heavy, something to use as a weapon if she should need it. And she thinks she might need it. Because there is no way that Sasha is going to have wanted Cecelia to break free from that closet. She'd left her there for days without food or water. She'd left her there to die.

Alone in the dark.

While she swanned around her house, playing happy families with her children. Only it doesn't sound so happy now. And Cecelia needs to protect herself. She needs to protect her babies at all costs.

Her eyes rest on the copper ornate bookends that sit in the centre of the windowsill next to the stairs. She places the books down flat and picks up the heavy sculpture tightly in her hand, poised to use it if she must, as she starts to make her way along the hallway. Towards the children's bedrooms. As she nears the bathroom, she can hear the loud gushing of running water. A violent, frantic splashing of someone in the bath, thrashing about in the water.

Then a loud spluttering and coughing.

The sound of someone gasping for breath. Choking.

'You killed him!' Sasha shouts. 'Now you're going to see how it feels.'

The venomous words send a wave of dread right through her. Who is dead? Zachery? No. No! Cecelia doesn't stop to think then. She is on autopilot. Terrified of what she'll see when she goes into that bathroom, but she knows that she must face it.

She must face Sasha, and when she does, she'll only have one shot. One attempt to catch the woman unaware. One attempt to strike out and hurt her. She needs to fight as hard as she can, for her kids.

Because the alternative is too much to bear.

Cecelia can't go back inside that cupboard to die all alone in the dark.

One shot is all she has, and she is going to grab it with both hands.

Literally.

Holding the metal bookend tightly, she runs into the bathroom. Her eyes fixed on Sasha as the woman turns from where she is bent, leaning over the bath. An expression of shock on her face as she realises that Cecelia has managed to escape. Cecelia was depending on the shock. On the few seconds of confusion to give her the upper hand. Cecelia is shocked then too, her eyes moving to the woman who is being held down under the water in the bath.

Her hands trying and failing to claw at the bath's sides as her body thrashes about in a desperate bid to break free of Sasha's grasp. She has no idea who the woman is, but Sasha is trying to drown her. Cecelia doesn't think as she lifts the iron object she's holding high over her head.

Sasha mirrors her movement.

Releasing her grip on the woman in the bath, she raises her own hands above her head in a bid to protect herself.

Sasha isn't quick enough.

The bookend smashes against her skull and knocks her sideways, sending her flying down onto the cold bathroom tiles.

'Mummy!'

Cecelia turns at the panicked screech from her children behind her as they run to her.

'Annabelle, Zachery!' Cecelia is crying now. Sobbing with relief that they are both okay as she reaches her arms out and pulls them both tightly to her. 'Mummy is here. Mummy is here.'

Only suddenly Cecelia has no idea where 'here' is.

She is in her home with her children. They are safe now.

But she feels anything but.

She feels as if she's just stepped into a parallel universe. A world that is no longer their own. It belongs instead to these two women. A lifeless woman strewn at her feet with blood pooling out from the cut in her head as it spreads out across the black and white tiled floor. The other woman, alive. Just. Who is this, clinging on to the side of the bath, gasping for breath?

42

CECELIA

'Annabelle, I want you to be a brave girl for Mummy. I want you to run to my bedroom and call the police. Press the number 9 three times. Tell them our address. We need the police and an ambulance. Can you remember all of that?'

Annabelle is staring down at the floor. At Sasha. She is staring at all of the blood as it seeps from the wound on her head.

'Annabelle, look at me. Look at Mummy!' Cecelia says gently. Holding her daughter's face and forcing her to look at her. To focus. 'Ring 9-9-9. Tell them to hurry. Zachery, go with your sister. Hold her hand.'

Cecelia doesn't wait for the children to answer her. She is too busy dragging the woman from the bath. Wearing Cecelia's dressing gown over her nightdress and a pair of slippers, the extra weight of her water-sodden clothes makes her feel heavier. That and the fact that she is dead-weight, lifeless, slipping in and out of consciousness. Her eyes keep closing involuntarily, though she is fighting her hardest to try and keep them open. They flicker every few seconds and she locks eyes with Cecelia, as Cecelia manages finally to pull her body out from the bath.

She places her down on the floor. Next to Sasha. The woman turns her head and sees her then, a muted cry leaving her mouth.

The sight of Sasha on the floor, of all that blood, jolting her awake. Alert again, she coughs loudly before throwing up a mixture of bath water and bile.

'It's okay,' Cecelia says, turning the woman onto her side so that she doesn't choke and she doesn't have to look at the sight of Sasha any more. A low groan comes from Sasha's direction and Cecelia realises that she hasn't killed her. Part of her is relieved that Sasha would survive. She'd hit her hard, but she'd only done that through instinct. To get her off this woman, to keep her away from her and her kids.

She hadn't wanted to take Sasha's life. But she didn't want the woman anywhere near her if she gained consciousness again. Cecelia had witnessed first-hand how unstable Sasha was. How much fury she has inside of her. How *she* is capable of ending a life.

They are still not safe here, Cecelia needs to get them all out. Away from Sasha until the police arrive. She thinks of the children, of Annabelle calling the police, and prays that her daughter is capable of dialling the numbers and asking for help. Because they are all in shock, all traumatised by the unravelling of tonight.

'Come on. You need to get up. I need to get you out of here. We're not safe,' Cecelia says, hooking her arm underneath the woman and holding her upright.

Sasha is twitching now. Her eyes are still closed but there is a tiny flicker of movement under them as if she is starting to regain consciousness.

'Move,' Cecelia says, louder this time. Firmer, letting the woman know that this time it's an order.

'Annabelle, Zachery?' Cecelia shouts as she reaches the top

of the stairs and sees the children run out from her bedroom. Annabelle is still clutching the phone in her hand.

'I couldn't call them, Mummy. The phone isn't making any noise,' Annabelle says.

'Shit! Okay, don't worry! You need to come with me now. Grab your brother's hand. Come on.' Cecelia guides the woman down the stairs and drags her towards the front door. Only it's locked and the key is no longer in the lock.

Sasha must have taken it. She must have locked the front door now that this woman was inside, with no intention of letting her out again.

'Mummy...' Annabelle says, pulling at Cecelia's top.

But Cecelia is distracted. She is leaning the woman up against the wall, needing some respite from the weight of her, from the heaviness of holding her up. The woman's head lolls to the side and their eyes lock. She looks like she is trying to tell her something, only her brain can no longer connect with her mouth, and she can't find the words to say it.

'What's your name?' Cecelia asks, trying to coax whatever it is out of her.

'Em...' the woman mouths, spittle leaving her lips. 'Emily.'

'Okay, Emily. I don't know who you are or what is going on here, but we need to get you out of the house.'

'My phone is in my coat pocket. You need to call Louise.'

Cecelia searches the coat rail behind the door, shoving her hand in to the pockets of the large coat hanging there.

She shakes her head.

'It's not there. Maybe Sasha took it?'

'Mummy...'

'What, Annabelle?' Cecelia says, feeling her daughter pulling urgently on her jumper once more.

'I think Sasha is awake.'

Cecelia listens carefully, hears the scrape of the wooden

stool that sits next to the bath. The groan as the woman is trying to haul herself up. Footsteps.

'We need to go,' Cecelia says, grabbing the woman tightly and making her way to the back of the house. Wondering if she can make it to the back door: they could go around to the side gate and out the front that way. She could get Annabelle to knock on one of the neighbours' houses and ask for help.

'Annabelle? Zachery.' Sasha's voice echoes down the stairs.

The children stare at Cecelia then with a look of horror on both of their faces.

'Move,' Cecelia whispers. Dragging Emily towards the backdoor.

Outside the cool air hits them. It's raining now and pitch-black dark. Cecelia makes her way over to the side gate and pulls it open, about to leave through it, only she imagines Sasha as she makes her way down the stairs. How she would pass the window at the bottom of the stairwell.

She'll see them.

And if she has the front door key, she'll be outside the front in just seconds.

Quicker than they can get there.

Turning back to the garden she eyes the summerhouse that's been locked up for winter. Knowing how full it is with all of their furniture and gardening equipment that she stored away inside. Wondering if it might be too obvious a place to hide away in.

Unless... she left the back gate wide open too. Tricking Sasha into thinking that they'd got out that way. That that was how they'd made their escape from her.

It was worth a shot.

'Come on,' Cecelia says to the children as she opens the gate wide; then, gripping Emily tightly, she leads her over to the summerhouse.

Praying that Sasha falls for the decoy.

43

SASHA

Sasha's head is pounding, and her vision is blurred. But, somehow, she manages to drag herself up to her feet and stand. Though she wobbles unsteadily as she stares down to the dark red puddle pooling out on the bathroom floor.

Blood?

It is smeared across the bathroom tiles.

Someone is bleeding?

Instinctively she moves her hand to her head and feels the warm, sticky liquid as it coats her fingers and still it takes her a few seconds to realise that the blood is coming from her. That she is the one who is bleeding. She stares at the bath. Watching as the water continues to gush from the taps, the levels rising rapidly, the bath is almost full. Almost overflowing.

Emily is gone. There is no sign of her.

Sasha wonders if she had been the one to hit her.

No. Emily had been underneath the water. Struggling to breathe, struggling to break free. Thrashing about as if her life depended on it.

Because it had depended on it.

Sasha had tried to drown her, just like Emily had done to Sam.

It was the only revenge fitting enough.

Only someone had struck Sasha from behind.

Cecelia.

Sasha remembers turning, the shock registering in her brain that Cecelia was still alive. That she'd somehow managed to find her way out of the cupboard. She'd seen the look of pure determination etched on her face as she'd lifted whatever heavy object she'd held in her hand, above her, before bringing it down hard on Sasha's skull. Sasha had felt an almighty explosion of agony, and then nothing.

Only darkness.

Now, she is staggering along the hallway, towards Annabelle's room. To check on the children. She assumes that's where Cecelia had gone next. To check on her precious babies. Please! Nice that the woman only seemed to show an interest now. Now that she thought the children were in danger.

As if Sasha would ever do anything to hurt either of them. The children loved her. More than they loved their own mother, she was willing to bet. And Sasha had enjoyed that. Having a family, of sorts, all of her own.

'Annabelle? Zachery?'

The bedroom is empty. The children have gone.

Cecelia's room is empty too.

Sasha panics, tearing through the house in search of her.

Taking the stairs because they couldn't have got very far. Emily would be holding them back. The pills would have taken effect, there would be madness there. Emily would be teetering just on the brink of it. Sometimes Sasha wondered if the madness was hereditary. Like a rogue gene passed down from a mother to her child. Because sometimes she felt as if she was going slowly mad too.

Seeing things that weren't really there.

She'd been able to do that all her life. It had left scars on Sasha, growing up. Knowing how different she was from everyone else around her. How she didn't quite fit. She knew why she had been plagued with night-terrors now.

She had been scarred.

Or as her mother had written in the letter she'd left her, 'saved'.

Saved from an abusive mother.

A parent who had murdered her sibling, a brother that Sasha had no memory of ever having.

Only now she wasn't sure if the visions were real or if perhaps they were memories. Because they had got worse since she'd come here to this house. Her nightmares had been more vivid too. They'd become clearer, as if playing out in high definition inside her head. The images of the little boy standing at the end of her bed. The boy floating in the bath water.

She was sure now that it was Sam.

The ghost of him. His restless spirit. Trapped here in this house, where it had happened. Waiting for justice for what had happened to him. To them both.

As if Sasha would be the one to get it for him.

And she would.

She could feel it, the anger whipping wildly around inside of her, like a tornado, sucking up all the good memories of her fake childhood and replacing them with the chaotic turmoil of those four missing years in this house. She feels rage towards Emily, for the life she's taken from her. For the life she'd so violently ripped from Sam.

For Emily ever thinking that she selfishly deserved a second chance, when Sasha and Sam weren't so fortunate to have that opportunity.

Emily had killed her brother. She was a monster.

She needs to suffer for that.

44

SASHA

They can't have got away.

That is her first thought as Sasha reaches the front door and sees that it's locked still. The key is still nestled in her pocket. They can't have gotten out.

They are still here somewhere in this house.

Only as she walks towards the kitchen, she begins to follow the cool breeze that leads her to the back door which has been left wide open. She steps outside and stares around the garden, searching through the darkness for any signs of life, but there is none.

It's only then she realises that the back gate is wide open. Sasha moves down the side of the house, guessing that this is how they'd made their escape. Making their way out onto the street, so that they could bang on a neighbour's door and ask for help.

They'd be inside one of the houses now.

But as Sasha scans the street, her intuition tells her that they haven't come out here at all. That they didn't make it this far, because wouldn't there be more lights on? Wouldn't there be a door ajar, or a slight twitch of a curtain?

Someone would be out looking for her.

No, the street is far too dark.

It is raining, coming down hard, and the wind is picking up. Sasha wraps her arms around herself in a bid to fend off the cold as she looks back at the house. She knows for certain that Emily, Cecelia and the kids are no longer inside the house. And if they are not in there, and they are not out here, then that only leaves one other option.

They haven't left the back garden.

Sasha marches back through the gate, closing it behind her.

'I know you're here!' she says in a loud whisper.

Loud enough for them to hear her as they cower close by, listening, but not loud enough to alert any of the neighbours. Her eyes have adjusted now to the darkness, and it helps that there is a warm hue of light gleaming down from one of the upstairs windows. The patio and lawn near to the house glows a pale yellow. She listens, hoping to hear a whisper or a crack of a twig, a shuffle of feet. Only all she can hear is the rain as it lashes down around her. Faster and heavier now, gathering momentum.

She eyes the summerhouse that sits on the patio's edge. The first place she'd run to in a bid to keep dry. Or hide from someone who wanted to harm you. Would they really be that obvious though? Making her way towards it, she thinks they might. The door is locked, a padlock is bolted through the metal catch. They couldn't have done that from the inside.

Unless that's what they want her to think.

That because the cabin is bolted shut that there is no other way inside, but what if there is?

Sasha moves, making her way around the entire perimeter of the wooden building, looking for another door or open window. But there is nothing. There is no other way of getting inside. They are not in there, she is almost certain, but even so she presses her face up against the window just to make sure. Just as the black sky flashes an electric white and a jagged forked line of lightning cracks down across the skyline, followed by a loud roar of thunder.

Fate. Another helping hand to find Emily and bring her to justice.

The summerhouse is lit up for a few seconds, long enough to allow her gaze to sweep the darkest of corners. To seek out the silhouettes of the two women and children that may be lurking inside. Hiding under the false security of the nightly shadows.

Apart from the furniture that is stacked neatly inside, it is empty.

No one is hiding in there.

She starts to doubt her intuition then, questioning the gut feeling that swirls inside her that tells her they are close. She has got it wrong, after all. They are not here. They are not in this garden.

She is about to go, about to give up and leave, because if she's been wrong about that then the chances were Emily and Cecelia did manage to escape. They would have sought out help by now and that meant that it would only be a matter of time until the police arrived.

She'd need to make her own escape.

Making her way towards the back gate, she sees another flash in the sky above her. Bracing herself for the crackle of lightning and the burst of thunder, she realises that the flash of light that lit up the sky briefly for a few seconds at the back of the garden hadn't come from the thunderous sky's electrical charge.

It had come from something far smaller and far less powerful.

Like a torch.

Zachery's torch. From when they'd been in the treehouse reading stories.

Sasha glances to the back of the garden, towards the old apple tree.

They are in the treehouse.

45

CECELIA

Cecelia and the children are huddled inside the treehouse. Emily is on the floor, slumped down in the corner. She is barely able to keep her eyes open. Cecelia is worried about her, certain that the woman has been drugged with the same thing Sasha had drugged her with before locking her inside the cupboard. Emily is barely coherent. Lying there, soaking wet from the bath, and her body shivering violently from the cold, and from the shock of almost drowning.

She will die out here, if Cecelia doesn't get her somewhere warm and dry soon.

The icy wind is relentless, continuing to rush in through the windows and slats of the small wooden building. Making the branches of the tree that they are suspended in sway violently. The only consolation is that at least in here they are sheltered from the pouring rain as the storm continues to build.

'Don't be scared, Mummy. Look, I brought my space rocket torch.' Zachery pulls the small torch that he'd concealed in his pocket and shines it in his mother's face.

'Zachery, no! Turn it off.' Cecelia tries to grab the torch from her son, to switch it off before Sasha sees the small ray of light emitting from it, only in her haste she somehow manages to smack it from out of Zachery's hand.

They all watch in horror as it rolls along the slatted wooden floor of the treehouse, past Emily, before it hits a ridged slat at the edge, hoping that it would bring it to a stop, only suddenly, as if in slow motion, it plummets to the ground.

The beam of light flickering as it falls, but as it hits the grass below, instead of smashing. Of breaking. Of the yellow beam extinguishing,

The light remains.

Pointing upwards now like a spotlight beneath them.

'Shit!' Cecelia brings her eyes back to Sasha.

Praying that she hasn't seen the small flash of light as she continues to walk towards the back gate. They had watched as she had searched the summerhouse to no avail. She is giving up her search for them.

But the flash of torchlight that had so briefly lit up the sky must have caught her eye, because she stops suddenly and turns towards the back of the garden. Just as another fork of lightning snakes down the sky towards them, flashing across the sky, illuminating the treehouse in a bold, brilliant white light.

'Keep walking,' Cecelia pleads, whispering the words so quietly as she does so, that she isn't even sure if the words have left her mouth.

'Keep walking.' She repeats the words again like a mantra. Like a prayer to the gods. Closing her eyes as she does so, as she senses the fear of her children. Cecelia pulls Annabelle and Zachery in close, instinctively clamping her hands over her children's mouths in case any sound pours out as the huge boom of thunder she knew was coming explodes directly above them.

There is silence.

For a few seconds no one speaks, no one moves. When Cecelia looks out again, her eyes scanning the patio and the grass down by the house, for any movement, Sasha has gone.

There is no sign of her. The gate remains wide open, and Cecelia prays that Sasha has walked out through it.

Only if that was true, why couldn't Cecelia shake off the impeding feeling of danger that crackles in the charged air all around them? She can still feel it, and she knows none of them is safe from this woman.

'Stay down. Stay quiet,' Cecelia orders the children, deciding that they couldn't move from where they are hiding until she was certain that Sasha had gone. Cecelia keeps her eyes on the gate. Her eyes scanning the garden, despite her vision being blurred by the heavy rain, by the constant movement all around her of the trees and shrubs dancing erratically against the wind.

It's only when yet another fork of lightning flashes its way across the sky that Cecelia sees the silhouette of a figure coming towards them through the darkness.

Moving with purpose as they make their way up the garden. Towards the treehouse.

It is Sasha. She has found them.

46

SASHA

'I know you are up there, Mother dearest,' Sasha calls out as she reaches the bottom of the apple tree and stands with Zachery's torch at her feet, shining it up at the treehouse that looms above her.

'We've called the police, Sasha. They are on their way!' Cecelia shouts down.

'They're on their way, are they? Is that why you're all out here, in the pissing rain, hiding in the treehouse?' Sasha laughs at that. At the desperation in the woman's voice, at her blatant, obvious lie.

'I disconnected the phone, Cecelia. I know that you are lying. No one is coming for me.'

'Why are you doing this? What do you want from me?' Cecelia's voice is quieter now, shrinking along with her confidence that they are going to get out of tonight unscathed. They are not. It's as if suddenly she's realised how vulnerable they are. Sasha is not going to back down now that she has come this far.

'From you? I don't want anything from you. You were just a means to an end, someone who just got in the way. I didn't mean to hurt Zachery, I didn't mean to do what I did to him that day,' Sasha says honestly, because she wants him to know that more than anything. That she hadn't meant that incident to happen in the bath with Zachery.

'Can you hear me, Annabelle and Zachery? I would never, ever hurt either of you. Not intentionally. Never intentionally. I have these memory lapses sometimes. Like I told you. These minutes of time where I don't feel as if I'm inside my body. I wake sometimes to find myself playing out my nightmares. Only now I know that they are not nightmares at all, they are chunks of distorted memories. From the trauma I lived through. Trauma from her. My mother.'

Sasha's voice carries her anger. Her fury. This is all Emily's fault. The visions Sasha sees, the night-terrors she is plagued with.

That is all down to her.

'That's what this has always been about, Cecelia. Me coming here, back to this house. It was always about her. You just got in my way.' Sasha finally speaks honestly, thinking about her time here in this house with the children. How welcome Cecelia had made her feel. Only that had all come to an end once Cecelia suspected Sasha to be capable of harming the kids.

So, Cecelia had to go. And, technically, Sasha wouldn't have killed her in the end. She was happy to just leave her locked in that cupboard and let nature take its course.

'What do you mean back to this house?' Cecelia says, picking apart the detail in Sasha's words as she tries to make sense of it all.

'To this house. My home,' Sasha says simply. 'I lived here before.'

'I don't understand...' There is uncertainty now in Cecelia's voice as she pieces it all together, and Sasha thinks that she is lying again. That she is starting to understand, only part of her doesn't want to.

'Oh, come on, Cecelia. Think about it. Think about what you said when you first told me about when you and Henry bought this house at auction. How Henry had hid the house's history from you until it was too late. You'd been so cagey about the details, not wanting me to know the secrets that lurk in the walls of this house, behind your expensive furnishings and fancy wallpapers. Even they couldn't hide it, though. Could they? That something really bad happened here.'

Sasha pauses for effect, knowing that Cecelia would have guessed it now.

'I already knew all about it. That's why I came here. Back here. To the house that I lived in once as a child. That's what's so funny about all of this. You, up in that tree with the children, hiding from me like I am the bad one. You really don't have any idea who she is, do you?' Sasha laughs again, but this time there is so much malice there that it sounds more like a cackle.

'She's your mother? She lived here too?' Cecelia's words come sounding small and strained.

Sasha had called the woman 'mother dearest.' Sasha had lived here before.

'They called it the house of horrors in the newspapers. That's what you didn't want to tell me. That there had been a murder inside that house. That a young, neurotic mother had bashed her tiny son's head in before drowning him in the bath. Sam. My brother. And I am the little girl that they found locked away inside the crawlspace cupboard.'

Cecelia is quiet. Sasha imagines that what she has just been told is taking a while to sink in. Because it's a lot, she knows that herself. It was only a few months earlier that she'd been in exactly the same position. Only she hadn't just been a bit-part in the story, she was the main character.

'That's the irony in all of this, Cecelia. That I am standing down here pleading my innocence and you are up there. Unwittingly protecting a child-murderer. The children are not safe up there. You need to send them down. I promise you, that if you do, I will not hurt them. It's only her that I want.'

'We're not going. No. Leave us alone.' It's Annabelle's voice as the child shouts down bravely. And despite herself Sasha smiles. Annabelle had always reminded her of herself. Headstrong and determined. Smart.

'Ah, props to you, Cecelia. For brainwashing them against me in record time!' Sasha laughs again, this time exaggerated and mocking. 'Send them down, Cecelia.'

Sasha is met by silence, angering her further. The children's treatment of her, their blatant dismissal. After all she'd done for the ungrateful brats. They'd chosen their poor excuse of a mother over her. Well, they'd had their chance at getting out of here alive. It wasn't her fault that they'd chosen not to take it.

Sasha turns on her heel.

Making her way back towards the summerhouse, as if to retrieve something that she'd seen there.

Returning just minutes later, she shouts up to Cecelia: 'I told you I only wanted her. Emily. But you didn't listen. So, don't say I didn't warn you.'

Taking the jerry can full of petrol that she'd found stashed down behind the summerhouse, Sasha slops the contents around the base of the tree and the treehouse ladder.

'If you won't come down willingly, I'll force you down. Last chance.'

47

EMILY

I am lying on the cold, damp wooden floor of the treehouse when I hear her voice. It grates through me, like clawed fingers purposely scraping themselves down a chalkboard, its only purpose the want to irritate others. I squirm at the sound, every single part of me bristling as I listen to the hatred she spouts, hatred for me. As she justifies her reasons to Cecelia for trying to drown me earlier tonight in the bath.

I see it in Cecelia's eyes. She instantly believes Sasha.

I am the monster that once lived in this house.

The mother who murdered her sweet boy.

I am everything that Sasha says I am.

The look she shoots me is so fleeting, so subtle, but I catch it regardless. I am used to the hatred that is slung my way. The disgust people feel towards me. I see how Cecelia wishes that Sasha had held me down. That Cecelia hadn't stopped her from filling my lungs with the water that would replace my final breath. She wishes for a second that death had taken me.

What she doesn't realise is that I wish for that too.

Anything so that I don't have to face Sasha's repulsion of me, now, as a grown woman. A woman I no longer recognise, as you'd well expect following the twenty-year void that stretched out mercilessly between us. Her scrawny childlike body now replaced by a tall, womanly one. Though it pleases me that she still wears her hair in the same neat brown bob I'd always insisted on giving her as a child.

I'd always wondered what she'd look like, when I'd thought about her. And I had thought about her so much over the years, despite acting to anyone watching and listening as if she never once entered my mind. Most days she was all I thought about. My first born. My darling daughter.

'Send Annabelle and Zachery down!' she shouts up, and I see Cecelia wavering.

Like any good mother would do, she is weighing up her options. Her only thought is to keep her children safe.

'Don't do it,' I whisper. Using all the energy I have inside of me, I sit up as Cecelia pulls the children in tighter to her in response to my movement, and I can't say I blame her. I see the way that she is debating right now whether or not they'd be safer down there with her, than they are up here with me. 'Don't listen to her. She has already tried to kill me tonight. She won't stop at just me, because she knows she won't get away with it. She'll use them as bait. Threatening to hurt them if you don't go down there too.'

'I told you I only wanted her. Emily. But you didn't listen. So, don't say I didn't warn you.'

I hear the sloshing sounds of liquid splash up against the base of the tree, before I smell the potent stench of petrol fumes as they float upwards to me.

She can't be? But even before I pull myself up from the floor and lean out of the open window, and see her holding the jerry can, I know that she is. She is emptying the contents of the petrol can all over the base of the tree, and the treehouse's ladder. These are the lengths that Sasha will go to, to get things her way. She looks so different on the outside, but inside, she is still the same.

Manipulative. Relentless.

'Stop, Sasha! Please!' I beg, glancing at the look of fear on the children's faces as I cling to the window's ledge in a bid to steady myself, because I don't just have the meds to contend with. The storm is howling now, the wind rushing through the tree, causing the treehouse to sway dangerously.

'Don't make me do it then, Emily. Come down. It's not them I want. It's you.' Sasha holds up the lighter. 'I want you to pay for what you did. I want you to suffer like Sam did. Like I did too. You are a monster, Emily. You do not deserve a second chance at freedom. You do not deserve this life at all.'

She is enjoying the look of sheer horror on my face as she runs her finger over the metal wheel as if threatening to strike it. This is not a thinly veiled threat; I know she'll do it. She'll take great delight in doing it. I step forward, knowing I have no choice.

But as I move towards the ladder, Cecelia grips my arm.

The words that come out of her mouth sounding as surprising to her as they do to me as she says them. 'If you go down there, she will kill you.'

She doesn't believe I deserve to die. Not here, not like this. That's something at least. Only I know different. I nod my head, because I already know what Cecelia says to be true. Sasha will kill me if I go down there.

'My life means nothing to me now. It hasn't meant anything to me for twenty years. Not since the children—' I stop mid-sentence, my eyes drinking in the sight of the two small, beautiful children at Cecelia's side as they grip her hands for dear life, and for a few seconds I wonder if she realises how lucky she is. How blessed she is to have them. There is something about the way that they look at me that awakens something inside of me. I can't keep doing this. Allowing myself to be punished over and over again for the sins of twenty years ago. I know in my heart that I do deserve a second chance. That whatever scrap of life that is left for me is mine to be claimed. And finally, I want to claim it at last.

'I can't allow your children to be put in any more danger than they already are...' I say, and step forward again.

My gaze catches the glimpse of light that flashes between the gap in the rooftops. A luminous glow running down the road outside the house. Sasha turns to see what I am looking at then too, just as one more final almighty clap of thunder fills the sky, and the dark skies melt away for a few seconds while everything around us turns white.

'If I come down, I want you to promise me that nothing will happen to this lady and her children. I can't allow any more children to die, Sasha,' I shout as I stare down from where I stand at the top of the ladder. My voice full of genuine sadness that it had come to this.

I see I have her full attention once more.

She glares at me, a sneer on her face as she answers me. 'Well, that's big of you, Emily! You don't want any more children to die. One was enough, was it? Only that doesn't bring Sam back, does it? It doesn't stop me from feeling so fucked up from witnessing what you did. Because since I've been back here, in this house, I've started to remember things. Broken fragmented memories of what you did—'

'Do you really think that I haven't suffered too?' I shake my head. 'You want the truth? You want me to tell you exactly what I did on that night? Why Sam died. Why you were locked away in that cupboard that night?' I shout, because Sasha had told me in the bathroom, just before she'd plunged me into that bathtub full of water, that all she wanted was to hear me say it. That she wanted to know what happened that night, first-hand, from my mouth.

'I tried my best. I am not the bad mother that you think I

am,' I start. 'There were times when I was so happy, so content, that I thought my heart would literally burst. Sam was always such a darling child. So easy, so loving. And really, he wanted for nothing. Even as a baby he didn't cry if I ran out of milk and needed to wait until the morning until I could get my giro. He patiently lay in the bed, while I struggled to get up in the morning, after lying awake all night crippled with what I know now was severe post-natal depression. He was easy. He got me through it.'

'And what about me?'

It was my turn to laugh at that. Because Sasha had no idea just how that sentence summed everything up about her.

'You were everything that Sam wasn't. You were difficult and demanding and always unhappy and sulking. And the truth was you resented the attention and love that I gave to your brother, and because of that, you purposely made it so much harder for me.'

'I was four years old...' Sasha interrupts me, only I have started now and I need to say it.

'You were broken, Sasha. Yes, even then. At just four years old. I had known it deep down, but as a mother I had refused to believe it. Because that's how we are built, isn't it? To love our children unconditionally, no matter what. To protect our children at all costs. And I wanted to protect you too.'

'Protect me? Is that what you call it?' Sasha spits and I see the venom. No matter what I say to her, she'll never forgive me. But I must try to make her understand. I must try and salvage something from tonight, even if it costs me the very little I have left for myself.

'Sam loved you so much, Sasha. You were his big, beautiful sister and his eyes lit up at the sight of you. Though to you, it was as if just the sight of him, just breathing in the same air as you, existing, riled something up inside of you. It was as if you could see his innocence. How good he was, how pure. How you were none of those things. You knew that. And you hated him for it. This is why I haven't ever spoken about it. It wasn't just through grief or shame. But heartbreak. I couldn't relive what happened that night, because just the thought of it broke my heart in two all over again.

'What do you remember, Sasha? His body floating in the bath? The blood all over the taps. Me dragging him out of the water while you stood sobbing behind me?' I spit. Feeling myself begin to shake with uncontrollable rage. 'Do you remember this tree. How I was out here on my hands and knees, clawing at the wet mud with my bare hands as I tried to bury his body. My beautiful baby boy, lying in a shallow grave in this garden like his life had meant nothing. Like he had meant nothing.'

I am screaming as I see Sasha falter.

She had remembered being out here.

That this tree held some significance.

For the first time in forever I feel the swell of fury leave my body. The anger I'd kept inside of me ever since, that I'd buried so deeply. I wanted it out of me. How dare she judge me? How dare she talk down to me?

'I've had so many years of therapy. Of specialists and counsellors and doctors trying to pick me apart and get inside of my head. To analyse me and work out why I had done it. One of the popular diagnoses they've tried to give me over the years is Dissociative Amnesia. They say that the trauma of what I did to Sam, of murdering him, of trying to bury his body in the garden to cover his death up, was too overwhelming for me to process. Too emotionally distressing so my brain simply blocked it all out.'

I will myself to say the next words. It was time for the truth. It was time to end this madness.

For both our sakes.

'I outsmarted them all, Sasha. They were all so wrong about

me. Because I can remember every single, minute detail about that night. I remember the feel of Sam's tiny body in my arms as I leant over the bathtub; I remember how warm his blood still felt as it seeped through my fingers from the gash in the back of his head, after his heart had stopped beating. I remember how the wet mud went dry under my fingernails, and how I picked it out in clumps as I sat there for what felt like hours, staring at the bloody cupboard door, listening to you crying inside. Shouting at me to let you out. When the police came, I told them that I locked you in that cupboard for your own protection.'

'For my own protection? Wow that's big of you.'

'Yes, for your own protection,' I repeat, shouting now.

I continue, because I need her to listen, I need her to understand why I did what I did that night. 'I locked you in that cupboard and I couldn't let you out, because I would kill you. And that was the truth. I think I might have been capable of murdering you too. For what you did.' I pause. The words pouring out of me now that I have started.

'I didn't block anything out, Sasha. You did. I just took the blame. It was you, Sasha. You killed Sam.'

48

SASHA

'You are a liar,' Sasha screams as she begins climbing, making her way up the ladder fuelled with the injustice and the fury of Emily's lies. She is disgusted at how desperate Emily is to try and redeem herself. How she will never admit to what she did. She will never show remorse for the heinous crime that she committed. That the woman is so sick and twisted she is prepared to fabricate stories about her. She is willing to blame a four-year-old child for doing something so evil, so callous, so monstrous as murdering her little brother.

'You are lying. Why won't you just admit what you did? Why won't you take responsibility for what you did? To Sam. To me. You are the reason that I have been plagued with the dark thoughts. And nightmares. You are the reason that I've always felt so broken; you are the reason for the detachment I've felt all of my life.'

Hadn't she felt it towards her own mother too, the woman who had brought her up as her own?

A woman who had done Sasha no harm that she knew of, yet still Sasha hadn't been capable of feeling love for her. In fact, there had been times when Sasha had despised her. For how desperate she always seemed in her attempts to get Sasha to love her back. Even in her death the woman had tried to soften the blow of the truth she'd confessed in her letter, by informing Sasha that she was the sole beneficiary of her will.

Sasha had inherited it all. The house. Her mother's belongings.

But it had meant nothing to her. It was just stuff. Things. None of it had ever brought Sasha any pleasure. It had pained her that even until her dying breath, her mother had never accepted that. Sasha couldn't be bought. Her mother couldn't just fix her like that.

That had been one of her mother's specialties. Fixing people who were broken. It would have devastated the woman to know that she had gone to her grave without succeeding. Knowing that Sasha was most irretrievably broken.

Broken because of Emily.

Worse still her mother had known the truth all that time. That's why she'd made all those excuses. That's why she'd smoothed the way for her at times, paying generous 'charitable donations' to the private schools she'd attended, when they had threatened to expel Sasha over her unruly behaviour. How, when Sasha had been sent home from playdates and sleepovers after damaging property or deliberately hurting her friends, her mother had paid the parents off. Sending them expensive gifts as a way of apology for the behaviour of her 'strong-willed, strong-minded' daughter. That's how her mother would justify the swell of anger that Sasha always seemed so unable to keep contained inside of her.

'I was always so angry. So pent up. And now I know why. Because of your abuse. For the damage that you caused. For the trauma I witnessed as a child. That is the truth. Not this crap that you're spouting right now. Trying to convince everyone that you're some kind of saint, that you have selflessly taken the blame for the last twenty years for a crime you never committed. Under what guise? Unconditional love for a child you hadn't even loved?'

'I did love you, Sasha...' Emily starts, only she falters, unable to find any real conviction to her words because they both know she didn't.

'But my God, you were so hard to love. I caught you once, in the middle of the night, hovering over Sam, clutching a pillow in your hand. Another time, I'd only left the room for just a few minutes and when I had come back you had placed him inside the crawlspace cupboard and left him in there crying. I made excuses for you. I always made excuses for you. Always turning a blind eye to things that you did and putting it down to jealously. To sibling rivalry. When the reality was, alarm bells should have been sounding off inside of me. But part of me didn't want to believe that you were capable of being so cruel.' Emily shakes her head. Sadness dripping from her words as she continues.

'As much as I wanted to, I couldn't switch that love off. Believe me I tried. Because there were times when I didn't like you. After you killed Sam, I felt partly responsible. I should have known, I should have stopped you. All I could do then was protect you. To shield you from a lifetime of being blamed for such a heinous act, because it hadn't been just a silly accident. You did it. You smashed his head open, and then held him under the water.'

'No! I wouldn't do that. I didn't do that.' Sasha stares up to where Cecelia stands then, her arms wrapped protectively around her two frightened children. She sees how it's too late, how they believe Emily's lies.

'You did it to Zachery too,' Cecelia says.

'No, that isn't what happened, Cecelia. I didn't mean it. You and the children made me feel so happy here. You welcomed me into your home and treated me like part of your family. Until suddenly you didn't. It was one stupid mistake, Cecelia.

That's all it had taken. One little slip. One accident in the bathroom with Zachery that day.'

'An accident? You tried to drown him, Sasha!' Cecelia shouted, not caring if she was interrupting the woman now. 'You're deluded, Sasha. Of course, I was going to ask you to leave. What sane parent wouldn't?'

'It was trauma. I don't know how else to explain it. The strange episodes I sometimes have, how I occasionally slip into a kind of trance. How I have no control when they come, the traumatic memories from my childhood. I didn't mean it. I only slipped the tablets into your wine to buy myself some more time, while I figured out what I could do or say to make it right again. Only I'd underestimated the strength of the pills for someone taking them for the very first time. Washed down with all that wine. And when you collapsed, I couldn't find a pulse. I thought you were dead. That's why I put you in the crawlspace cupboard. I panicked. I didn't want the children to see you.'

'Ahh, how sweet of you,' Cecelia snorts. 'Always thinking of the children. You must have heard me when I regained consciousness?'

Sasha doesn't answer. She'd heard the moaning and banging, and she realised Cecelia was still alive. But by then she'd come around to the idea of not having to deal with her any more, because she knew she'd already gone too far. If Sasha left her in there and pretended not to hear her, then technically, she hadn't killed her, had she!? Technically, she'd let nature run its course and the problem deal with itself. Holding Emily's head under the water in the bath tonight had been a different mind space completely. That had been uncontrollable hatred pouring out of her. Wild fury at the evil that resided inside of the woman. The sense of injustice that she wouldn't accept responsibility for what she'd done. She wasn't going to get away with that now. She was going to say it. She was going to say what she did and that she was sorry for it.

Sasha is almost at the top; only Cecelia and Emily aren't looking at her any more, they are looking behind her. At the commotion that bursts into the garden below.

Shouting first, then the flash of lights and movement. Swarms of people running.

The police.

They are here for her.

'You called them?' Sasha looks at Cecelia and then over at the children. Wondering how they managed to call her bluff. She had disconnected the phones and taken both Cecelia's and Emily's mobiles from them.

It is Emily who shakes her head.

'No. We didn't. She did.' There is a look of something smug gleaming from her eyes as she looks down to see who has led them here. Sasha turns, catching a glimpse of Louise standing below her.

Sasha feels the warmth of fingertips against her cheeks. Looking back up, Emily hovers over her.

Crouching now, a softness in her eyes as she speaks.

'I forgive you, Sasha.'

'No!' She shakes her head. The force of the movement leaving her unbalanced. Her need to get away from the woman's insincere touch. Her feet are slipping, sliding from the wet rung of the ladder where she stands. Sending her descending backwards. Hurtling towards the ground at speed.

FLASH.

Red wellington boots sinking in the mud. She is standing at the foot of a tree and looking up. Then she's climbing.

This tree.

As the rain pours all around her just as it pours down now.

Sasha lifts her foot and places it on a tyre swing. Her hand reaching up for the rope.

Above her is a big red juicy-looking apple.

If she tiptoes, she can just about reach it. Just a few more inches.

Her fingers scrape at the flesh of the apple.

Then she is falling fast.

THUD!

Pain in her head explodes as she hits the ground.

She lies there, startled. Staring up at the darkened night's sky as the grey clouds, illuminated only by the moon, dance above her.

Her hair and clothes caked in mud. Her face is wet from crying.

She can't get up. Winded now, the air expelled from her body.

Everything hurts, but her head is banging.

Reaching up she touches her scalp before pulling her hand away and seeing the blood on her fingertips.

A woman nearby is shouting now. Her voice angry and hysterical.

She is down in the mud, clawing her hands through the wet earth as the tiny boy lies next to the makeshift grave.

Crying hysterically.

BAD GIRL. BAD GIRL.

Sasha lands with a thud at the foot of the apple tree. The stench of petrol all around her.

A sea of faces looking down at her.

And that's when she sees him.

Sam. The ghost of him.

Standing at the foot of the apple tree, where she'd last seen his body.

She remembers what he looked like. That yellow straw-coloured hair. That freckly little nose. Though no one else seems to see him, and for a second Sasha wonders if he is really there. If he is an illusion. Her mind playing tricks on her.

There is a look of sadness on his face. Sad for her.

Emily's words spinning inside her head. *'You did it, Sasha. You killed Sam.'*

He was never helping her bring Emily to justice, she realises as her breath becomes shallow, the pain in her body slowly turning numb.

It was her that he wanted brought to justice all along.

49

SASHA

Don't look at him. Do not look at him.

Focus.

I keep my gaze fixed on her instead. The healthcare assistant as she hovers in the doorway of my small, cramped room. Her beady eyes mirroring mine as she impatiently waits.

Watching.

They are always watching.

As they pass my doorway, pressing their faces up against the window, as they crank the bedroom door open a few inches in the middle of the night, and peer in through the crack to check that I am still in my bed.

Sometimes they even follow me to the bathroom, waiting outside the door until I am finished.

There is zero privacy in here. I am a goldfish on display, treading water in this tiny glass bowl. Waiting for my audience to dip their fat hand inside and contaminate my water as they feed me.

Pill after pill after pill.

That's how they manage us crazy people. People like me,

who see people who aren't really there. Though I am trying so hard to not see him.

Do not look at him. Do not give yourself away.

But I catch sight of him, from my peripheral vision.

Sam.

As he stands still like a statue, there in the corner of my room. Standing in that very same spot since the first day that they locked me away in here.

His presence no longer bringing me any comfort; the sight of his bright blond hair and tiny freckled nose only torments me now.

More so, that angry expression that is fixed to his face.

'Come on, Sasha love. I haven't got all night.' Her smile appears friendly, but her tone is hard.

She has no interest in helping me, she is simply here to do her job. To go through the motions and ensure that I'm taking my medication before reporting back to them.

The doctors who think that they know me better than I know myself. The ones that hold all the power to determine whether or not I am mentally stable.

Opening my mouth, I dutifully place the two pills on my tongue before swallowing down the tepid glass of tap water, without hesitation.

Not for her, for me.

That's the real reason why I do as I am told. Taking my medication so obediently, without protest.

To block him out.

It pains me to say it, but I learned that from the best.

From her.

Emily.

I let out a long, steady breath as I wait for the tablets to start to work their magic. Hoping that the air expelled from my lungs will take all of the toxic thoughts I have about her along with it.

I must get them out.

I've learned that the hard way. How the bad thoughts only fester, otherwise. Slithering around inside of me like a silent, deadly parasite.

They do not serve me. They poison me instead.

Since that night when I confronted her, it's as if the memories that were locked away inside a box in my mind have been shaken wide awake.

They come mainly in dream form, in flashbacks and fragmented recollections.

Me back at that house, just a small, frightened girl.

Emily, with that flash of madness in her eyes.

Dreams of Emily hovering over Sam as he'd slept, not me. Of her clutching that pillow in her hands.

That time I'd seen her place him inside the crawlspace cupboard and leave him there alone, crying for hours.

The night she'd tried to bury Sam's body, after she had drowned him in the bath. She was right: I had been selfish. Reaching up for that apple, while my brother's body lay cold on the ground beside me.

Only hadn't I felt as if my insides were starting to eat away at my own flesh for survival because Emily hadn't fed me for days and I had been starving?

No. These visions are all just part of my imagination.

My mind is playing tricks on me.

Disassociation.

I'd accused her of that.

How it was common for people like me who have committed such despicable, violent crimes. A form of detachment, a method of survival.

Saved.

I think of the word that my mother used in her letter.

My real mother: the woman who brought me up as her own. The woman who despite my indifference to her had loved me so fiercely anyway.

She had tried to save me in her own way.

The only problem was that some people just can't be saved.

Not from fate, nor from the people they are born to.

Sometimes safe isn't enough and the truth of who you really are means more.

I know who I am now.

The tablets are working.

My eyelids feel heavy, involuntarily closing and allowing the darkness in that I so desperately crave.

Ready for the nothingness.

Those few short blissful hours of him locked out of my head, unable to get to me.

I know that he'll be there, waiting for me, when I awake.

But for now, I sleep.

50

EMILY

I stand at the front of the bus and hold the iPhone that Louise set up for me over the large round yellow button.

'It's all contactless now,' Louise had explained. 'The payments are taken electronically. Directly through your phone from your bank.'

These machines are so clever, knowing exactly how much money to take. Though it still seems so bizarre to me how people rarely use real money any more. That they use fancy phones like this one that Louise bought for me, instead. Everyone has them. Everywhere I look I see them permanently glued to people's hands.

They are not just fashion accessories, you can do all sorts on them, Louise had said.

Surf the web. Do your food shopping online.

All the things which seem so alien to me.

The world has gone mad.

What's wrong with doing all these things in person? We're not robots. We need interaction with real people. Surely it's not healthy to interact so much with what is essentially a tiny computer screen.

'You can watch your favourite TV programmes on them too. If you're out and about. So you don't miss them,' Louise had added, when I'd turned my nose up at all her other suggestions. Though that hadn't won me over, either.

'What's the point of staring at a tiny screen, when I can watch it on the big TV when I get home?'

I move my phone again and wait for the beep.

What did she say again?

Tap on. Tap off.

Her instructions engrained in me as I had stepped onto the bus.

'If you don't remember to tap off at the end of the journey, Emily, you'll get charged for the whole route and you only want eight stops. Remember, tap off.'

Maybe these smartphone things are not so smart after all, because I don't think my phone is working properly.

I turn to look, to seek her out, past the queue of impatient-looking faces that all stand in a row behind me, only I have lost her in the crowd.

Panic starts to set in.

I can't do this.

The driver, who up until now has sat staring ahead out the windscreen as if he's redundant, turns and looks at me. 'You're holding everyone up, love.' He nods at me to go and sit down, so I do just that.

Making my way to the back of the bus, still unsure if I've made the transaction.

I take a seat by the window.

The crumpled piece of paper with the address scrawled on it is clutched tightly in my hand.

64 Maple Street.

Part of me still unable to believe that I am really going back there. That this time it is by choice.

This time I have been invited.

Eight stops, Louise said, I am to count them.

Concentrate.

I block out the noise of all the loud chatter and conversations that are going on all around me. I am good at that. Blocking out the noise. Christ only knows, I've had enough practice.

I see her then. Louise, smiling and waving me off just as the bus starts to pull away.

Part of me wants to tap on the glass and mouth, 'Look, I did it! I paid my fare, I'm on the bus.' But I simply wave back instead.

I was wrong about Louise. I can admit that now.

She is a good, kind person. One of the rare few people that genuinely does want the best for me. And being rehabilitated, fully, back into society is the best for me, she had insisted. She'd promised me that she would do everything she could to help me, and so far, she has more than kept her word.

She has found me a flat away from the unit, away from the other healthcare assistants and support workers.

Today, after she set up my new phone, she'd insisted on walking me to the bus stop.

If it wasn't for Louise, I wouldn't even be here right now.

I am sure of that.

How if Sasha had reached the top of that ladder that night, she would have killed me.

Louise had been onto her long before me.

Sasha had asked too many questions. About the house back then, about the children. That's when she'd roused Louise's suspicions.

Later, when I'd accused Louise of doing all those bad things to me, stealing my journal, hiding that rotten meat underneath my bed, planting the newspaper clipping inside of one of my books for me to find, Louise knew that there was only one other person who could be capable of doing all of that to me.

She'd thought for a while that moving me into the low-secure flat had been what had triggered my audio hallucinations once more. That the move had been too overwhelming. That was why I'd started hearing the crying girl again.

Only she figured out that the only other consistent change was her. Sasha. Masquerading as Charlotte.

How despite me not recognising her, her presence had stirred visceral memories buried deep in my subconscious.

An instinct of some kind, a vague familiarity.

Louise had started to keep a closer eye on Charlotte. And on me. Turning up at the flat more often, always unannounced and unexpected.

After my tablets went missing, and my behaviour spiralled, she'd started watching the security cameras at night too.

Waiting to catch her out; and it hadn't taken long.

She'd seen us that night, leaving in an Uber. She'd called the company and demanded the address that they'd taken me to, and then she'd called the police.

The calvary arrived just in time and the rest, as they say, is history.

Which is a funny saying really, isn't it? because we never really leave history back there in the past. It always finds a way of repeating itself.

I saw it that night, in Sasha.

How she had grown to become just like me.

She inherited it all.

The bad dreams, the visions, the trances.

She'd said as much, hadn't she? How she sees things that aren't really there, how she re-enacts things without meaning to.

I shouldn't have lied. I know that deep down.

I shouldn't have told them that it was Sasha who killed Sam.

Only I knew that I had no choice.

She would never let me live my life in peace. She'd find some way to get to me, to make my life difficult. I know that, because I had seen it in her eyes as she held me down in that bath. How she wouldn't be content until she had killed me.

In a way, I have done her a favour of sorts.

Being locked away for all those years has helped me. I am different now. I am better.

One day, perhaps, Sasha can be better too.

I count eight stops, and as the bus comes to a halt I see them. Cecelia, Annabelle and Zachery, all standing at the side of the street, just as Louise had said they would be. Their excitement is contagious and I can't help but laugh as they wave and smile as they see me through the window.

I move to the front of the bus and hold my phone over the yellow scanner so I can 'tap out', just like Louise had told me to. Only I still can't hear the beep, but the way that the driver nods at me to leave, tells me that perhaps it did, only I couldn't hear it.

Over all the noise she is making.

The crying girl.

Ignore her and she'll go away, I tell myself as I step off the bus and make my way towards Cecelia and the children.

'Ignore her and act normal.'

This is my second chance and I refuse to let her ruin it for me.

A LETTER FROM CASEY KELLEHER

Dear reader,

I want to say a huge thank you for choosing to read *The Babysitter's Secret*. This is my fourth psychological thriller, and I have to say I thoroughly enjoyed the dark, twisted turns that this book took as I started to write Sasha and Emily's story. If you did enjoy *The Babysitter's Secret* and you would like to keep up to date with all my latest releases, just sign up at the following link. Your email address will never be shared and you can unsubscribe at any time.

www.bookouture.com/casey-kelleher

The first things that came into my mind when I started writing this one was a creepy Victorian house, a disturbing bathtub scene and Emily, trapped in a room hearing voices. I had no idea whose voice she was hearing or why, but I knew that her story would be a dark one. Sometimes, during the writing process we see our characters in our minds, and hear their voices and, more often than not, the characters end up taking on a life of their own. Taking us off in a completely different direction to when we first started. Which always makes the process more exciting and made me really love writing this one.

I'd love to hear what you thought of *The Babysitter's Secret*, so if you have the time, and you'd like to leave me a review on

Amazon it's always appreciated. (I do make a point of reading every single one.)

I also love hearing from you, my readers – your messages and photos of the books that you tag me in on social media always make my day! And trust me, some days us authors really need that to spur us on with that dreaded daily word-count.

So, please feel free to get in touch on my Facebook page, or through Instagram, Twitter or my website.

Thank you

Casey Kelleher

www.caseykelleher.co.uk

 facebook.com/officialcaseykelleher

 twitter.com/CaseyKelleher

 instagram.com/caseykelleher

ACKNOWLEDGEMENTS

Many thanks to my amazing editor Susannah Hamilton. It's been an absolute pleasure working alongside you with *The Babysitter's Secret*. As always you really helped me pull the story together so perfectly and I'm really looking forward to working on our next one together.

Special thanks as always to the amazing Noelle Holten – PR extraordinaire! There are not enough Long Island Iced Tea cocktails in the world to show my appreciation. And to all of the Bookouture dream team, and to all of the fabulous authors in the lounge.

Special mention to Emma Graham Tallon and Victoria Jenkins for being such amazing friends and for keeping me sane/encouraging me to procrastinate during the writing process.

Thanks as always to my bestie, Lucy Murphy. (Last time I'll be using that name in one of my books, soon-to-be Mrs Pash.) And to my sister-in-law, Laura Cooper. I can't tell you how nerve wrecking it is to have people reading my books for the first time. So, I'm super grateful to you both for not only being so supportive but for also being super speedy and not making me wait too long!

Thanks to my niece, Sasha for letting me borrow your name. I love you lots and I'm very proud of you. And to Annabelle, I really hope you love this story.

Huge thanks also to Colin Scott and for the Savvys for all your fantastic advice and support.

And to all the lovely readers in NotRights/Gangland Governors. TBC, UK Crime book club, The Fiction Café book club, Bitchy Bookworms, Psychological Thriller Readers – and so many more groups! For reading, reviewing and sharing my book! I really appreciate all your support.

As always I'd like to thank my extremely supportive family for all the encouragement that they give me along the way. The Coopers, the Kellehers, the Ellises. And to all my lovely friends.

To my sons Ben and Danny. You know you actually have to this read one now that it's dedicated to you!!

To my husband Danny. You are my rock! I couldn't do this without you. Not forgetting our two little fur-babies/writer's assistants, Sassy and Miska.

And to you, my lovely reader, I say this often, because it's true: You are the very reason I write, without you, none of this would have been possible.

Casey x

Made in United States
Orlando, FL
27 May 2023

33552822R00171